THE WORD
OF THE
ROCK GOD
SECOND EDITION

BROOKLYNN DEAN

Brooklynn Dean Books

Other works by Brooklynn Dean

Fiberglass Galaxy
Amethyst
The Woman in Red Heels
2288
Deification
Grieving the Spirit

CHAPTER ONE

"Man," Craig scoffed, his fingers strumming down the line of strings on a second-hand guitar. "How is it even possible that my neck cracked?"

"Loading the van drunk," Max answered, a small laugh slipping through his lips.

"Yeah, funny."

"At least we found a replacement."

"Yeah, and it's shit. Listen to it." He huffed.

"Easy," Max said, chewing on the edge of his Dixie cup. "I'll go get you a drink," he added as he hopped down from the back of the couch.

"Whatever, man," Craig said, rushing his hands through his hair before focusing on the foreign guitar again.

With the doors now open, the small bar was filling quickly. Max's eyes glanced around at the line of people waiting to get wristbands or red x's. They moved to their left where the stage stood just four feet about the ground. A crowd had already formed near its edge, tight with no gaps between shoulders, and it separated further as it moved back toward the bar.

Arguably one of Max's favorite parts of playing in a new city was the ability to walk amongst the crowd anonymously. Every night he was unknown, another faceless mass in a mass of faces, and every night he was reborn, the stage lights giving shape to his blurred features, the microphone providing authority to the once whispered voice.

He liked these moments when he could walk inside the bar and maintain his anonymity. He liked the feeling of being no one to them, of being no consequence when his shoulders brushed against someone in the crowd. He liked the way they only glanced at him, offering a lazy smile, when he apologized.

When he met with those same faces after his thirty minutes of mattering, he felt flattered in the new appreciation. It stayed with him, but what once seemed so perfect under the neon spotlights felt strangely hollow in a dark hotel room. It may have been the extreme contrast of an empty bed, cold and isolated, to the crowds that surrounded him after a set. So many bodies pressed so closely together, each in their own separate effort to see the look on his face when his eyes fell onto theirs—it created a heat that rivaled the sun. But for what purpose?

Though he wanted to believe each person standing before him, each person just learning his name for the first time, would remember what he said when he was standing four feet above them, he couldn't deny the validity of the thoughts that crept inside his mind during those isolated hours. Whether he was safe inside a bed or hours into a dark drive to a new city, his eyes heavy as his mind drifted to and from consciousness, Max questioned his impact. Was anyone there for the music? Were they all there for the art? Or did they merely seek the opportunity to feel important in the few seconds they stood before someone with a dream made reality?

Those thoughts, those newly formed opinions that twisted positive experiences into troublesome memories; those thoughts always made him aware of just how hollow all that praise might have been.

It was disheartening if he chose to believe it. But if nothing else, disillusionment and three a.m. were the perfect cocktail for artistic release. At least he'd get some new songs written.

Placing his elbows over the golden rod that lined the bar, Max leaned forward, waiting patiently for the bartender to make his way to him.

What mattered most on nights like this, the absolute best part of any evening, was the connection Max felt when he'd bend his knees, almost eye level with the crowd at his feet, and he'd see smiling lips forming the same shapes as his. The admiration within their eyes was obvious, but it mattered very little to Max. He found importance in the hope that radiated within their eyes, and the way it blended with their vocalization of his words to create something somehow corporeal. As it rose up from the lungs that sang for him, from the eyes that adored him, from the hands that reached to him, Max marveled over the power of the spirit and how easily it could prove itself with one, simple sensation——a chill that ran down his spine like a shot of adrenaline.

Often times, he'd remove his earplugs, hoping somehow over the speakers and his magnified voice, that he'd hear their voices, too.

Nothing made him happier than taking a hand that had been reaching for him all evening. When he felt the tingling energy passed from their hand to his, the energy that told him for certain he mattered to this person—not his spot on the stage or the sound of his voice. Only something so pure as the connection shared between two souls, two like-minds trying to desperately to understand the emotions that built up inside them separately, but felt entirely alike, could produce something so electrifying as the jolting energy passed between their palms.

Nothing but the deep and incomparable connection two people, or five, or one hundred, shared when they spoke the words that mattered most to them—when they spoke words that healed their internal wounds, similar to the wounds he'd had when composing them. Those words, with their protective energy, became a safety net to the people who admired him, and in return, that admiration became his shield. It was an understanding privy to only those inside the net, and explaining it to someone who'd never felt their own emotions sung from someone else's lungs was a pointless endeavor.

It was why he chased that sensation wherever he went. It was why his words meant more to him when they danced on someone else's tongue. It was why he loved the way they sounded when pronounced with different accents in different tones of voice.

Whatever he'd been feeling when he composed the lyrics was almost entirely irrelevant in those moments. The specifics of that situation didn't matter at all. The beauty of those moments, the purity of such connection, was found inside the emotion of it.

That shared emotion, invoked inside someone else when

he wrote the way it felt to him, was the most innately human experience of any other. It reminded him, through the tears in the eyes of those who felt it, through the sincerity in their voices when they sang it, that everyone is linked, but through something far more powerful than just DNA and chromosomes.

"What're you having?" The bartender pointed to Max.

"Two tequila shots. Doesn't matter what brand."

Setting a twenty dollar bill on the bar, Max used his fingers to push it closer to the bartender's side of the counter. The small lights above them caused the glitter speckled over the recklessly applied blue nail polish to shimmer in the otherwise dim area of the bar, and when the man standing next to him took an obvious notice of this, Max withdrew his hand quickly.

It wouldn't matter in an hour, he reminded himself. In an hour, that stage would make everything odd about a regular person somehow seem interesting and attractive.

He smiled when the bartender turned back and placed the two shots on the bar.

"Both for you?" The guy chuckled, eyeing Max's frame and shaking his head.

"No," Max answered as he took them, attempting to position his hand in a such a way that his fingertips weren't so exposed. "I don't drink."

His head downcast as he moved away from the bar, Max turned directly into the body behind.

"Oh, I'm so sorry," he said quickly, a sudden heat dancing beneath the skin of his cheeks.

"I'm fine," she answered in a voice so melodic it lured Max's eyes upward immediately. He blinked, head shifting as if to remove him from a trance. Her eyes, in the reflection of the yellow-burning lamps, appeared almost golden. She exhaled a small chuckle, her brows lifting, then she looked to the glasses in his hands. "It looks like we had some casualties, though."

Max's brows creased briefly and then his sense of self awareness was revived. Looking down, seeing that both drinks had been expelled from their glasses by the sudden force, Max's shoulders fell. He turned back to face the bar, setting the glasses down.

"Two more?" The bartender chuckled.

He nodded, smiling thinly.

The woman leaned over the bar. "Those are on me." She looked to Max.

"Oh, you don't have to——."

"Both for you?" she asked, and Max's eyes narrowed briefly. She couldn't have heard what the man said, and she didn't seem to be mocking him.

"No." He smiled a bit. "They're for my friends."

"Not a shot guy, huh?"

"You could say that," he answered, not wanting to see the aversion with which his sober lifestyle was often met in these types of places on the beautiful features of his new acquaintance.

"Hm." Her eyes narrowed, falling away from his bright blue eyes and raking over his body—the leather jacket draped over a simple orange shirt, and the thin silver chain tucked inside its collar. "I'm going to guess you like something sweeter." She smiled.

"Oh, no, I just——."

She tapped on the bar. "Add a Dirty Shirley and a Manhattan to that."

"You got it," the bartender said, setting the two shots on

the bar and turning back to the array of bottles on the shelves behind him.

Max reached toward his back pocket, ready to remove another bill from his wallet, but her hand intercepted his.

He looked down to the connection quickly. Heat seemed not only to radiate from her hand, but also move into his. He felt the sensation as tangible as her hand itself, feeling the way the heat seemed to roll off of her like waves and creep inside the pores of his skin as water seeping into the sand.

"I said it's on me." She grinned.

"No, I ran into you. I couldn't——."

"You could, you can, you are." She raised her brows toward the bartender as he set the other two drinks in front of her. "This one…" She lifted one of the glasses, filled with a clear liquid, and offered it to him. "Is for you."

"Oh, I don't…" He bit his lower lip briefly. "Are you sure? I feel bad taking these as it is."

"Don't feel bad," she said, taking his free hand into hers again, the warmth caressing his skin before slithering inside it, and placed the mixed drink in his palm. "I'm happy to support the arts," she winked.

His brows creased as he looked into irises still, under closer inspection, the color of a paling sun. She didn't seem the type to listen to his music, or to even know he was a person who created any at all. But if she was supportive of the music, he thought it best to politely accept her offer. Surely, Craig would drink it.

"Well," he swallowed somewhat thickly, worried over how swollen his tongue suddenly felt, then he smiled to her, "Thank you. I appreciate it."

"Well, I appreciate you," she grinned. Something devious inside the knowing glance she gave the glass, she added,

"Enjoy."

He smiled once more, watching the way her lips never parted when she returned the gesture, giving her an air of nonchalance he hadn't been able to manufacture with her. Her eyes lingered on him briefly as she turned to face the bar, her velvet dress allowing her to slip easily onto one of its stools. When their connection was lost entirely, Max stepped away from the bar and headed back toward their small prep room.

His eyes roamed the area before the stage. As always, he marveled at the way the people closest to it were packed together and how the space between shoulders increased when proximity to the stage decreased.

The most intriguing thing about having so many bodies tightened into such a small section, however, was that it had no real boundaries. There were no walls, no barriers, no chains. It was as if the floor, where it aligned with the stage, also had a ledge from which to fall, and they stood almost on top of one another just to avoid the dreadful decent.

While it was endearing to see such a collective, there was always a disheartening factor. Much like the duality of man in general, there were opposite forces at work inside a group of men.

Packed together, shoulder to shoulder, closer to strangers than in any other scenario, nine out of ten faces were illuminated by the cool lights of phone screens. In an otherwise dimly lit bar, the technology cast on their faces made them appear robotic—unmoving facial structures, monotone voices grunting "yeah" and "uh-huh" without ever really hearing what was said to them. An entire generation on autopilot.

Max smiled sadly, reminding himself that in just an

hour's time he had the opportunity to pull them from their illusion of connection, how he'd wear his heart on his sleeve, right between his thick leather bracelet and his silver one, exposing his soul to them, feeling them come to life in the remembrance of a similar feeling. He liked being the one to remind them that whatever sadness they connected to in his solemn songs was temporary, and he loved seeing their expressions light up when the following one-hundred-eighty seconds of his soul reminded them that there was hope beyond the struggle.

He couldn't imagine the woman he'd just met standing in this crowd. He couldn't imagine her dancing freely to his music, or even smiling widely enough to sing along. There was something so strange about her— off putting but for no real reason at all. She was attractive, clean, and quite friendly. Maybe it was something inside the fiery touches that created the discomfort. Maybe not. Maybe it was Max's shy nature that felt immediately intimidated by someone so bold. He couldn't be certain.

His eyes lowered quickly, confusion creasing his forehead. He looked over his shoulder toward the bar. It didn't feel like she knew who he was, but the feeling of someone's focus on him while his feet were level with theirs was unusual.

Causal interactions were rarely causal when so much of who one is internally is at everyone's fingertips, and respect wasn't earned through merit. No, not these days.

These days, respect was given to anyone with a handsome face or melodic voice. If someone had both, the way Max did, gaining such a position of importance was even easier. Still, there was a darker side to such recognition.

Were his defined jawline and radiant blue eyes what originally drew people's interest to his music, or were they the sole reason for the interest? Did it matter what he said? What he sang? Would it matter less if he looked differently?

When he reached the door to his green room, Max leaned his shoulder against it, causing a few of pieces of its chipping paint to separate from the rusted metal. He inhaled once through his nose rather deeply. Then, trying to let go of the troublesome thoughts bombarding him about himself, his followers, and his new, nameless friend, he released it.

Licking his lower lip into his teeth, and shaking his head at himself, Max used his shoulder to push the door open and went back into the room with Craig.

Placing the glasses on the table next to Craig, he said, "One's for Phil."

"Yeah, yeah," Craig said, quickly throwing back one of the shots.

Max turned away from him, the mixed drink still in his other hand. His steps were lazy, eyes focused on the fizzing inside the glass. He pulled it close to him, hunching his shoulders around it as he leaned over it to sniff.

His eyes moved to their corners, chin turning in Craig's direction slightly. After turning back, he brought the glass to his lips, wondering if it was the curiosity of the drink's taste or of the person who ordered it that felt so tempting. Still, he hadn't had an opportunity like this before—one that practically forced the liquor into his hand. And with no Philip around to guilt-trip him. Maybe it worked as some sort of fate. Maybe he needed to drink. Just a little. Hadn't alcohol helped so many of the great musicians before him? Maybe it hadn't helped them, but they all certainly partook, so it obviously didn't hurt.

As he tilted the glass, he felt the fizzing of soda tickle his lips. He smelled the alcohol, but it wasn't very strong, not overwhelming at all. He opened his lips and let the liquid spill over them.

Craig sat with his elbow on his knee, looking up to Max sideways. "What's with you?" he asked sharply, his lips curling.

"Nothing," Max said, turning and sitting on the decrepit couch. Feeling so out of place with the glass in his hand, Max was careful to keep his hand over its liquid, as if its color confirmed or countered anything, and his eyes fluttered about around Craig, the inside of his lip stuck in his teeth.

Though he tried his best to be innocuous, the battered couch whined against the sound of his jeans. A large hunk of foam spilled out of one of the cushions.

"Got some Sprite?" Craig's brows raised.

"Yeah." His brows creased as he looked to it. "Or maybe 7 Up. I'm not sure."

"You didn't order it?"

"Uh, no…" He stammered. "No, a woman did."

"A woman did?" Craig slid against the arm of the opposite couch. "She coming up to the party after?"

"No."

"Why not?"

"I didn't invite her."

"Again, why not?"

"Because I'm not going to be there——."

"Man, we've been to three stops and you've already got a notebook filled with lyrics and poems and whatever else you sit around writing. You need to lighten up."

"Well, if it makes you feel any better, this isn't just Sprite in this glass."

"Yeah. Thanks, Sherlock," he said. "Let me see."

"What? Why?"

"To make sure you're not getting roofied, little girl," he

teased, taking the glass.

Max shook his head, his lips pursed.

After taking a sip, Craig's lips curled. "Awfully sweet," he said, handing it back to Max.

"I don't think it's too bad," Max said, lifting the glass hesitantly. He took care to drink from the side Craig hadn't, and his eyes glanced around a bit before he tilted it enough to taste the drink again. He could handle this.

"Okay," Philip said as he entered, "Drums are set and I checked your guitar and mic."

"Thanks," Max said. "There's a shot for you."

Philip's eyes glanced over to the table near Craig, his hands moving to his hips. "Uh-huh," his head tilted, brows creasing as he looked to the glass in Max's hand. "That's not water, I take it."

He shook his head slowly.

"It's vodka," Craig said, standing to leave the room and check his own instrument.

Philip's eyebrows raised as he looked at Craig, then back to Max. "How many did you have?"

"Just this one," Max said.

"Okay." Philip eyed him for a moment longer, watching him lean his head forward and brush his hand into the thick blonde locks of his swept back hair. "Any particular reason you decided to imbibe tonight?"

"It was offered," Max said lowly, the fingernail of his thumb picking at a small chip in the glass.

"It's been offered plenty of times in the last nine or ten years. Didn't answer my question."

"I don't know. This girl…" His lips closed and a breath left his nostrils.

"Oh, so it's a girl. Okay. I thought we learned our lesson.

The type of girl you meet at shows isn't usually your type of girl. Or I guess we should say you're not usually their type of guy. One super slow, super sad song per set is more than enough. I really don't need—."

"No, it's not like that." He exhaled, looking down to the drink. "I mean, she was nice, really pretty, but something was off about her."

"Off like what?"

He shook his head. If his reasons for feeling uncomfortable were warm hands and gold eyes, Philip would think he was crazy, or worse, very drunk. He didn't need his friend to worry, not right before a show, and there was no reason to, anyway. Even though Philip seemed to forget that they were the same age, Max was a grown man. If he wanted a drink, it wasn't anyone's decision but his own. If he felt uncomfortable, he knew how to steer clear. Everything was fine. Max wasn't going to let this strange need to protect him that Philip's had since they were eight take his mind away from his drums.

"I'm good." He smiled to Philip.

"All right." Philip tossed a water bottle to him. "Have a drink before we go on."

"I have a drink," he said.

"You have vodka." His brow tweaked. "Really don't need you slurring your words or staggering up there."

Max nodded, twisting the lid loose as Philip went back toward the side stage.

Max leaned against the door frame, watching his bandmates as they prepared to take the stage. He looked down to the bottle of water in his hand and debated briefly about switching to a different clear drink instead. After all, he spent his time backstage in jeans and T-shirts, never drinking anything stronger than coffee, and feeling uncomfortable every time someone swore. What was he doing singing to crowds of dark eyeliner and darker clothes, bringing his guitar to life in heavy riffs, and practically screaming into the microphone if he wasn't going to live up to that image?

He exhaled through his nostrils, eyes on the ground as he pulled up his shirt. His chain moved with the fabric, falling against his now-bare chest. He never took it off. But he wondered if he should stop wearing it on stage.

Unconsciously, his fingers moved to the chain at his neck, and he slid the crucifix across it. Why was he here? Really, what was his purpose? It wasn't this representation of all that was deviant. It wasn't spikes and chains and anarchy. He felt inside himself that he was here to write music, to shape words into sentiments, not just sentences, and use that creative force to inspire something in others. He just wasn't sure he ever knew what it was meant to inspire—especially if what he looked like mattered more than what he said.

He frowned, his eyes falling to his hands as his left brushed over his right. Some retained heat from the woman at bar remained inside its tissues, slithering around inside him like an invisible serpent.

His eyes lifted with his head, and he peered around the door to the direction of the bar. If he squinted, he could see her. She sat alone, one leg crossed over the other, her velvet dress clinging to the curvature of her body, as she stirred two straws into her drink. She didn't fit in amongst the crop tops and corsets surrounding her, but it wasn't for anything conspicuous or extreme. She simply wasn't the same.

His brows furrowed as he watched Philip move to the

stage, a myriad of screams and calls filling the air, and then he slammed his sticks against his drums a few times.

It was time for them to go on, time for him to sing the hymns of his heart, and he hoped, for everyone there who didn't know him, he'd at least reach one of them with his words.

The lights flashed in time with Philip, each kick of the drum at his feet pounding against Max's chest in time with his heartbeat. He watched Craig rush onto the stage, heard the screams of the people at his feet, and then, waiting for his exact cue, that perfect moment, Max walked slowly, head hanging, shoulders slouched, up to the microphone. Lifting his chin as he rolled his head, he let his tongue escape his slightly parted lips. He brought his hand to his cheek, leaning his face into it as his eyes closed, and when the Craig's arm rushed down the strings of his second-hand guitar, making it cry out almost deafeningly to the mass before them, Max's head shot up, eyes widened, and he gripped the microphone before him with a sudden jolt of fearless intensity.

The stage was set, the actors performed their roles, and now it was time for Max, focal point of the setting of sexed up, drugged out rockers, to be who he really was.

His lungs expanded, all hope of connection vibrating his vocal chords as his eyes scanned the people at his feet. He loved the small venues with no barriers because he loved the chance to be so close.

Taking the mic from its stand, Max moved around it, bending his knees before the crowd. He sang in time with two girls, their hands reaching for him, and he used his free hand to hold onto them.

Watching him from her spot at the bar, Malum's eyes narrowed. He looked as a preacher providing sermon to repentant souls about to die. The way they reached for him in desperation, their mouths crying out for his attention, for one second of the feel of his eyes on theirs looked exactly the way harrowing souls in hell would look if they were somehow given a glimpse of God. It was impressive. He was ahead of schedule—that is, if the schedule they intercepted was accurate.

Resplendent eyes shimmering even in the darkness, she focused her gaze, not on Max, who now stood on the opposite side of the stage, someone's phone in his hand as he danced to the beat of Philip's drums, but onto the stage light at his feet.

It shook, vibrations from her eyes urging it away from its set path. All at once, it spun, hitting Max directly in the eyes. After his attention was on the light, it shifted again, this time toward the crowd. Its blue light moved beyond the lifted phones and snapping photos, over the heads of the flock beneath him, and into the bar area.

There, cast in shining blue, sat the strange woman who practically burned his hand with a gentle caress. Her eyes on him caused his head to rear back in surprise. His brows creased. He'd never been able to see someone so clearly in such a small, dim venue, and certainly not while he was on stage safe inside the small rectangle of the only light inside the place.

He inhaled sharply, looking over to Craig and then to Philip. Neither were affected. Neither seemed to notice. He looked back to the crowd as the song finished and his confusion was hidden in the darkened seconds of between-song-silence. Thank God he wasn't singing when that happened. Even the thought of messing up a performance was almost as disappointing as if he'd actually done it.

The lights came back up, and his eyes moved directly to the back, but the people inside it were draped in blackness.

It was a fluke, he figured, and picked up the guitar at his feet.

Screams rose from the crowd when they saw him slip the strap over his bare skin. Smiling a bit, he leaned into the microphone, and the next song commenced.

He preferred the songs that didn't require his musical talents because he liked being eye level with his audience. He liked singing in tune with them, seeing their faces light up when he looked into their eyes. However, the songs that needed his guitar playing were enjoyable for other reasons. Typically they were softer songs, songs that mattered most to him, songs that were more his spirit than his creativity. He liked being able to move his eyes slowly from face to face, to see them truly reacting to the words when the song was slow enough to really hear them. He liked the calm he created in them. Their phones were down, their heads were up, eyes lifted toward the ceiling as if they were peering up into the heavens and Max, draped in the sheer blues and soft pinks of the stage lights, was an angel parting the darkness of the night and easing them into a hypnotic three minutes of pure human to human connection.

In these modern times, attention was everything. Not just for the way it'd become a commodity, but for what it meant when it was shared by individuals. After all, Max considered, his left hand strumming at the gentle chords while his lips pressed against the cool metal of the microphone, the only real way someone could prove their devotion to their partner was by locking their phone and tucking it away when they sat across from one another.

All of these people, most who hadn't known he existed seven minutes prior to this moment, were giving him their attention. There wasn't one phone lifted, not even to record his singing. It was unusual, the intensity of it, and he wondered briefly if this was what it had been like to be a performer of the 80's, the 90's even. He felt he might collapse under the immense pressure of so many eyes.

Still, it was miraculous. So many people truly lost inside the moment, truly experiencing it. They weren't seeing him through the lens of a screen nor were they watching the sounds escape an image of his lips, no. They were seeing him, watching his mouth as the words were produced. How powerful.

As his gaze slowly moved from eyes to eyes, they found their way to the back of the bar again.

There she was, there were her eyes, as focused on him as theirs were, but she wasn't entranced, not in the way everyone below him seemed to be. No, her eyes communicated with him, sending him images of himself above the sea of people. How reflective those golden irises were. How shining inside the darkness. It seemed to break where it met her, her heat radiating through the bar and surrounding him with a gentle embrace.

A shaken inhale sounded against the microphone, and Max quickly looked back to his audience. They hadn't noticed the slip up. In honesty, it probably added some sincerity to what he sang. Not that the words were disingenuous, he'd simply relived them so many times that the painful experience that was their source felt more surreal than remembered.

Not in this moment. In this moment it felt as if he were far from the stage in some random city in Ohio. He felt he was back in his hometown, hours away, and trapped inside the small room with the woman who'd broken his heart. He could see her face clearly, hearing the words she'd said that night as if she were standing next to him on the stage and speaking them into his microphone. You're so stupid for someone so smart. You're throwing this away for God? Who is God in this day and age? God is nobody. God is nothing. Max had disagreed. He still did. Whatever Jessie said that night, no matter how clearly the memory echoed inside this strange exploration of his lyrics, Max's faith never faltered.

He'd give up anything before he lost his soul, and that was a lot of the message masked inside his harsh vocals and heavy guitar.

Focusing on the music as he tried to blink the memory away, Max's eyes fell again onto the faces that had been blurred behind the memory of Jessie's. He was in the small bar again.

Time seemed to slow, even as he turned his head. Everything moved in single frames of vision. He felt each tiny muscle move beneath the skin of his forehead, the confusion trickling over his features in slow pulls instead of one great force of emotion.

His tongue brushed over his lower lip, head turning back to the direction of the bar. Golden eyes still gazing at him, she somehow escaped the time loop everyone else was caught inside. He blinked, and by the time his eyes were open again, the crowd below him looked up to him in real time. The chords of the guitars weren't muffled, the beat of the drum wasn't slowed.

That woman, he thought, watching her as she quickly moved from her bar stool and rushed toward the door, she had something to do with this. But how?

He cleared his throat, blinking a bit rapidly to moisten

eyes that had grown dry in the elongated moment he hadn't blinked inside.

His chest rose perceptibly heavy to everyone in the crowd, but their eyes still gazed up to him lovingly. It was as if they hadn't noticed any misstep in his music, they hadn't seen the transcendental slip in time. He swallowed thickly, letting the air escape his lungs in another shaking mess of syllables that felt more like gasps of air than actual words, but the two girls at his left foot still sang on with him.

He smiled to them when his eyes found them, and finally, for the first time since the gentle melody began, one of them used the fingers gripping her phone to lift it.

As she moved, others moved. A sea of mannequins coming to life before his very eyes, but they didn't stare into their phones to see him. They raised them, white lights shining from the tops of pink and silver and black rectangles, a modern flame in the age-old performance of connectivity, and he felt suddenly at peace with everything he'd done. Everything that led him here— whether it was his heartbroken past, his private school background, or the shallow deviancy he felt when standing in a room full of smoke and sweat— was a small pebble in the cobblestone street of his life's path. He knew in that moment that this was where he needed to be, this was where he was meant to be, and seeing so many eyes, the windows to so many souls, was the image meant for him.

He glanced up to the corner of the bar quickly, swallowing between words the immovable mass of nerves this strange woman caused him. An understanding seized him inexplicably that she hadn't been what caused this strange slowing of time, but that she was, indeed, somehow related to it.

At least he couldn't see those off putting golden eyes anymore. He looked back to the people beneath him, comforted by the loss of her focus, and somehow sang more powerfully than he ever had before.

Standing at his merch-table, Max watched the headlining band with reverence. There was something about the way they moved, each member's body so in tune with the music, that made every show entrancing for him. He almost forgot where he was for a moment.

He hated missing their last song. His place at the side of the stage was always claimed, but this particular venue's rush to clear the building as soon as the show was done was made extremely clear. So he stood in the back, still glancing up to his fellow musicians while he folded T-shirts and put them into a large cardboard box.

"Maxwell," Philip said, patting his shoulder. "Almost everything's away, huh?"

"Yeah."

"Cool. So, if I head up to the room with, uh…" He turned to look toward the bar, and Max saw a tall man with shaggy brown hair wink to him. After tapping his finger on his lip for a moment, Philip said, "I think his name's Blake. I'm not sure. I'll figure it out."

"Yeah, go for it," Max said, chuckling. Philip chased men the way Craig chased women, always leaving Max to handle any business related side of their craft. "I'll get this out to the van."

"You coming up right after or are you finding a coffee shop?"

"What do you think?" He smirked at Philip playfully.

"I think I'm gonna be looking through a notebook of new poems tomorrow morning."

Max nodded to him, smiling.

"All right. I'll see you later."

"See you," Max said, turning to grab the second box from the floor behind him.

"Hi," a gentle voice said, causing a slight jump in him when he turned back to face the table.

Max stood frozen, eyeing her cautiously. Her eyes were gray, not golden, and her hair was curled and blonde, not dark and straightened, but her face was almost identical to the woman he met at the bar.

"Hi," he said, looking down shyly. "Sorry."

"Don't apologize." She smiled, extending her hand. "I'm Bonum."

"Bonum?"

"Yes." She smiled. "Odd name to you, I'm sure."

"No, it's nice. Very pretty."

"It means 'good'."

He smiled because he felt something so innately good around her.

"Did you enjoy the show?"

"I did." Her brows jumped, "I enjoyed the softer song, the one about the young lady who left you."

"Oh." His eyes lowered, and he bit his lip briefly, then he looked back up to her. "Thank you."

"It's very poignant, but its message is quite powerful."

"Its message?" His eyes narrowed. He was careful with the words he chose while writing that one. Nothing threatened to expose him as a fraudulent bad boy like the reason the subject of that song left him.

Her eyes fell to his neck, her head tilting a bit when she

looked to the small crucifix on his chain, and she smiled. Then it shifted to the opposite direction when she stared into the bit of his chest tattoo that peaked out from behind his leather jacket. Reaching for him, she pushed his jacket aside so she could see the entire piece. He looked to his chest, then up to her. She pursed her lips, brows raising, and she scoffed disappointment. "Well," she said, eyes looking down when she released his coat. "You don't follow Leviticus, but at least your chastity is still intact."

He recoiled, brows raising in shock. "My what?" A nervous laugh left his lips in a sharp breath. "I'm not—."

"Your song." She smiled, standing normally again. "'Waiting', right?"

"Right," he bit the inside of his lip, another heavy breath leaving him shakily as he looked around from his lowered head. When he made certain no one was in evidence, he looked up to her, "Right, okay. But how…" His brows creased. "How could you know what that was about?"

Her brows lifted, eyes widened. She looked as if she had to really consider how to reply. "I have a talent for interpretation," she said, then leaning forward she whispered, "But I don't think it would hurt the young people of your flocks to hear that such a commitment is still okay to make." She winked.

"My flocks?" His brows creased again, hand moving unconsciously to the pendant on his chain.

"Those people," she said, "they were here for you, you know that, right?"

"No, they—they were here for Changing—."

"You felt it tonight," she said, and his lips parted.

His eyes widened, a strange sense that this woman knew more of him than she could be able to know, even from an internet search, caused the hair of his arms to stand on end.

"You did, didn't you?" Her eyes widened excitedly. "You felt that sensation of time shifting around you?"

"What? How do you know about that?"

"I saw it." She smiled.

"I didn't see you." His brows creased.

"You didn't need to then."

"Do I—I need to now?"

"Does it feel like you need me now?" Her brows creased, a genuine concern evident in her voice.

"I don't— I don't even know who you are."

"It's okay." She smiled, placing her hand gently on top of his. A cooling tingle washed away from her hand and spilled onto his, filling him with a sense of calming relief he hadn't known existed. "I know you."

"How—?"

She smiled widely. "Silly. You're a rock star." She winked.

"But that's not—that's not how you know me, is it?"

"You're an excellent poet." The gray inside her eyes moved, but it wasn't the glistening of lights inside irises. The color itself moved, rolling throughout the circular iris like bouts of clouding smoke. Maybe something cleaner. Maybe the fog after a cleansing rainstorm.

"Who are you?" he whispered, mesmerized by the vision. She pulled her hand away.

"Just a friend," she said, her face so serene that Max felt any worry he had about her slip into nothingness. Her body began to turn away from him, and she smiled. "I'll see you around, rock star."

"Wait," he said, rounding the table.

Pausing, she looked to him, turning only her head toward him, not her body.

He inhaled through his parted lips, neurons firing at rapid paces, trying to find the appropriate words to say. He felt he knew her, that there was some unspoken connection lingering in the spaces between them, that the air wasn't invisible or empty. Something within her, maybe a surrounding aura or some easily perceived energy, was caressing him. He felt it as distinctly as a hand against his own or lips touching his cheek. Something carnal, but chaste. Something holy, but not entirely spiritual.

"Why do I feel like I know you?"

"Maybe some part of you does," she offered without providing any real answer. She grinned, but nothing mischievous. Max was certain she was incapable of anything so impure.

Maybe it wasn't the face of the earlier woman he'd dreamt into existence. Maybe it was this face, so similar to hers, that understood him so completely—and after his experience with Jessie, more than he'd ever wanted anyone to again.

His brows pulled together a bit, his head shaking. Somehow he felt entirely exposed standing before her, but no matter how deeply her eyes gazed into him, he felt no discomfort. Vulnerability, when presented to Bonum, felt uncharacteristically safe.

By nature, the baring of his soul had always proven to be much more terrifying than the baring of his flesh, but even in the recesses of his mind, standing on stage, witnessing eyes raking across his chest and stomach made him feel some sort of embarrassment.

When the lips of young girls would be drawn into their mouths, when their eyes bore the signs of carnal desires, he felt somewhat corrosive. Why should he display the parts of him that could be so easily desired, and to what effect? He felt sinful. Even the woman at the bar, her eyes on his neck, his jaw, his hands made him feel that his entirely covered appendages were sexualized. Maybe it's why, despite her kindness, he felt uneasy. Maybe something about Bonum made him realize that.

Regardless of the way it felt with everyone else, the subtlety of the exposure, or how magnified it felt with the earlier woman, it was entirely different here in this exact moment.

Standing before Bonum, his flesh meant nothing. She could see him entirely without clothing and he'd feel no shame. He could perceive somehow through no words and no gestures that his body didn't matter to her. Even his face, so praised by the masses who listened to his creations, and doted on by those who hadn't heard a single song, wasn't the focus of her eyes when they looked directly at it.

She saw him for who he was, not what he looked like, and in this world of deceit and gimmicks, illusion and disenchantment, that meant more to Max than anything the last decade of touring ever provided.

It also seemed to confirm, in some unexplained manner, that his spirit was in fact intact, that it existed, a part of him as true and tangible as his arm, and, trapped inside a lifestyle of materialism and pleasure, confirmed that Max was still correct to deny such endeavors for the sake of his soul.

All the while he stood before her, silently staring, eyes flickering back and forth between her serene left and calming right, the words stayed within Max's mind. He parted his lips to speak, but nothing would pass through them. Nothing was clear enough to voice into existence. All he could perceive was feeling, not thought or action, and he felt the muscles in his face struggling to fight the impending tears that threatened to form under the magnitude of such a bond.

He swallowed thickly, breaking their connection as he exhaled through his nostrils loudly, then he looked back up to her. "Thank you," he said, though he wasn't certain why.

The corners of her perfectly pouty lips rose ever so slightly. Her eyelids blinked over the shining silvers of once gray skies slowly, very slowly. She reached for him again, this time, her hand pushing beneath his jacket and settling down on the dark black evidence of bloody, scabbing, permanent and purposeful scars on his chest. He felt his heart beat rapidly, and she looked gently to her hand and smiled.

"I feel it as strongly as you do," she said, looking back up to him. "Don't ever forget what you are inside this."

Their eyes connected for a moment longer while he felt her hand, and its icy calm, slip away from him.

She smiled again, tender and sincere, and then, as she turned to walk away, she took his hand in hers. Squeezing it once, she released it as quickly as she'd taken it, then her eyes blinked forward and were lost to him.

His focus stayed on her as she made her way through the crowd, still huddled before the stage as if tightly bound by some great electrical cord. When she vanished inside the crowd, he looked down, lifting his own hand to the tattoo over his heart.

He licked his lips as he turned back toward the table, brows still furrowed as he looked over his shoulder in the direction she'd gone. He looked down to the boxes on the table, his hand still pressing against the large Roman numerals on his pectoral, when something caught his eye.

There, lying on the black sheet over the table, was a small, but almost blindingly shiny, circle of silver. He picked it up, determining now that it was a pendant, and his lips parted. Looking over his shoulder again, seeing no trace of Bonum, he exhaled quickly, looking back to it. Saint Gemma. Patron of those who seek to resist temptation.

Everything was different after that show, after Bonum. The feel of the cardboard box was different, each tiny particle somehow obvious beneath Max's fingertips. Nothing as a whole mattered the way it did prior, only tiny the pieces of varying matter that created this perceivable world.

As he carried it out the doors, Max understood this place in an entirely new viewpoint. Each individual standing in the group, each soul, though they dressed similarly, moved the same, all staring either to their phones or to any of the bands' vocalists, were all so vastly different.

When he watched them earlier piling in through the doors, taking the same small step closer and closer to the table where they extended the same wrist for the same hot pink paper bands, Max saw them as a collective force.

When he noticed the way they all rushed to the stage, hands spreading widely to grab hold of it to claim a spot, Max found it comforting that so much human activity seemed to be hardwired into the brains of strangers, of people of varying ages, creeds, sexes.

Max realized, as he opened the back doors of their van, that he'd always approached crowds as simply that—a crowd. He never seemed to take close consideration to the fact that every person standing within the sea at his feet was thinking something entirely different. One might be singing his words, but what was she thinking when he bent down to her and took her hand in his? What was the person next to her thinking? Were there people thinking they were going to check the band out when they left? Were there people counting down the seconds until their set was done? Regardless of how similar they all were in their stance, their minds were running rapidly, no two thoughts the same.

How many of them benefited from the solemnity of his slow song? How many were cathartic when they tried to scream their pain away with him? How many didn't hear the words at all? How many didn't care?

He set the box on the wiry carpet of the van and pushed it further inside. How many of those young souls might benefit from words not so delicately written? What would happen to the individual in the crowd, even just the one who needed it, to hear that it's okay if he or she didn't participate in all the temptations spiraling around him or her?

He licked his lips, contemplating his own choices—not the actions, or inaction, but of the way he'd written the experiences after.

Masking the truth of the scenario, fearful of the reactions to his personal conduct, not wanting the torment of being a joke because of it, Max wondered if any of his so-called morality mattered, then, at all.

He took his tattered teal notebook from the back of the van before closing the doors, then he stood aside. Looking across the road, as if by divine miracle, was a tiny twenty-four-hour coffee shop. He wouldn't have to wander the streets tonight, nor would he have to settle for sitting on the curb outside the hotel to get a few minutes alone to create.

After looking down both sides of the empty street twice, Max crossed it, all the while contemplating the weirdness of its lack of headlights and the silence of the sidewalks.

Even when nothing was open, most cities at midnight bustled. Even if was only two men walking down the road, or just the sound of cars on side streets, there was something to signify life. All the bars were still open, clubs were playing music with heavy bass lines loudly. But he heard nothing. There wasn't even wind.

He stopped before he entered the coffee shop, his left hand, still tingling from Bonum's cool touch, pressed against the thick ridged metal handle of the glass door. Looking around once more, determined to find even just one sign of life in this town, Max saw only the lights of the club he'd just played in turning off. The darkness made darker without the buzzing of their golden orbs. Golden orbs, he thought, brows creasing slightly. How they shined in the dark corner of that club.

He shook his head, pushing the door and entering the shop.

"Hi," the man smiled to him, standing up and setting his phone on the counter beside him.

"Hi," he said, looking to the man's name tag, "Tyler."

"Whatcha having?"

"Largest coffee you have, please."

"Sir, I am not sure you realize what you're getting into." His left brow arched over his playful eyes and he turned to the wall. "See, you've got your small, your medium, your large…" His eyes went back to Max. "We do super larges, extra super larges, and…" He leaned forward a bit, muttering from the corner of his mouth, "The only thing that gets me through these night shifts." He stood straight again. "The Mega Ultra Large."

"I think I can handle it," he said, chuckling.

"All right," Tyler said, flicking his wrist to take one of the Mega Ultra Large cups from its stack. His brows raised as he clicked the marker in his hand. "Just don't be running around here, bouncing off the walls. Some of us…" He nodded his head toward an open door to the side of his station. Max could see someone's head slumped over against the wall inside. "Like to get paid to sleep." He looked up to him, "What's your name?"

"Max," he said.

"Mhm," Tyler said, scribbling his marker against the cup. "Seven dollars, twenty-four cents, please."

Handing him a ten, Max dropped his change in the bucket labeled "GET ME OUT OF HERE", and chuckled.

"Don't think you're getting a free refill for that," Tyler said, his hand on his hip. "You're pretty, but you ain't that pretty."

Max smiled, his eyes dropping to the floor shyly as he shook his head.

"There you go, Max," Tyler said, leaning over the counter as he placed the cup in front of him.

"Thanks, Tyler." He smiled.

"Oh, no, thank you." He grinned, watching Max's black jeans closely as he made his way into a small booth by the window.

Though he sat with his back toward the counter, Max couldn't help but feel the focus of eyes still on him. His brows creased. It was that strange attention again— that attention that came without appropriate setting. Here he was, eye level with another person, and that person seemed all too eager to engage with him.

He glanced over his shoulder. Tyler had resumed his seated position, but now he was talking on his phone. When his eyes shifted to Max's, he smiled. It felt wholesome somehow, as if everything that happened in the last few hours since he left the stage were in perfect harmony with one another.

He looked down to his notebook, flipping hastily to find a blank page. The crisp white sheet waiting for his innermost thoughts, Max took a deep breath in. He reached for the Mega Ultra Large cup and brought it to his lips. Taking a giant swig of the caffeinated drink, he leaned over his paper, assuming the position, and lifted his pen.

When it pressed into the paper, it took control. This was how writing always went for Max. He lost himself to it, giving himself over to the power of his pen, letting the flood from his fingers wash over the page and leave in its wake all the thoughts the many faces of the day stirred about within him.

Everyone he met, they felt close in a way that had never made sense, not until tonight. Tonight, after meeting Bonum, after meeting his friend from the bar, it all became clear. Their faces were no longer blurs lost to sea. He saw each of them inside his mind as sharp and contrasted as a photograph, but not one taken on a phone, lost to the circuitry of hand-held computers and the delicacy of glass screens. No, he saw them as real, tangible portraits— snapshots flashed into physicality. He could hold them, touch them, and in some strange way when he wrote about them, the nerve endings in his fingertips fired as if he were.

When he remembered the girl in the crowd, the one who knew his songs, he could see her face even more clearly than he had in the smoky room of flickering lights in darkness. She had pink streaks in her raven hair. He blinked his eyes, shaking his head as he marveled over how he suddenly knew this. He didn't recall seeing them in the moment, but here, with his pen against the page, he could count exactly how many she had. He saw her shimmering brown eyes, the small bow curve of her upper lip, even the speckles of glitter that shined across them in the ever-changing lights were deeply defined.

What if she needed it? He thought, and a flicker of Bonum's face entered his mind. He stopped, looking down to the page. What if she needed to hear him say it was okay for her to refrain? What if it was her, the one person in a sea of fifty who already admired him, who needed to witness before her eyes, hand in hand, his lips forming the words he hadn't been able to write so clearly?

Max's shoulders hunched in, a terrible pain shooting inside his stomach. What had he really been afraid of all this time? Of some guys behind the safety of their screens hurling the same insults at thirty years old that they had in high school? Of yet another girl leaving him because she couldn't wait? What was so wrong with the choices he'd made? Why did he feel he had to hide his nature away inside metaphors and overly manufactured hooks? It seemed in opposition of how it should be that, in this society, a deviation away from deviance wasn't seen as a positive attribute.

His message, the message of that slow song, maybe Bonum understood, but Max doubted that girl in the crowd did. Maybe he should've been more honest in his choice of words. Maybe instead of saying, "I can't wait forever," he should've quoted her directly. "I'm twenty-four. I'm not marrying anyone any time soon, and if you think I'm spending years waiting for you when it's so easy everywhere else, you're delusional."

It wasn't poetic. No one Max ever found interesting seemed to be. And no one ever told him when they said opposites attract that it was to such extreme extents. Then again, he considered, maybe it was his own fault for looking for morality in places that not only encouraged sin, but dressed it up in small skirts and drenched it in sweet liquors.

Still, reworking the lines that broke his heart didn't have to be as cryptic. Maybe making the reason for his ex's inability to wait clearer would've helped that girl so desperately reaching for him. Maybe sharing his reason for such a decision would have.

He licked his lower lip, brows tightened in a blending of guilt and disappointment. With the hand that held his pen, he reached for the cup. As he took another drink, his other hand moved for his pendant.

He stared at the page, determined now, to be more concise with what he said. He wouldn't ask Philip for advice on restructuring. He wouldn't ask him when to throw a "fuck" in for edge. Maybe being bombastic for the sake of it just made him a hack.

He'd write who he really was. Maybe Bonum would enjoy the product of that. Maybe she was right and someone might even benefit from it.

When he leaned back over the page, allowing himself to get lost inside the memories of the night, Max's pen pushed against the paper. It moved to its own accord, as usual, sailing smoothly from line to line. It was miraculous how differently it felt now that he was determined to hide less. He refused to be so shy any longer.

As his memories moved from face to face, seeing not just defined features, but also more clearly defined emotion, pure joy in the smiling faces, awe in the eyes of those who watched him open his lungs and scream for the first time, his attention was brought to a familiar face.

His eyes popped open. He lifted his pen. He wasn't sure what that woman with golden eyes made him feel.

He bit the inside of his jaw, lips open while he took a

deep breath in. Whatever it was, he was almost afraid to see it become clear when he wrote it down.

He blinked, shaking his head. After taking another drink, he tried to focus on the other faces, on the faces that didn't seem to thrill him as much as frighten him.

He couldn't.

Opening his eyes again, Max pursed his lips. His nose scrunched. Why would he feel afraid of her? Oh, yes, those warm hands. He wondered if he really was losing his mind.

Still, he had to admit, there was something disconcerting about golden eyes. He imagined they were contacts, but what if they weren't?

Again, he shook his head, lifting his hand to his hair and scratching at it. Focus, he thought.

Letting his eyes flutter closed again, his pen pushed down into the paper. He wrote of his disappointment in himself, of his guilt for claiming such morality while hiding it, of wondering why he clung to it so dearly when nothing of the world around him could be approved by it. He thought about the temptations, everything Bonum and Saint Gemma must expect him to face, and he wrote about his curiosity for it— What might the effects of two shots to his brain feel like? What might the sting of a needle in his arm do? What did the flesh of someone beautiful feel like against his own? Without his conscious consent, images of hands on his arms emerged from the dark recesses behind his eyelids. The weren't sharp at first, no recognizable features, but as they roamed along his biceps, the imperceptibly of their fingernails suddenly became black. When they brushed over his bare shoulders, he felt the heat exuding from them, and when they gripped him, tugging him downward, he found himself lying over a beautiful face, familiar but still unknown. When the idea of what her crimson lips might feel like against his own, he realized, leaning into her more closely, that her eyes were golden.

His eyes opened quickly again. He thought about the golden eyes, the beauty of the face surrounding them, and then the delicate wrists and bare arms exposed outside of her form fitting dress. He began to wonder consciously what her flesh might feel like, but stopped himself mid-thought.

Looking down to the paper, he saw, damning in its jet black ink, that he'd been writing all the ways such thoughts had been making him feel.

He frowned. These were not the types of writings he did after shows. These weren't things to be considered. The importance of his writing, his lyrics, his poetry, was understanding sanctity in a realm of sin. He didn't want to see his friends destroy themselves with never-emptying cups of booze, and boredom induced drug hazes. He worried that his best friends gave so much of their physicality away, so many pieces so widely scattered through the different cities of different countries, that eventually they might lose themselves entirely. The idea of seeing them, hollow cheeks and purple under-eyes, was as poetic as it was tragic, but knowing the subject of such profound art made its poignancy more wretched than powerful.

He looked around the empty shop, eyes catching Tyler's glazed over expression as his finger swiped mindlessly at his phone. There was no one here. Maybe there wouldn't be anyone in his hotel room either.

Exhaling loudly as he closed his notebook, Max frowned to its ripped cover. Scolding himself as he shook his head, he grabbed it, took his coffee cup, and exited the booth.

"Good night, Max," Tyler said when he saw his only customer begin to push the door open.

"Good night." He smiled.

Without thinking, Max crossed the street. He caught himself when yellow lines met his downcast eyes. He paused, looking to the road on either side of him, but it remained empty.

His brows raised as he shook his head at himself. He couldn't believe how out of it he was. His lips curled when he considered that one drink. It had hours to pass through his system, there was no way he could retain any effect it might have had on him. Or could he?

He passed the van, deciding not to drive it just in case, but kept his notebook with him. He wanted to write something significant this night, something that wasn't lost to him each time he considered the woman at the bar. How eerily she gazed at him during those quiet, slow motion moments of his music. Maybe the harsh lights and hollow insides of coffee shops weren't the best source of inspiration. He hoped the comfort of soft sheets and warm pillows might help him focus.

As he approached the hotel, Max's mind shut down completely. All the worry he had for himself now lost upon the sight before him. There, sitting on the curb in front of the hotel, was an after effect, no doubt, of Craig.

"Hey," he said softly, sitting down next to her.

She responded by lifting her head and sniffling.

"Are you okay?" he asked, swallowing thickly.

He hated seeing the remnants of great nights soured, of broken faces, heads in hands, contorted legs, ripped fishnets adorning knees pushed together, the artistry of a young girl's make up washed away by the salty rivers of regret, of hurt.

"Oh, God," she bellowed, throwing her head back in

exasperation. She jumped up quickly, but he followed.

"Wait, where are you going?" he asked, taking her wrist gently.

"Home." She sniffled, jerking her arm from him to dig around in the small clutch for keys.

"You might not want to drive when you're upset," he offered, careful with his wording. He knew to tread lightly, considering how many times he approached the hotels in various cities, how many times he stumbled onto a sight like this one. "You want a little coffee?" he asked, head lowered, eyes looking gently up to her, as he offered his Mega Ultra.

She snorted a laugh. "No, thanks."

He licked his lower lip into his mouth briefly. "Well," he stammered a bit, trying again, "Maybe just talking would—?"

"Yeah, I'm not gonna talk to you about what an asshole your band mate is."

"I mean…" He shrugged slightly. "I know he's not the greatest guy—."

"You don't even know which one I'm talking about."

"Trust me, I do." He nodded.

"It's not your job to fix it," she said harshly, but when she looked up to him she smiled. "But thank you for trying."

She zipped her bag when she retrieved the keys, and walked past him.

He turned. "Wait, are you sure you're okay to drive?"

"One glass of wine. I'll be fine."

Max smiled sadly as he watched the lights of an old red Chevy flash on and then off. He stood there, making sure she was safe inside, before he turned to the hotel.

Hopefully the debauchery was over. He really needed solace, and he hoped an empty hotel room wouldn't be too much to ask.

It was.

When he opened the door, his lips parted in the shock of the overwhelming number of faces. He couldn't believe they all fit. No wonder the rest of the city seemed so calm. All of its inhabitants must've found their way here.

With his grip still on the handle, Max took a step back, intending to close the door, and use it as a chair back. Maybe he could write in the hallway.

"Hey," Craig called to him, interrupting his plan.

Max's shoulder fell, his head falling back a bit.

"Listen, man," he said, pulling along a woman whose shoulders were caught inside his arm. He pointed to Max with his first finger, the others still wrapped around the neck of a beer bottle. "There's a girl here, she's perfect for you. I told her no way you'd show up. Told her that stick in your ass ain't coming out for nothing or no one," he chuckled, "But here you are!"

"No, Craig," he said wearily, shaking his head. "Who was the girl in the fishnets, by the way?"

"What girl?"

"One outside really upset, calling you, uh, something less than kind, we'll say."

He looked to the blonde inside his arm. His lips pursed, then he looked back to Max. "Beats me. Thought this was her. She must've been really mad, huh?" He snorted.

"Yeah, what'd you do?" Max tried again.

"Nothing," he said.

"Nothing he'll be doing again," Philip interceded, wrapping his own arm around the girl. "Come now, honey, we'll find you something fun to get into."

"Hey," Craig said, "she's the something fun I wanted to——."

"Stop." Philip lifted his finger, staring at Craig.

Craig lifted both his hands defensively, and when Philip ushered the girl back into a group of women, he looked to Max. "I hate that Mama Bear look he gives. Makes you feel that whole 'I'm not mad, I'm disappointed' thing."

"Yeah," Max deadpanned, still intending to leave, but when he turned his head away from Craig, his eyes caught the nightstand between the two beds of the hotel room.

Throwing his arm around Max and guzzling a few swings of the beer, Craig said, "Listen, this girl, she's been asking about you since we got here. Super hot." He closed one eye, freeing his pointer finger from around the neck of the beer bottle as he scanned the party. "There she is," he said, pointing to a beautiful woman with long dark hair and eerily gleaming eyes.

"Oh," Max said, wiggling out from under Craig's arm. "I don't know—."

"No," he said sternly. "No, I'm sick of you being a buzzkill. I'm sick of Philip keeping you a buzzkill. No. He ruins everyone's fun, but I saw him sneaking into the bathroom with that dude from the bar. No one can have fun but him."

"Blake is sober," Max said, looking back to the nightstand. He reached for his pendant. This time he bypassed the crucifix which had always brought him so much solace, and took hold of Saint Gemma.

He licked his lips, glancing over to the golden eyed woman briefly, confirming that she hadn't seen him, and he began to move away from Craig.

"Dude, don't be lame," Craig said, as Max, still eyeing the woman, rushed over to the nightstand.

Retrieving the small Bible inside it, Max headed, as

quickly as he could through the tightness of the crowd, toward the attached room. When he neared the door, he caught sight of the woman again, this time walking toward the plethora of alcoholic beverages scattered across the bar— the bar that sat directly between Max and the adjoining room's door. He backed up, not wanting her to see him, and when he hit the wall, he turned his head to look at it. Seeing a door there, he looked back to the woman, her steps bringing her closer and closer to him, and he quickly grabbed the knob and slipped inside the door.

Locking it before he turned on the light, Max hoped he wasn't where he thought he was. Sure enough, with a flick of the switch, it was confirmed. He'd just successfully locked himself inside the bathroom.

Some thuds from outside the door caught his attention, he looked to it, hearing some giggling, and a familiar voice of some strange seductive kindness. He held his breath, convinced he had to mask it, for the loud music and chattering of the hotel room was muffled inside this small, white space.

When it sounded like the voices left the door, he breathed something akin to relief. It wasn't exactly relieving to think the woman from the bar wouldn't find him inside this room because there was a part of him that remained unapologetically intrigued by her, but the strangeness of her motions inside the time loop, her golden eyes especially compared to the silver skies of Bonum's, made him consider her a person who should be approached cautiously. And right now, with his thoughts so focused on the ideas of sinning with her that he couldn't even write a single standing lyric after the intensity of such a show, just proved that he wasn't in the best mindset to try to get to know her at this moment.

"All right," he exhaled through his open lips, rushing a hand through his hair.

Flipping the lid down on the toilet, Max sat down on it sideways so he could put his feet on the edge of the tub and use his lap as a desk.

"What did she say," he muttered to himself, flipping through the pages of the Bible. "Leviticus…Leviticus…"

He bit his lip when he found the book. His brows pulled together. He felt he should know this already. Can't blame that one on the vodka, though.

His finger scrolled down the page, the blue glitter shimmering in the harsh bathroom light as he read a single word in each line. Words like "speak," "atonement," "slaughter," all rushing quickly past his eyes.

Though he wasn't reading it, entirely unsure of the words' context, he found it strange that each one seemed to play some significant role in his feelings this night.

Yes, in a manner of speaking, he spoke for a living. Even when he wasn't actively using his vocal chords, the recordings of their productions rang out in the night through some teenager's earbuds. Whatever he did through music, whether his lyrics or his guitar, spoke to the people willing to hear.

A thud against the door pulled him from his reading. Max inhaled once through his lips, staring to it, imagining the people on its other side, and how much fun they were having. He wondered if there was actually something wrong with him, if searching for meaning inside a book whose origins and ideals were less than certain was actually an endeavor of insanity. Still, he reminded himself, the core values of such a text, of simply being a good person, held some weight. The problem, he supposed, was that the definition of good was mostly obscure and quite relevant to the individual, group, collective.

The group outside this bathroom door did not imagine themselves sinners, condemning themselves with each swallow of alcohol further and further into the depths of a fiery afterlife. Why did he imagine it as such, then?

He licked his lower lip into his teeth, trying to imagine the feel of those small bones against the tender flesh as that fizzing soda-vodka combo. No, it wasn't nearly as painful, though it had felt rather harsh on its first swig, but wasn't that the trickery of such things? If sins felt bad, after all, no one would commit them.

He exhaled through his nostrils, returning his gaze to the book. As he read about becoming guilty, of touching something unclean, his hand lifted to his lips. His teeth chewed at his lip, at his nails. His nail picked at the drying skin on his lips. So drawn into the text, Max hadn't even realized how slouched over it he'd become until he felt a tight pain seizing his back.

He sat up, looking around the small room before deciding to just slip off the toilet and sit on the floor. He leaned against the tub, arching his back over its ledge enough to correct a bit of his cramping muscles, then he sat up, pulled his knees into himself, and placed the book, once again, inside his lap.

His brows creased as his blue eyes scanned the text again, deciding not to be lost inside any specific passage that didn't seem logical to Bonum's complaint. Finally, after pages of flipping, when he located Leviticus 19, something stuck out to him. He looked down to his chest, seeing only the orange of his T-shirt instead of the tattoo. His eyes flicked back to the text.

"Ye shall not make any cuttings in your flesh for the dead,

nor make any marks upon you," he muttered aloud as he read. His hand rose to his chest and he brushed his palm over his tattoo. His lips pursed as his narrow eyes moved away from the book, onto nothing in particular, and his fingers strummed momentarily.

Who was this woman showing up to a rock show, scorning him with biblical references, and leaving him symbols of her faith? Surely, she couldn't have known about his own faith, even if she deduced a lifestyle choice of abstinence from one of his songs. It was such a risky way to approach him. It was risky to approach anyone that way.

Again, he found himself questioning, Who was she?, but he concluded he'd most likely never know.

Then his brow lifted. Lips curled downward in contemplation. This wasn't the time of the Bible. This was the time of the phone. And he tossed the holy text aside to remove the most worshiped tool of texting from his pocket.

All he knew was her first name, sure, but it wasn't a very common one. Social media must have some insight into who she was, and even if it ended up being only one account with one photo, Max knew he wanted to see it.

Typing "Bonum" into any search engine, however, provided him nothing but photos of delicious looking cupcakes, falling leaves in front of autumn skies, and a plethora of faces. What did he really expect to find when he searched the word "good", though?

He exhaled, tossing his phone aside with the Bible. He looked at the two objects, so separated by time, and frowned.

Maybe as one moral code faded, it was only natural for another to grip the souls lost in the crossfire. Maybe as one god phased out, it was only natural to see it replaced.

He picked up his notebook, but he didn't open it. He was

ashamed of what he'd written, of the intimacy he'd imagined with someone whose name he didn't even know. He wondered if Craig ever considered that— the closeness he so often shared with people he could only be more separated from if he actively tried. But he shook his head in the negative direction. He was certain Craig didn't consider much beyond the cheap thrill of a cheap thrill. Maybe Philip did, however.

He looked down to the notebook, swiping his hand over its battered covered. The tip of his pointer finger caressed the soft pulls of white tuft the large fold in the hard green cover expelled. Everything, he considered, even something as simple and as common and as unappreciated as the cover of a notebook was more than what it appeared on the surface.

In this case, what was inside this particular exterior was a bunch of unorganized thoughts— the ramblings of someone regurgitating the same holy song and dance he'd been force-fed his entire life, concluded by lazy, wanton, half-sentences about lechery.

He felt like a false prophet, like one of those self help speakers who tell people that they need to free themselves from materialism to achieve bliss while they shovel every last cent of their paychecks into his pocket.

He pursed his lips, leaning his head back as he opened the notebook, resigning himself to only re-read what he'd written already, but before he knew it, he fell asleep.

CHAPTER TWO

"Dude." Craig beat on the door. "Let's go. What are you doing in there?"

Max opened his eyes, his cheek was hurting.

As he sat up from the side of the tub, he heard the sound of air fluttering against paper. He looked down to the notebook which fell from his lap. Lifting one hand to rub at ridges left in his face, he used the other to turn the page of his notebook. Spit branched out the letters of the words he'd written in blue pen. He didn't even remember writing.

He groaned a bit, rubbing his eyes. He wanted to read what he'd written, but was a bit afraid to, so he grabbed the notebook as he stood and tucked it under his arm when he opened the door.

"You didn't seriously lock yourself away in here because of a girl."

"What?" He scoffed, pushing past Craig. "No."

"You didn't even talk to her."

Grabbing his bag from the floor and lifting it onto the bed, Max rummaged through it until he found a fresh shirt.

"Come on, man." Craig pressed. "Why not hang with her?"

"I don't know," he said, throwing the orange shirt into his bag. "Bad feeling, maybe."

Craig rolled his eyes. "You and these feelings. What you should've felt was the warmth of her body against yours instead of the cold porcelain of the fucking toilet on your face."

"I didn't sleep on the toilet," he said lowly, eyes to the ground as he zipped the bag.

"Whatever, man." Craig threw his hand in Max direction, and went inside the bathroom.

"You good?" Philip asked, walking up to Max and holding his head in his hands.

"Yes," he said, pushing at one of Philip's hands as he recoiled. "I'm fine."

"What were you doing in there all night?" Philip asked, his brows creasing when he saw the imprint of the bathtub on Max's left cheek. "God, what is this? Did you sleep on the toilet?"

"Why do you both assume toilet? No, I was on the tub."

"Why?"

"I don't know. That woman from earlier was here and Craig said she was looking for me. I just felt off."

"So, you hid in the bathroom?" One of his creased brows tweaked, giving his concerned parent expression a hint of amusement.

"I wasn't hiding," he groaned. "I was…reading."

Lifting his hand as he emerged with the holy book, Craig chuckled. "Yeah, most guys take porn in with them."

Philip smiled a bit to Max, then he turned to dig some clothes from his bag. "I'm gonna take a quick shower, then."

Max grabbed his own bag from the bed and slung it over his shoulder.

"Where you going?" Craig huffed, the edge of a hangover sharp on his tongue.

"Just wanna get some coffee," Max muttered lowly. His head stayed down but his eyes moved up to his friend's.

"Bring me a muffin!" Philip called from the bathroom.

"We're leaving in thirty," Craig announced, throwing a wadded up ball of jeans into his bag.

"All right," Max said, heading for the door and exiting the room.

As he boarded the elevator, he considered the next stop in this next city. New faces, new bodies. New crowds inside invisible lines. He wondered how many of the myriad he'd met last night would still care about him tomorrow. How many would he have in a week?

When the doors opened, he exited with his eyes to the ground. Something nervous inside him again, he chewed on the nails of his left hand. His brows tightened. He felt it again, that strange sensation of someone staring. Not here. Certainly not now. This wasn't the appropriate setting for such acknowledgment. It was the exact contrast of the perfect time.

His eyes glanced around the hotel lobby, taking in the sounds of heels clicking against its bright, shimmering floor, the way the sun shone onto the black shoes of a businessman's wardrobe, the sounds of phone alerts dinging. No one's eyes should be on him here.

When he slipped inside the coffee shop, he breathed something akin to relief, and then he chuckled at himself. What had he really been expecting to happen in the ten feet between the elevators and the shop entrance?

Chalking it up to the nerves left over by the odd

interaction last night, Max ordered his coffee as cheerfully as possible, trying his hardest to be unafraid of allowing his eyes to meet those of the employees, the other customers. He sat down in a chair nearest the entrance and waited for Philip and Craig.

Unable to think about anything but that distinct sensation, that tangible focus, that let him know someone was watching him, Max   barely touched his coffee. His lips were curled inside his mouth, shoulders shrinking by the second as his blue eyes danced across the lobby. For a moment, he thought he saw the long dark hair of the previous night's woman, but further inspection of the individual, and most specifically her eyes, proved he'd become completely paranoid.

Every time he saw the black dresses, black nails; every time he felt a gust of warmth in the room-temperature area, his head whipped into its direction.

However, every time though, it was not who he expected it to be. And every time he couldn't tell if he was relieved, or let down.

"Where's my muffin?" Philip asked, walking briskly to the table. Tufts of his black hair were sticking out in all directions, small drops of water falling from them when he moved.

"Sorry," Max said, shaking his head. He pushed a small brown bag toward Philip when he sat down across from him. "I got so distracted."

"By what?" Philip asked inquisitively, reaching into the bag and withdrawing what appeared to be a plain muffin. He lifted it in his hand. "What's this?"

"Oh, they have chocolate chip—."

"And this isn't one because—?"

"Because," Max said, accentuating the word playfully. "That one has cheesecake inside it."

Philip's chin lowered a bit, his smiling lips parting as his brows raised. "It's the cruelest thing in the world."

"What is?" Max's brows creased, but his smile remained. Of all the things about his best friend he loved, his habit for impersonating tele-novella stars was probably his favorite.

"That you're straight."

"Yeah?" Max chuckled. "Well, that woman last night must not mind."

"Yeah, what's with that? She scared you into sleeping on the toilet," he said through his chewing.

"I wasn't scared," Max said, scoffing as he fell back into his chair exasperatedly. "And I wasn't sleeping on the toilet." He inhaled quite deeply before expelling the air harshly, then he leaned forward again. "She was the same one who bought me that drink."

"Okay," Philip said. "You're shocked she was at the party, then? I mean, I don't think that's so surprising."

"She didn't feel like…" Max shook his head. "I don't know. Why was she looking for me?"

"They always have a favorite."

"Who?"

"The women who come to these shows. Sad for her she picked the loner monk guy, but it's always so tragic when I meet the ones who desire me enough to know my birthday and favorite food, but pay so little attention to who I actually am that they still end up shocked when they find out I'm gay." He tsked, shaking his head as if he were offering condolences.

"Do you ever think about that, though?"

"About what?"

"About people knowing so much about you. About why they even want to."

His brows lifted, lips pursing in consideration. "No, I haven't really. It's just the way it always is, I suppose."

"And something being the same as it's always been somehow justifies it?"

"People need to be justified for wanting to know about the people who've brought their favorite music, or art, or literature into existence? Ask me anything about Kurt Vonnegut and I could tell you. Why? Because Slaughterhouse Five is my favorite book. Simple as that."

Max nodded, his head turning away in consideration of it. It still didn't answer why someone like the woman in question would take such an active interest in him. He hoped it was closer related to the kindness she expressed to him than the sense of unease that followed her regardless of it.

"All right," Craig's grumbling voice called from the lobby. "Let's go."

Still unnerved, Max sat in the back of the van biting at his fingernails. The glittery paint adorning them chipped away as he chewed, and when he got a taste of the polish, he quickly withdrew his hand.

"What's with you, man?" Craig asked, glancing in the rear view mirror.

"That girl," Philip offered.

"What girl?" Craig's brows creased.

"That one that gave him all those strange vibes last night."

"Oh, God," Craig groaned, his eyes rolling. "Well, she's about four-hundred miles behind us now. Think you can get it over before the show tonight?"

Max shook his head, eyes transfixed on the transparency of the window. He wasn't looking through it. He wouldn't have been able to say whether they'd been driving through barren farmland fields or a great metropolis. All his focus was on the menacing face he'd seen in the shadows of the bar and how bright it seemed in the daylight.

"She was at the party last night," Philip informed Craig.

"What?" Craig scoffed a small disbelieving laugh. His eyes moved from Philip to Max. He turned his head this time, seeing the man's face and not his reflection. "You serious?" he asked when he looked back to Philip.

"Sure am." His tongue clicked against the roof of his mouth as he looked back down to the magazine and turned the page.

Max's teeth were now acting as a vice grip on the inside of his lip. "What if she's there tonight?" He asked.

"She's a girl," Craig scoffed. "You scared of her or something?"

Philip tsked him, turning to look at Max, then back to Craig. "Don't be sexist."

"Come on, man," he said. "Being afraid of a girl's like being afraid of you." His eyes went back to Max's reflection, "Was she tall? Broad? Muscles?"

"No," Max said, lips pursing at Craig. "She's the one you said was looking for me."

"Oh, really?" Craig chuckled. "She was small."

"Yeah," Max said, brows furrowing slightly, eyes still staring at the glass before him. A tiny crack in the window caught his eye. It was small, thin, almost entirely unnoticeable, but it certainly had the potential to shatter the entire glass fixture it crept inside.

The sound of Craig's voice snapped Max back into the

conversation. "Yeah, I think you're good." Craig laughed.

"Well, I think it's best to trust your instincts," Philip said. "If she gave you a strange vibe, then we'll have to steer clear of her at the show."

"All right, well, let's say she's there tonight," Craig considered, "What's the game plan supposed to be?"

"Let's just hope she's not," Max said. His eyelids fluttered a bit. "Just wake me up when we get there."

———

Malum's back pressed against the bar. Her tongue swiped over her teeth as she eyed the people pushing through the door.

"Gonna need your ID if you want a drink, Miss," the bartender said.

"I'm afraid I don't have one," she said, looking to him over her shoulder, "But you're going to put a cherry vodka and Sprite in my hand anyway."

As she turned back to face the crowded room, she turned her hand over and opened her palm. Before she even had time to see Philip lugging his drums onto the stage, she felt cold glass in her hand.

She winked to the bartender. "Don't let me run empty."

He nodded his accordance.

After using her tongue to fetch the little black straws in her drink and take a sip, Malum's nose scrunched. It was far too sweet for her tastes, but if the prophetic Rock God would enjoy it, she'd find a way to make it work.

"Oh, barkeep," she called, releasing the glass from her fingers. It clanged against the resin counter, affording her the attention of anyone in proximity to the bar. "Less Sprite, more vodka."

"Sure," he said, discarding the drink and mixing a new one.

She heard the glass connect to the bar again, but let it sit next to her elbow. Her eyes were fixated on Philip; on his dark eyes and even darker hair. She wondered what color his skin tone really was behind the blues and purples of the neon lights around them, wondered if the way he held his chin so strongly was an act or a natural expression. How difficult, she considered, might he be to separate from her mark?

Her hand rose slowly, fingers reaching for the small straws. As she twisted them inside the glass, the ice bouncing off of its confines, her eyes narrowed. Craig, a sight in his own right, carried his guitar to the stage. Biceps bulged when he reached for the tangled mess of wires at his feet, veins rising beneath the skin of his forehead and neck when he visibly swore at the disaster. What a charming mouth he had— its appearance was as delightful as the words that spewed from it. Ah, yes, Malum thought, He's the ticket in.

She lifted the drink to her lips. A crimson smile connected to the glass, alcohol brushed over her tongue.

She sat it back down with another clang.

"Not enough vodka." She exhaled her exasperation, and then she turned to face the bartender. "I'm going to need enough alcohol in there to make the drinker very easy to handle. Do you understand?"

He nodded, discarding yet another drink, and refilling the glass to her standards. This time she kept her eyes on his task, the golden irises of her manifested form becoming lost in the black pools of widening pupils.

Oh, were the lights dimming so soon? She'd have to pay

attention if the Rock God himself were about to journey onto the stage.

Darkness encompassed her. She smirked, eager in anticipation, and finally, with the percussion of two loud pounds to the drum, the stage lit up.

Her crimson lips smiled something deviant when her mark walked onto the stage. Even donned in plain jeans and his leather jacket, Max encompassed the presence entirely. His voice was serene as a messenger's should be— allowing any philosophy to pass into the ears of youth like warm, heated butter, and his angelic face, defined jaw sitting beneath vast depths of shining sapphires, was the perfect disguise for something vile.

Oh, what fun she could have with him. What a perfect little puppet he could be; her own personal marionette.

His hand brushed downward, the strings of his guitar vibrating within the small space, filling it with sound. Malum watched the mass of young souls beneath him, their faces illuminating in the shadows by their devotion to their god.

How easily God had been replaced. How seamlessly musicians who were once mere idols began to fill the void left by the loss of God. Yes, he was their savior, their voices syncing with his, speaking his words in perfect time with him, chanting their devotionals and basking in his glory. He was as close to divinity as they would ever come, and they raised their hands in worship of him.

Malum smiled, for she felt the vibrations, too. They rustled at her feet, edging nearer and nearer to her, pounding at the fleshy prison her spiritual being was currently locked in. Grinning as she let it pass through her, Malum stared up at the new king, the Rock God, and laughed in satisfaction as she watched the hands of children, once open-palmed to the divine now shift into the sign of horns. They were praising a ruler they didn't even realize existed, and what a clever entry the devil created in allowing their loss of faith to prove his nonexistence.

When Max's lungs opened, when the words spawned from his soul passed through his lips, Malum's teeth gritted together. There was no denying it, his voice was downright heavenly. But she knew she could change that.

Golden irises focused on the stage lights at their feet. Here and there they'd pull a shimmering blue beam out of orbit and light on her face, just when Max's eyes might be in the appropriate place to catch her staring devilishly. She saw his eyes widen when he first caught sight of her, and she watched his chest rise more pronounced and fall heavily in the discovery of the face. Then gold stared into purple, and the violet hues of another stage light allowed Max to see Malum a second time. A lyric caught inside his throat, parted lips expelling only a sharp breath into his microphone. He was certain of what he saw, but looked over his shoulder to Philip for confirmation.

When their eyes met, Philip's brows only creased briefly. He was entirely oblivious to the plight of his friend, for Malum was careful to hide herself from his sight. Craig, however, was granted the privilege of seeing her face, doused in low lighting and shades of pink. Unwitting Craig would be her ticket to a cautious Max.

Max consciously loosened his brows, eyes scattering across the sea of the living at his feet.

They're here for entertainment, for release, he reminded himself. Don't lose focus.

He turned his head away from the microphone for a split second, breathing in the scents of sweat and smoke, his eyes closing as he released it all. When he faced the choir beneath him again, he smiled warmly, seeing so many faces cleansed of the anxieties of their generation, freed by three minutes of his creation.

This was bliss, he thought, This has to be paradise.

Reinvigorated, his lips opened smoothly, disguising hymns as romance, sex, and drugs. His tongue pressed perfectly against his teeth, each word pronounced with a wholesome intent his image rendered entirely unassuming. What a powerful place, he considered, for one man to claim as his destiny.

When the song finished, Max's eyes traveled from glistening window to glistening window, all shades of blues and browns and greens, taking the time to acknowledge each soul behind the orbs with reverence before his vocal chords vibrated the melodic words, "Thank you."

A genuine sensation of gratitude passed through his being when he perceived, as physically as emotionally, his importance to the people who stared up to him. Recognition reflected back to him from inside the eyes of strangers. They knew him. They knew his name, and they knew the sound of his voice. They knew the colors of his eyes, and the shapes of ink inside his skin. They knew him, but he knew nothing of even one of them. What a concept.

His senses heightened in the appreciation for all that was before him, all that promised to comprise his existence. What was he beyond the physical sound of their straining voices? What was he if not the tangible heat their reaching hands released? Was he the audible panting of his colleagues' lips and the stinging of broken flesh against the ridges of guitar strings, or was he something more than anything eyes could perceive?

The sound of Philip's drumsticks connecting seemed muffled, miles away from him, not inches from his feet, but the clicking was enough to pull him from this moment of awakening. Without the time to properly consider why such an understanding flooded through him on this night over any other, Max struck the strings of his guitar with the teal pick between his fingers, and his eyes, as they lifted from the sea of devoted vocals, lighted on golden eyes for the third time this evening.

Suddenly unafraid of such a questionable presence, Max opened his throat as his chin lifted, eyes peering into hers whenever the lights allowed them to connect.

Whoever she was, whatever she wanted, Max understood that he was something different to her than anything he was to anyone else inside the bar.

There was no admiration in her eyes, no sign of relief from the troubles outside the soundscape, and her lips, scarlet and shapely, never uttered his words.

He watched her arms cross in front of her, a smirk turning the corners of her mouth upward as she peered up from her menacing stance. It was the last time the lights fell on her.

———

"Hey, there, handsome," the familiar voice said.

Max turned around to see her hands on the table. She leaned over it, eyes gleaming as they looked up to him.

"H-hey." He smiled, nervously at first.

"I was looking for you last night." She grinned.

"Oh, yeah?"

"Yeah," she said as a smirk formed on her crimson lips. "I thought you'd be at a party in your own room." Her eyes rolled playfully.

"I, um, I try to write after shows. Something about the atmosphere always inspires me."

She eyed him knowingly. "You don't trust me, do you?"

"I don't know you." He tried to smile, but his eyes moved away from hers quickly. "I mean, you have to earn trust, right?" He looked back to her nervously, a thick roll of sticky spit falling down his throat. "And you're traveling to all the same cities I am." His brows furrowed. He hadn't meant to say it. When he looked up from the shirt he was tucking inside the box, his lips bounced around a bit but were unable to form any type of apology.

"Only the last two." She grinned. "I travel for work, and I wasn't able to stay for the first, so when I realized Changing Nuances were in the same city as me again, I figured I'd come listen."

"Why did you have to leave?" he asked inquisitively. Sacrifices Surrendered was the second band to play, sure, but each set was fairly brief.

Her brows lifted, eyes widening over her pursing lips. "Oh, I received a call," she lied, so used to the action the deceit slipped out of her perfectly pouts lips like silver.

"A call kept you away from a thirty minute set?" He forgot his effort to hide his suspicion.

"You still don't trust me," she said.

"Oh, no. It's not that. I just——."

She leaned forward, whispering, "That wasn't a question." She leaned back. "Do I seem that devious?"

"I don't know." He exhaled as he laughed, eyes on anything but hers. "I mean, it's not you specifically. It's…"

He huffed. "I'm just overly cautious maybe. A little apprehensive at times."

"Someone hurt you," she said solemnly, watching the way his hands folded the clothing so reverently.

His eyes sprang up to hers, but his expression was stoic. "Don't tell me you were analyzing my lyrics."

"Listening, yes, but not enough to gather that." She'd been informed quite some time ago about Max, about who he was, and what she needed to become to him. She couldn't have very well said that, however, so she went with: "You give yourself away."

"I do?"

"Uh-huh," she said, rounding the table. Taking a few of the shirts, she started to fold them. Kindness always worked with these types. "Just look at the way you're standing, the way you fold the shirts. Everything is gentle, so reverent. It's like you go out of your way to make sure everyone around you is happy and enjoying themselves, but the truth of it," she looked over to him as she put a shirt in the box. Appearing perceptive never hurt either. Most of her marks were easily persuaded away with looks and charm. Not Max. His type wasn't built for her side, so she had to, as much as it physically pained her, try to be the exact opposite of what she was. "…Is that you're just like that naturally."

His lips, tight and protective, began to loosen. Though they remained closed, a smile formed on them, and he looked away from her shyly as he put the shirt in hands in the box.

"All that from the way I fold shirts," he said timidly.

"Just the fact that you're folding them at all," she said, placing another in the box.

He smiled up to her. "Thank you."

"You're welcome."

"You—Your contacts are really something," he said, hoping she wouldn't perceive the shaking of his voice.

"Who says I'm wearing contacts?" She winked.

"They're gold."

"Pft, they're brown ," she retorted, placing the final shirt into the box.

He closed it. "Brown eyes are beautiful, sure," he said, looking up to her and biting his lip in the nervousness of what he wanted to say. "I mean…" he looked down. "Blue eyes, green eyes, it's hard to find any that aren't magnificent in their own way, right?" He laughed nervously, their eyes connecting, allowing him to absorb the true nature of the flickering golds. "Yours aren't just brown, though."

She smiled, leaning forward, bending at the waist so her chest tilted somehow seductively over the box, "Yours aren't just blue," her brow raised, and she watched a bit of the internal barrier he'd built in defense of her lower. His eyes gazed into hers, no perceivable expression on his face, but its serenity entirely clear. She smiled, gazing back into his eyes, and then, suddenly enough to jerk him from his focus, she stood straight and lifted the box she'd been leaning over. "Where are we going with these?" She asked cheerfully. The taste of such tone made her want to gag.

"Oh, you don't have to—."

"I insist," she said, shooting him a stern, but warm, look.

"Okay," he said, lifting the other two boxes. "Thank you. Our van's just right outside."

"Your friends don't help you with this?" She asked as they walked through the club.

"They get distracted easily," he said, glancing over to both bandmates slamming glasses into the bar before throwing back their heads and taking shots.

"Yeah, Craig seems like he enjoys his vices," she chuckled. While separating him from Craig wasn't a priority, if she had to plant seeds about both bandmates in order to plant them about Philip, that'd just have to do. She wanted to try to find some other method, however, because Craig's overarching personality made her quite happy.

"He definitely does," Max said, using his back to open the door for her.

"What's your other friend's deal?" she asked, watching him as he opened the back doors of their van.

"What do you mean?"

"I mean, he seems like he's got two sides to him."

"I don't think so," Max said, brows furrowing as he slid his boxes into the van.

"I mean," she said, handing him the box in her hands, "he was there at the bar taking shots, but last night it almost looked like he was babysitting."

"He likes to have fun," Max said, turning to face her after closing the doors. "But he doesn't like to see anyone get taken advantage of."

"Ah," she said, leaning her shoulder against the van, arms crossing in front of her. "I take it Craig's good for that."

"Definitely." Max frowned.

"You don't like seeing it either."

He shook his head. "No."

The wind blew causing his shoulders to shimmy in the chill of it.

"Aw," she said. "Are you cold?"

"It's a little chilly," he said, lifting his hands to his jacket, "Here—."

"Stop." She smiled, taking a step toward him, extending her hands for his. The heat was caressing him, wrapping itself around him, before flesh ever connected.

"I run warm," she said.

Staring at his hand where she'd stopped it just near the lapel of his jacket, her thumb brushed along the painted nails.

"Oh…" he started, feeling the need to justify such a fashion choice, but she interrupted.

"You know," she said, "in sixth century art, the devil was always depicted in blue." Her chin remained lowered when her eyes blinked up to meet his.

"Oh," he said, brows creasing as he stared to his nails.

She smiled as her crimson lips closed, and she petted his nails. Grinning when she looked back to him, her chin lifted as she leaned into him, she asked playfully, "Is that why you chose that color?"

He exhaled a small laugh, eyes moving to the ground. Wearing such a color with this concept in mind created an urgency for polish remover to well up inside him. He felt blasphemous in some odd way, like he was participating in something satanic without even intending to. He looked back up to her, fearful eyes suddenly softening when he saw the way she looked at him. It was stern, unreadable but in a seductive way. No one had ever looked at him like this, like he might be someone bad, someone dangerous, someone who wasn't so gentle and soft. "You," his brows creased, a thrill rushing down his spine. "You think I'm the devil?" He exhaled a nervous breath, the word causing his tongue to sour when it formed it, but the way she eyed him contemplatively—studying every feature from his blonde hair to his blue eyes, his defined jawline, and his leather jacket, was too exciting to deny.

"Hmm," she said looking back up to him, "maybe."

He smiled, looking away shyly while she used her hold of

his hand to move it around her. Taking a step closer, she used her other hand to coax his other to her waist, and when he smiled up to her nervously, she said, "I told you, I'm warm."

With the simple statement, Max allowed his hands to move around her, feeling the soft velvet of her dress beneath his fingertips as his hands brushed over her sides.

She moved against him, warmth exuding from her body, her arms where they curled around his shoulders, her torso where it pressed against his own, even her cheek when she leaned it against his hair.

"Wow," he said, fingers curling on her back to grip her more tightly. He couldn't believe how undeniably good she felt, not merely for the heat she provided in the chill of the cold, but for the sheer comfort only being so close to another person could offer.

She brushed her hand through his thick locks lazily, heat spilling from them and cascading down around his head. It danced around him like curling smoke, wrapping itself around his neck, filing through his hair, and caressing his face.

He shivered against her as a chill coursed down his spine, and she pulled him closer in response to it. This time, his face buried inside the crook of her neck.

It was remarkable how safe he felt inside her arms, as if no one else who'd held him in such a way had ever caused him pain. All the fear of being close, all the worry of how badly it might hurt to experience distance again, melted away against the intensity of her fiery flesh.

"You're a sweet guy," she whispered, masking her devious grin beautifully by the softened tone. Still petting his hair with one hand, she squeezed his shoulder more tightly with the other. "I'm sure someone has taken advantage of that in the past."

"Yeah," he breathed against her, pulling her more tightly into him as the fear of such a recurrence reminded him of its possibility.

"I won't," she said sternly, and quite believably. She gave herself credit, her type was naturally prideful, but how could she not inherit such a trait when her father was the father of lies?

"Well, now I wish I would've hung out with you at that party last night."

"Yeah?" She smiled, leaning back so they could look at one another, but their bodies were still pressed together. "Well, we have tonight."

"No," he said, looking down. "We're leaving tonight."

"Sleeping in the van, huh?"

"Yeah," he said. His brows pulled together as his hands began to loosen and fall away from her.

She smiled, leaning into him, but before she could say anything, she withdrew. "I think your friends are coming," she said.

He hadn't seen or heard anyone, but sure enough the sound of the bar door opening behind from behind forced him to take his eyes away from her. It wasn't Philip or Craig exiting the venue, but by the time he turned back around, all he could see was a hint of her figure moving across the road. His lips pursed, confusion racking at his mind.

"Wait," he called, "I don't even know your name."

"It's Malum," she answered, turning to smile at him, and then vanishing across the road.

"Hey," Philip said, startling Max as he threw an arm around him. "Ready to head out?"

"Yeah," Max said, looking across the road one last time. His brows creasing in the seemingly psychic nature of the previous moment. "Yeah, let's go."

Walking around the van, Max climbed into the driver's side.

"I'll help you get out of the city," Philip said, slipping into the passenger's seat with a fluffy green pillow. "Then I'm out."

"I'm out now," Craig said, throwing down a balled up blanket and lying across the bench seat in the back.

"It's fine," Max said. "I got it."

"Nah." Philip yawned. "I got you."

"Thanks," Max said. He smiled so lightly Philip could tell it was forced. Or maybe it was just the number of years they knew each other that allowed him to perceive it.

They drove in as much silence as the low music and sporadic GPS directions allowed. When Craig's snoring became audible, Philip spoke.

"So tell me what's wrong," he said.

"Nothing's wrong." His eyes fell immediately, but the taste of denial lingered on his tongue.

"Something was wrong last night and you're behaving exactly the same way."

"Nothing was wrong. I just…I saw that girl again. Malum."

"Malum?"

"Yeah, lot of people in that area must have weird names. I met someone named Bonum before we left the bar."

"Did she give you odd vibes, too?"

"No," he said, fast and small.

"Okay, so she did."

"She didn't. She was nice."

"And this Malum isn't?"

"She is. That's what's so confusing. She's been nothing

but nice to me since we met. We talked a bit today…"

His eyes widened. "Stalker."

"No, she travels for work."

"What does she do?"

"I'm not sure." His lips pursed.

"Oh, honey, you're so naive."

Max scoffed. "No, she had to leave the first show before she saw Changing Nuances, so she came to this one."

"Oh, so she's a fan." He gave Max a knowing face. "Like I said, you're so naive."

"Okay, yeah, a fan of them, but she was here for work."

"Sure, she was."

"Regardless, I think she wanted to…hang out."

"And you didn't because you get a weird vibe, or you did because she's nice?" Philip laughed.

"It sounds like you're talking to a sixteen year old." Max scoffed. "We went to the same school. We had the same upbringing. Why did we end up so different?"

"Because you're a wimp." Philip grinned.

Max shook his head, smiling a bit.

"No, okay…" Philip continued, repositioning himself in the seat so he was turned to face Max. "I guess, my entire life, I knew who I was, and I knew that every one of our teachers, our parents, they all believed that I was wrong for being that way. I would've too if Marcy hadn't been eleven years older than us. I mean, she'd come home from college and sit me down and talk to me, me at eight and nine and ten years old, about the different philosophies she studied, about psychology, science. There was so much more to who human beings were than what we were always taught, and I was exposed to all of it during those formidable years—those years when being good and righteous and Christian and moral were instilled in you so deeply." He exhaled. "I was fortunate enough to never have to buy into any of it. You were forced to."

Max's lips pulled together, considering how blasphemous speech almost always seemed logical. After all, the things he believed in would never be able to be proven— Or *disproven*, he reminded himself. With that in mind, living according to the code just in case of the afterlife such an institution expected would be the safest route to take. But if none of it was real, then he'd miss out on so much—specifically with Malum—for nothing.

"Plus," Philip added playfully, "We went to an all boys school, which gave you no chance to be interested in anything, uh, we'll say romantically, but it provided me with all the interest one guy should be able to have for a lifetime."

"So, I'm just a robot, then? That's what you're saying?" Max looked over to him, his thumb tapping at the wheel. The glow of the red light on Philip's face made him appear more sinister than he was capable of being, but maybe it had something to do with the demonic meaning so often cast onto the color. Then his brows creased. What had Malum said about art and the color of the devil?

"No, you're not a robot," Philip said. "If you were, we wouldn't be friends, right?"

"Yeah, okay." Max smiled a bit through his tight lips. "Good point."

"You're okay, Maxwell." Philip said, nestling into the pillow.

"Hey, wait," Max said. "Before you go to sleep, can you look something up on your phone really quickly?"

Philip huffed, sitting up and taking his phone from the cup holder. "You're lucky I love you. What is it?"

"The color blue in the sixth century."

Philip's eyebrow quirked. "What?"

"Or something about blue in the sixth century and…and, um…" His lips closed and his shoulder lifted a bit. He muttered, "The devil."

"Oh, God." Philip groaned. "I'm too tired to ask why. Let me look."

Max smiled shyly.

"Hmm, okay, well, the first result is this picture." Philip looked at the road, then at Max. "It's a sixth century mosaic." He turned his phone, and Max looked at it quickly.

"Hmm." Max's eyes went back to the road, narrowing when they came back to the phone. "Can you screenshot it and send it to me?"

"Sure," Philip said.

"Does it give any description?"

"It just says that the two angels are most likely representative of Michael and Lucifer, that Michael, pictured with lambs, is in red, leaving the blue angel depicted with goats to be interpreted as Lucifer."

"Okay," Max said, pursing his lips. "Thanks."

"You're sure you're all right? This is weird."

"I'm all right." He smiled to his friend as another light turned red. "Get some sleep."

"Night," Philip said, reclaiming his relaxed position as he curled up into the pillow and closed his eyes.

Philip as Michael, Max considered as he watched his friend, falling gently to sleep, draped in the red hues of the light once again. It made perfect sense to him.

CHAPTER THREE

When they pulled into the hotel parking lot of yet another new city, all three men were wide awake.

Craig insisted they stop for a gas break, even though they had well over half a tank, and managed to emerge from the gas station with two phone numbers.

It baffled Max that someone with so little to like about his personality almost always had the attention of someone of the opposite sex, but since he felt no competition with the man six years his junior, he didn't dwell.

Philip, the natural caretaker that he was, went inside to get Max coffee, and though Max was thankful for the heavenly beverage, he wished it was as good as that Mega Ultra had been.

That night was so different from any other, so separate from the last ten years, so separate from last night. The only thing remarkable since was Malum, and the way any unease he'd felt about her vanished.

It was odd, he realized this, because so much of why she'd been there relied on coincidence, and he quickly considered the opposite side of chance: Fate.

For whatever reason, that night seemed to be a night of signs. Trapped inside some powerful vortex, perceiving only Malum's movements as fluid within it, Max saw the attention of the people at his feet as miraculous. And being introduced to this woman, no matter how odd she felt at first, on the same night had to be some part of his destiny.

He didn't believe in soulmates, and he reminded himself of this fact as they unloaded their bags from the back of the van. No, of the childish behaviors he exhibited, of all the unprovable beliefs he held, the concept of one person being created entirely for him, or him for that person, was too illogical to accept. After all, unless they were born at the exact same moment on the exact same day, one person would have to be born without their other half even being alive, or in most cases, even being conceived. Unless one were to believe that God— or the universe, he was starting to believe he wasn't entirely sure anymore— knew of every person at every time for all of eternity and already assigned such seemingly random spirits to one another thousands of years ago, being born specifically for another person just felt dumb. If he had a preordained destiny, he hoped it would involve something far more meaningful than how much some other person loved him.

He walked slowly into the hotel lobby, following Philip and Craig on autopilot as his mind roamed. Regardless of how unbelievable the concept was, Max somehow still hoped it could apply.

He blinked lazily as he followed behind them, eyes absorbing each curve of the smoky baby blue patterns in the creamy floor. For as calming as the color was, he could no longer stop himself from associating it with some unadulterated evil. He looked at his nails and his lips curled. Why did Malum even have such a knowledge? Perhaps she studied art.

"All right," Philip said, turning to Max. He snapped his fingers in front of shining blue irises which were staring off into the nowhere space to his lower left. "Hello," he said pointedly.

"Yeah, sorry," Max said, looking up to him and taking the card-like key presented to him.

"You need a nap. Thank God we don't go on for seven hours."

"Yeah." Max chuckled lowly, looking downward again.

When his band mates began to move away from the reception desk, he followed, again on autopilot, eye raking over the colors of the floor, the plush chairs, the wallpaper. When they moved across the wooden shelves that created a border between the lobby and the hotel restaurant, a surprising, yet entirely welcome image caught his eyes in place.

"Max?" Philip called from the hallway of elevator doors. "What are you doing?"

"Um, I'll just be a minute," he said, never turning his head to face them. His eyes, fixated and unblinking, were caught on Bonum.

"Hey," he said, brows creasing as he approached her.

"Hey, there, Rock Star." She smiled widely.

"What are you doing here?" he asked lightheartedly.

"I travel for work," she said, extending her hand. "Sit with me! Let's chat."

"Okay, but, um, yeah." He pulled the chair back, smiling as he sat. "Sorry. I've just been driving all night, and I'm kind of tired."

"Oh, don't let me keep you, then——."

"No, it's okay," he said. "Oddly, I feel very happy to see you."

"You do?" Her smile widened. "Good. I'm glad." Her gray eyes stared into the wholesome blues, his reaction to her proved he was still on the correct path, then her eyes fell to the chain around his neck. "I see you found Gemma."

"Oh…" He looked down briefly, clasping the pendants. "Yeah. Yeah, I did. Thank you for that."

"You're welcome. It never hurts to have a saint around."

"Definitely doesn't hurt," he said. "So, what kind of work do you do?"

"I'm an auditor."

"An auditor? Like, you work for the IRS?"

"Not quite." She smiled, "I don't mean to be boastful, but my higher up is much higher up than anyone in that department."

"So, who do you audit?"

"People," she said. "Special people. People of great importance. I just check in from time to time, make sure they're still on the right path." She smiled serenely, a slow blink of her gleaming eyes, and Max was entirely captivated.

He stared to her, his lips parting slightly. No one had ever seemed so stunning to him, not even Malum, but this was an appeal entirely different from hers.

While Malum was thrilling and seductive, Bonum, with such similar features, seemed too bright to be desired in any manner that wasn't based on pure connection. Just as Max felt his body didn't matter to Bonum, Bonum's didn't matter to Max, and her beauty, therefore, became some paradigm-shifting symbol of everything that felt right in the world.

"So how's your career, then?" she asked. "Written anything new lately?"

Max blinked, her words pulling him from his trance. "Oh." He looked away, a bit embarrassed. "Oh, yes." His brows creased, guilt crept inside him, shame from all that lustful imagery. "I mean, no. Not anything I like."

"Maybe I can help. I'm excellent at this type of thing."

"No," he shook his head. He couldn't imagine anything more terrible than Bonum reading what he'd written. Except maybe lying to her. "I mean, it's honestly not good at all. I'm starting from scratch." A nervous chuckle left him, then he lifted his bag from its spot on the floor near his feet. "I should get up to the room, though. We have another show tonight and I've gotten no sleep."

"Well, if you're ever stuck, we seem to be in the same cities quite often. Perhaps we'll cross paths again."

"Yeah." He smiled as he stood. Taking a moment to focus on the curvature of her face, the color of her eyes, just in case he would never get to see it again. "I'll hopefully see you around."

"See you around." She smiled.

As he walked to the elevator, a new wave of inspiration hit him. He hit the button vigorously, wanting to get to the room as quickly as possible so he could compose from it.

The numbers above the center elevator illuminated slowly. First the thirty-seven, then what felt like an eternity later, the thirty-six. Suddenly, all of his urgency was dwindling. He threw his bag to floor, crouching over it, rummaging through it until he found his notebook.

The pen had fallen from its spiral binding, and he frantically scoured through clothing and toothpaste, gel, and shampoo, in search of it.

An elevator dinged before he could find it, but he chose to ignore it. Instead, he sat there, in the middle of the hall of elevators, writing.

The sounds of the opening doors were only background noise. Voices were muffled. Nothing was relevant but the paper in his lap and the pen in his hand. His fingers urged it forward, not with determination, but with some sort of divine inspiration. Maybe muses were real, he considered, And maybe Bonum was one of them.

She filled him with such strong emotion, the same way Malum did, but the feeling was in total opposition. When he'd written of Malum, his pen formed words of such disobedience, such want, such ideas of darkness that twisted his perception of them into something so desirable that even the letters of the alphabet appeared violent. Bonum, however, inspired only the most elegant of words, the most melodic rhythms. It was nothing of the urgent thrills of Malum. It was only comfort, warmth, light.

When his hand stopped moving, when he felt he was at the end of his bout of creative release, Max looked down at the pages. Brushing his fingertips over them as he read what he'd written, he smiled.

The doors opened in front of him, and Philip rushed out, hands on his hips.

"It's been, like, an hour. What are you doing?"

"Writing," he said, looking up to his friend apologetically.

"Please go get some sleep. If you suck on stage then we all look sucky."

"Okay." He laughed, tucking his notebook inside his bag and following Philip to the elevator.

He felt her before he saw her.

Heat pressed against him, curling around his shoulders, and then the tapping fingertips as they walked over his back. "Hey," she said, leaning over the bar and smiling.

"Hey." His brows raised, a smile growing on him. "Malum! What are you doing here?"

"Honestly, I wanted to see you," she said, rapping on the bar and raising two fingers.

Max watched the bartender nod to her, and then he looked to her curiously. "This place has a strict curfew with shows, so make sure you find me right after."

"I can't stay for the show unfortunately." She appeared solemn, but the fact of the matter was that his voice was too heavenly, his lyrics too pure, that even though the grand catalyst already happened, she emerged from it by the skin of her teeth, so hearing much more from him was like rushing her face repeatedly over the jagged blade of a saw. "But I'm in this town a lot. I know some people."

"You're a good one to have around then," he said.

"Yeah, maybe," she grinned mischievously as the bartender sat two shots down.

"They even know what you order, huh?"

"Yep," she said, reaching for the shots.

"That's, uh, what you got in Ohio was…brown." He looked to the clear liquor.

"Brown?" She made no effort to hide her grin. She knew this man was innocent, but she didn't expect someone who worked so often in bars to have so little knowledge of alcohol.

"Oh, I'm—." he paused, considering whether or not he should admit how little he partook, but figured he'd already given himself away. "I'm really not much of drinker."

"Well, it's only one shot." She looked over to him, eyes gleaming above her smirk.

"A shot of what?"

"Stop," she said, reaching for the salt shaker and looking at the bartender. "Couple limes."

He nodded and brought them over in a cup.

"If you think about the alcohol it'll feel harsher than it is," she said. "But if you get out of your head, you'll like this. It's fun." She licked her flesh between her thumb and forefinger and shook the salt shaker over her hand. "You do the salt, then the shot." She offered him one of the glasses, smiling, and after a brief pause, he took it. She nodded. "Then the lime."

Across the club, in search of his band mate, Philip opened the door to their green room, and peered around the venue. His eyes moved around from person to person, neck twisting the effort to see around the crowd forming in front of the stage. Then he spotted him. With a woman.

Philip watched the woman raise her hand to an obviously uncertain Max.

Leaning toward her hand, Max looked up to her hesitantly, before he took the salt, and thusly her hand, into his lips. He felt her heat absorbing into his lips, dancing across his tongue. His eyes fluttered closed briefly, enjoying the almost liquid texture her heated hand gave the salt, but also trying, without acknowledging it, to differentiate the taste of the condiment to the taste of her skin.

Removing his lips from her hand, he leaned his back, rushing the tequila to the back of his throat hurriedly. When his head leveled, he winced, eyes screwing shut, but he felt Malum's heat on his cheek. Opening his eyes, he saw the lime in her hand, and quickly leaned forward to bite into it.

His hand rose to hers, keeping the lime steady against his lips, his tongue rushing against its sour relief.

"There you go." She grinned, something Philip read as quite mischievous as he studied the pair with narrowed eyes.

Max exhaled through his mouth when she threw the shriveled fruit slice back into the small cup of limes and shook his head.

"Okay, let's try again." She chuckled, sliding her shot over to him.

"Oh, no, I shouldn't—."

"No, that was worse than it needed to be," she laughed, taking the salt and shaking it this time over the creamy flesh of her collarbone. "You took too long between steps. Rapid fire this time," she said, tilting her head to the side so that her clavicle was more exposed. She lifted the glass to him, raising a brow when she smiled.

He inhaled deeply, nodding as he took the glass. Moving down from his bar stool, he took a step closer to her. Her hand slid up his arm, resting against his neck and urging him into her with it. His free hand moved to her waist, feeling the same instinctual urge to connect to her as his face moved closer and closer to such a desirable destination.

A small hum left her throat when his tongue connected to her skin, and though, in that one swipe, he'd removed the salt, he couldn't prevent his lips from closing over the bone.

Applying a slight pressure to his neck with her hand, Malum urged him to remain where he was, and while it was more than an appealing offer, Max felt the need to withdraw.

He didn't let his eyes meet hers when he pulled back, quickly taking the shot.

As soon as he swallowed, he saw the lime between her fingers, and used to his careful grip of her hand to pull the fruit into his teeth.

It was enough for Philip, who could never explain his absolute need to protect Max from such common and seemingly harmless situations, and he stormed to the center of the bar. Watching the pair as they chuckled, Philip noted that their arms never left the other's body.

After Malum tossed this second slice aside, her hand moved to his cheek, her fingers brushing over his defined jaw, and he followed suit by letting his hand move around her waist to connect with his other.

They leaned into one another, his thick, blond hair brushing against her forehead when he began to tilt his head, their lips so near he could feel her heat tingling across his nose and chin. She brushed his cheek, tilting her own head, eyes excitedly devouring the image of such piety giving in to the intoxicated desires of any other man in the bar.

"Maxwell!" Philip called, pulling Max's focus, and subsequently his head, away from Malum. "Do you not see Billy on the stage?"

"Oh, right," he exhaled, smiling toward Philip and gesturing that he understood. He looked back to Malum. "I'm sorry. I have to go get ready."

"It's fine," she said. "I have to head out anyway."

"Yeah, well, um, how long will you be working?"

"A couple of hours," she said, hopping down from the bar stool.

"Well, you know Craig always has parties after shows, so

if you wanted to come, we'll be in 1024 tonight."

"You'll actually be there?" She smiled.

"Yes," he said. "If you will be."

"Okay," she said. "I'll try my hardest."

"Cool," he said, taking his unfinished glass of water, and stepping away from the bar. "I'll, um…" He stepped toward her, kissing her cheek shyly. "I'll see you later, then."

"See you later." She grinned, leaning back against the bar as she watched him walk toward the scowling Philip.

She exhaled loudly through her nostrils. Philip was starting to really annoy her.

———

Malum hung out by the bar while the first band played. She couldn't claim to actually enjoy it, but at least their bassist was a hollow shell of human flesh all too eager to spread his festering diseases in the pursuit of quick release.

She wanted to stay and watch Max, make sure no one else got to him before she could really get to him, but squandering her talents on sitting through the closest thing to gospel some heavy metal screamo band could get wouldn't benefit her when she had an obstacle like Philip hanging around. She saw the way he intercepted women from Craig, and now watched him take Max from her. She knew exactly who Philip was. Everyone in Max's position had someone like Philip—someone to watch out for their friend when their natural naivety would render them susceptible to someone like Malum. This just simply would not do.

She exhaled exasperatedly, her conjectures about the drummer from the first night she'd seen him now clearly confirmed. Taking two shots of her own, ignoring the salt and lime, she watched the first opening band, taking in the messages of such songs, the sins of the flesh, the drug hazes, the spirits, and closed her eyes. She let the debauchery of the band calm her, wash over in waves of comfort, and push away her anger about the dreaded Philip.

When the demonic growls of their guitars ceased, when the singer's scratchy, slurring voice stopped, she inhaled deeply the scents of cigar smoke and weed. She could smell the sex happening in a bathroom stall, feel the burning sensation of liquefied heroine stabbing into someone's forearm. It all felt so good, her lips parted in the ecstasy of it. Then, the metaphorical rain fell heavily on her parade-like happiness as she sensed Philip moving to the stage toward his own drum set.

She watched him, swallowing one more shot of tequila, as he pulled his seat up to the instrument, determined to stay long enough to see the prophetic king walk onto the stage.

When Craig joined Philip, testing his guitar, Max's, and the microphone, she grinned. No one in that crowd below would guess, behind that chiseled face and bright green eyes, that Craig was as villainous as he was alive. Every orifice oozed selfishness, lechery, deceit, overindulgence. He was the very picture of a soul destined for hell, and at such a young age, too. Quite impressive. It's a shame he hadn't worn off on Max just a bit. It would've made Malum's job a lot easier.

Still, the fact that Max remained so holy was actually beneficial to her. It meant her enemy wouldn't need to keep such a tight leash on their messenger, and this meant more opportunity for her to tie her own chain around his neck.

She took another shot, "Last one," she grinned to the bartender as she watched Philip pound his drums. Craig's guitar sounded, and before she knew it, the radiant visage of

Maxwell Lenett strolled onto the stage.

She had to admit, the way the lights fell on him, illuminating the brightness of his eyes, and shadowing his heavy jaw, he was truly beautiful. Too bad such beauty was always assigned to the other side. That was one thing she never understood. Why should everything good and holy materialize in such manners when it so often was hidden inside plain, less appealing packages? For as manipulative as everyone claimed the devil was, no one could deny that God sent his own warriors to earth in perfect packaging. After all, who would take heed to any warning that wasn't spilled from a perfect pouting mouth? Who would care about what someone said if they hadn't first been captivated by how they looked?

It didn't matter. Max was beautiful, sure, and he was holy and pure, but Malum had a date with him, a date she hoped would end with opposite concept: the concept of the devil falling to earth as the most beautiful angel anyone had ever laid eyes on. After all, why did Max, so conservative in action and garb, insist on draping his nails in the color of sadness and evil?

One way or another, this night should surely solidify his place in life—she was the only one who could help answer that eternal question, that question plaguing him continuously every time he put his head to pillow, his hand to paper, or his lips to microphone. If all he believed in wasn't a part of his image, did it really matter anyway?

When his lips opened, the heavenly sound of his vocal chords spilled into the room. She could see, as she made her way toward the door, that the time loop had undoubtedly taken effect. Everyone stood motionless, phones away, eyes focused, watching Max, truly watching him. They were listening, young minds being morphed not only by the purity of his voice, but also by the morality of what he said.

The drums pounded into her head like vice grips as she pushed open the door and moved out onto the street.

Oh, my little angel, she thought, catching her breath as she peered in at him through the door, I'll make you into a Rock God yet.

Max tripped over his chord a few times. Once he had to look away from the microphone for fear of throwing up.

He was quick to cover the mishaps, usually a few well-timed head bangs could cover slipping or almost falling, but the way the alcohol lodged itself inside him promised he'd throw up if he tried to slam his head around so roughly.

Strangely, though, he didn't feel bad. Sure, his stomach twisted here and there, and when he bent down to be eye level with a few people in the crowd it made his vision blur, but once he stopped moving again, everything was fine.

Besides, he reminded himself, only considering such things in the brief pause between songs, or during a particularly large guitar solo, he'd seen both his friends and countless strangers consume a lot more than two small shots and be almost entirely unaffected.

Okay, maybe he was being naive. Maybe going almost twenty-eight years without more than a sip of champagne at his cousin's wedding is why so little affected him so greatly. Still, even with no tolerance at all, he felt certain this isn't what it should feel like.

As he stood from his spot before the crowd, moving back around the microphone to take his guitar again, the music slowed. It was time for that song, the great heartbreak. Time for him to expel small pieces of his soul through his lips.

He blinked slowly, eyes needing more effort to focus on the faces below than normal, and then he opened his lungs.

Strangely, in the course of the gentle music and solemn melodies, somewhere between *Maybe no one ever waits these days* and *maybe I should change,* a violent wave of the emotion seized him. Suddenly, he wasn't present on the stage, but he was that twenty-three year old who stayed up all night inside a rundown hotel room, pouring every ounce of feeling onto a piece of scratchy toilet paper in the flickering light of a dingy green bathroom. Suddenly, everything he usually felt when performing this song, after countless performances, felt closer to him than it had in years.

His voice cracked a little when he sang the words *can't stay, can't wait,* and he had to look downward briefly as he strummed the strings of his guitar. When he looked back up, lips to microphone again, his eyes remained downcast, but obvious to the diligent flock before him was the one small tear that rolled over his left cheek.

He wasn't sure why he was crying. He wasn't sure if it was the emotion of that song, the subject of it and how much he loved her, or something entirely separate. Maybe it was just the alcohol. Maybe it was Malum.

———

"What happened up there?" Philip whispered, placing a hand on his shoulder when he came back into the green room.

"I don't know. Think drinking can make you emotional?" He scrunched his nose, rubbing at his forehead.

"You had, like, two drinks." Craig scoffed, bending over

his guitar case to gently place his instrument inside. Max watched him. Strange how he could be so protective of something inanimate, but so careless with things that were sentient.

"Yeah, most likely," Philip said. "Which is why you shouldn't be doing it."

"It's fine," he mumbled, lowering his head. He looked up to Philip through his lashes, something akin to a troublesome child who hated seeing his parents' disapproval, but planned to continue their disappointment anyway. "Better get to the table, huh?" He smiled weakly.

"Yeah, let's go," Philip said.

He felt better standing there, signing his name to CD cases and T-shirts, seeing people smile, or hearing how something he'd written helped them. He was certain nothing could ever feel better than that, even in his discovery of so many new things this week.

Near his table near the bar, a woman sat with her back turned toward him, careful this time not to be seen. She had no drink. She was careful not to touch the bar at all. The crashing of an intoxicated man into the stool next to her caused her a great deal of discomfort, but she was assigned this great duty, and refused to allow failure to even be an option. Whatever the prophet did, wherever he went, she had to ensure he was still on the correct path.

"'Waiting' is an amazing song," she heard a young girl say to Max and the grays of her eyes sparkled silver.

"Thank you." He smiled, spreading her shirt across the table to sign it.

"We could see it meant a lot to you." An older woman with her hand on the girl's shoulder said. "The emotion was really there."

"Yeah." He chuckled a bit. "Honestly, it's not super rock star to tear up, is it?"

"I think it is," the girl in front of Craig said. She was older than girl in front of Max, but not by much. "Means that whatever you were saying in that song was important."

"Yeah." He smiled, looking down.

"What's it about? She couldn't wait for you to come home from touring or something?" The younger girl said.

The message of that song was important, or at least it used to always feel that way. He thought of Bonum, of how easily she understood what it really meant.

He inhaled deeply, taking all the courage he could summon to look up to her. "No, she, um, she didn't want to wait to be married to experience…the physical aspects of being of being in love." He bit the inside of his jaw briefly, eyes flickering aside from his lowered head. "I did." He looked back down to sign the CD Craig now slid over to him from the other girl.

"You did want to wait?" the younger girl asked.

"Yes, and because she couldn't change my mind, she left me."

"Oh, wow," the younger girl said, pulling the signed T-shirt against her.

The older woman, when Max looked back up to them smiled her approval, tightening her hold of her daughter's shoulder a bit.

When they walked away, and he looked to the other girl, no more than seventeen, her short shorts, tiny shirt, he smiled as he handed her back her CD. "Don't feel like that's all you have to offer, okay?"

She recoiled, eyes widening.

He felt so assumptive in saying it, so judgmental. He

opened his lips to take it back, but she spoke first.

"Oh, my God. I…don't know how you—I mean…" Her brows creased, but her eyes had grown glassy. She lowered her chin, saying lowly, "I don't think that's all I have to offer."

"Good," he said. "You're more than that."

She smiled, a shaky exhale leaving her nostrils as she thanked him.

"What the fuck?" Philip leaned into him, brows furrowed as he watched the girl walk away.

"I don't know," he said. "Just felt like she needed to hear it."

Bonum smiled from her position at the bar. Max was coming into himself quite nicely since the time loop, and she was ecstatic to see that, not only was he still writing for something righteous, but that he was learning not to hide it as intensely.

Unfortunately for Bonum, these confessions, these displays of tears, came from Max's tryst with the intoxicating Malum. Unfortunately for Malum, it was her intoxicating influence, meant to sway him away from such righteousness, that somehow furthered it.

Neither knew of the other's proximity; Malum underestimating the frequency of Bonum's check ins, and Bonum, having never been inside a bar on the same night as Malum, wasn't aware of her presence with the prophet at all.

What worked in Malum's favor, though it made her job more difficult, was that innate purity of Max's spirit that radiated such wholesome energy it covered the small changes alcohol caused in human beings, small changes more easily perceived in those of lesser moral character. Max's moral character, the shining ray of hope, inside dark smoky bars was as close to divinity as a man could get. But she, with her own touch of something divine—a twisted divinity, but divinity all the same—was more than confident in her ability to corrupt it.

"Hey," Max said, moving hurriedly in front of his friends as they tried to leave the merch-table. "Help me tonight, guys. Come on."

"Sure." Philip smiled, patting Max's cheek before turning to the hanging shirts behind them.

"You guys got it—." Craig started, but Max put his hand against his shoulder. "Dude, I gotta get the room set up. I wanna get to the party."

"Yeah, well, so do I," Max said.

Craig's brows lifted, his chin tilting as his head drew back a bit. "Oh, you do?"

"Yeah. Just help me this time, please."

"Well, all right, then." Craig chuckled, a pleased smile curling across his lips.

"Thank you," Max said, and the two moved to collect the rows of stickers and CDs on the table.

"We gonna have some shots or what?" Craig asked, a sly look still painted on his face.

"No, we're not," Philip answered as he turned around, setting the shirts on the table. "You've had enough, huh?" He looked to Max.

"I'm fine," Max muttered dismissively, but his eyes wouldn't rise to meet Philip's parental glare.

"He's a big boy," Craig said. "He's fine."

Philip glowered to Craig before his features fell. Suspiciously, he eyed the bar, the crowds leaving, the few stranglers still lingering near the the stage as they finished their drinks. He didn't think he saw her, but he hadn't really gotten a good look from halfway across the bar.

"A few shots wouldn't hurt—." Craig started again.

"He's already *had* a few shots," Philip scowled, flipping his wrists so the T-shirt in his hand snapped through the air.

"Hey, man, don't get mad at me. I didn't give them to him." His brows jumped, eyes moving to Max. "Wait, you got a girl here?"

Max just shook his head, eyes on the table of products beneath them. Flipping through the stickers, the CDs behind him, Max was starting to wonder if he was merely a part of the mirage celebrity and fame placed before those trapped within the barren, unending wasteland of mature, mundane work, or if he had spent so much time inside it that he, himself, had become some sort of hologram. Looking at his likeness plastered on a spool of countless stickers, stickers placed on cell phones and notebooks and bathroom stalls of high schools, he certainly felt like more a commodity than a person. Thank God he met Bonum, a person who seemed to believe he was much more than just an image, a person who believed that who he was was far more important than what he did. Even better, the prospect of seeing Malum, yet another blessing; another woman far more intrigued with who he was off stage than who he was on it.

It didn't matter now, though. What mattered was avoiding Craig's bullying and bypassing Philip's over-protectionism.

"It is a girl!" Craig laughed, slapping his back before picking up the box in front of him. "Listen, between you and me," he whispered, turning away from the table, and subsequently from Philip. "A few shots never hurt in that endeavor."

Max looked over to him, disdain surely as evident on his

curling lips as the worry was in his pleading eyes. "Yeah, thanks," he said, smiling unconvincingly.

Craig just laughed as he took the box out to the van.

———

Max was overjoyed to be at this party, a frightening concept because it was an entirely one.

He stood awkwardly by the bar, attempting to lean on it, then changing his mind, tucking a hand in a pocket, then removing it. He tried picking up his glass and holding it, really just as some sort of comfort item, but the fact that it only contained water made him feel even more uncomfortable with it.

He didn't think any effects of the tequila were lingering inside his mind, but he decided this moment would've been better if they had.

Whether it was his light-weight status, or the expectation of what alcohol should do in the mind of someone who'd never been intoxicated creating some sort of placebo effect, he wasn't certain. But after just one shot of tequila, Max felt undeniably more comfortable with Malum's closeness, even going so far as to taste a bit of her flesh deemed too sacred to touch on his previous girlfriend until they'd spent a significantly longer amount of time together. After the second, Max felt like he could kiss her. A complete stranger. A stranger who'd, when they first met, despite her kindness, felt off to him. Furthermore, the two shots combined seemed to make the expression of his feelings, even those that had been locked away inside lyrics for years, much easier. It made his morals less embarrassing, and his intuition heightened.

Yes, he thought with absolutely certainty, A drink in this

matter might not hurt. But just one this time. The other effects, like motion sickness and stumbling, weren't ones he much cared for.

Armed with the accessories of the occasion, a glass of "whatever is clear, flavored, and mixed with Sprite", Max wandered slowly through the distinct groups of people forming in little huddles between the two rooms. When someone approached him, he'd engage politely, eyes always scanning the area behind them, flicking to the door, ever searching for the one face that seemed to stand out so easily in a dark and crowded room.

After quite some time with no luck, he resigned himself back to the bar, leaning over it defeatedly. He bit the inside of his lip, brows lifting, as he stared to the drink. He hadn't had a single sip, but now, it looked appealing. Weren't blackouts a thing? Strangely that seemed better than the rejection of the first person in quite some time he felt he could depend on. He scolded himself for attaching such hopes on someone he barely knew at all.

He exhaled exasperatedly, straightening his back as he focused on the condensation forming on the outside of the glass, palms flat on the table, arms extended.

Fine, he thought. What could it hurt?

Picking it up, raising it to his lips, Max took a drink. He leaned back over the bar, never releasing the glass, but debating further if another drink was appropriate. He decided against it.

"Lying's a sin, you know?" a smooth voice said behind him.

He turned, blue eyes meeting golden ones.

He smiled, but his brows pulled slightly. "What?"

She leaned against the island, eyes on the drink beside

him. "You said you weren't really a drinker."

"Oh, I'm just trying it out." He leaned against the bar, attempting to play it cool.

"And how's it going for you?"

"Well, I haven't gotten sick or done something stupid yet, so okay, I guess. It just doesn't taste like the one from the other night." He looked to her. "Whatever you ordered for me…I liked it, but can't recreate it."

"Here, let me see." She reached around him, and his shoulders fell a bit as the heat from her arm caressed him. She looked to him as she took the glass, their eyes connected, bodies brushing against each other, and everything seemed to move in slow motion. She smiled, leaning back now that she had the drink, and Max felt suddenly cold in the loss of proximity.

She took a sip. "Oh," she said. "No, you didn't use the right vodka."

She threw her head back, finishing the drink, then sat the empty glass down. As she reached across the bar, Max watched the bottle she took.

"It's cherry vodka," she said as she poured it into the glass, then the Sprite. "Here, try this one."

"Oh," he said, lifting his arm hesitantly toward the glass before letting it fall. "One was probably enough."

"Yes, one is enough, but you only had one sip of the other. This is your one." She smiled, her brows lifting.

"O-okay," he said, smiling slightly before he took the glass.

She watched him, golden eyes fixated onto his. She leaned against the counter with an ease that was somehow demanding in its comfort, and then she lifted a brow, looking impatient.

"Okay," he said again, a genuine smile gracing his lips this time, and then he brought the glass to his lips. The same tingling sensation of fizzing pop brushed against his lips, and then he took a drink.

"Better?" she asked.

"Better," he echoed in agreement.

"Good," she said lowly, an obvious air of seduction in her eyes when she cast down her chin and gazed up to him through her long, dark lashes.

When she took another glass from the counter and poured herself the same drink, he looked to his own and had another sip of it.

She lifted her glass toward him with one hand, her other moving the tall chair of the bar closer to him as she moved onto it fluidly, and she grinned, "To no interruptions this time."

Max licked his lip, looking around the hotel room. When he saw no trace of Philip in this area, he smiled back to her. "Cheers."

She watched him intently as he took a larger drink of the mixture, eyes narrowing over her glass of the same concoction as she took a small swig. Her lips curled at the sweetened taste. Good thing she knew what he'd like and decided to build up a tolerance for it.

Max, as he drank, considered how little he had worried under the affects of the shots. He felt he could've said anything he thought without fear of the inevitable reaction to it. Maybe, here with Malum, he should chug this drink, then maybe have a second, and a third. It would make talking to her much easier considering the "disappointing" discovery she was sure to make if she stayed around as long as he intended. He'd felt ever since his first heartbreak that hiding these values was necessary. It made sense in theory. Here with Malum, in the practice of it, it felt wrong. Even if he wasn't lying, per-se, an intentional omission could still be seen as betrayal. As the once-receiver of betrayal, he definitely didn't want to put that turmoil onto anyone else. Beside this, she'd have to find out about certain commitments anyway. After all, in a time when God was dead, the only religion left to practice was sex. Undoubtedly, Malum leaving him for the same reason Jessie did would hurt more after a few weeks together than it would right now, but how did that saying go about losing love or not loving at all?

He looked over to her, watched the way her tilting head made her stares seem somewhat dreamy, and took another drink.

"So quiet tonight," she said. "You didn't hurt your voice, did you?"

"No." He smiled. How considerate she was. "Just thinking."

"About what?"

He breathed a small laugh, looking down to the drink in his hand. "I might need another of these before I tell you."

"Well, then," she said, taking the vodka bottle and refilling his only half-full glass. When she sat it down, she looked back to him cheerfully, met with his raised brows and almost-smiling lips. "I'm curious," she shrugged her shoulder.

He chuckled, bringing the glass to his lips and drinking. "Oh, no," he said, taking the bottle of Sprite and filling the cup until its contents spilled over.

"Oh, no." She chuckled, playfully mocking as she grabbed a few napkins and placed them around the bottom of the cup. "Gotta drink it now." She laughed.

Seeing no other alternative, Max leaned over the glass carefully to level the mixture.

He still felt nothing, though. He wanted a little bit of that edge, not as much of it as before, but just enough that he could tell her how badly he wanted to see her tonight, how he already couldn't wait until the next time they ended up in the same city, how he wished she could follow them to Charlotte tomorrow. With this in mind, he took another drink.

"You're far enough gone that you can't pour a drink," she said, smiling, "So I think you've got enough liquid courage in you to tell me what you're thinking."

"I'm thinking." He exhaled, looking down nervously, but when he did, he noted that slight distortion to his vision that only occurred when his head moved. Obviously some effect was taking place, so why didn't he feel braver? "I guess, I'm just thinking about you."

"Well, I'm right here." She placed her hand on his, the heat reminding him of a protective blanket when it absorbed into his flesh.

"Right," he said lowly, smiling as he looked down to their connection. He wondered if it felt less and less hot—and by less hot, he simply noted that it didn't feel like his flesh was searing away from his bones this time—because of his slightly-inebriated state. Maybe he was just building a tolerance.

"Don't be shy," she said teasingly.

"I'm not shy," Max said, looking down to the drink. Not wanting to say what would inevitably end their budding relationship was quite different than being shy. Whether he said it or not, Max figured he'd let the vodka decide and took a fairly large drink.

"Okay, so what is it?" She leaned in, and Max looked to

her. There was something about the way their eyes connected, something that affected him the way Bonum's did but in a somehow different way. It was faster, more urgent. It felt the opposite of calm, but where it'd felt intimidating the first night he saw it, now it was starting to become exciting.

"I guess I'm just thinking…" He smiled, looking away. Shaking his head, he finally looked back to her. When he did, he got too caught up in that thrilling intensity, and with his brain now soaking up even more of the new substance, he wasn't able to say any of the things he'd considered. Instead, "Your eyes are really messing with me," just flew out. She smirked when his eyes narrowed. He leaned closer to her. "They really are gold, aren't they?"

"Yes," she said lowly, another seductive glisten inside them as she lowered her chin. There was something about the way she peered up through her dark lashes, the contrast of that deep black to those shimmering pools of gold. Their gleam, he realized during this close inspection, seemed always half seductive, half heinous. "Do they frighten you?" she asked, the grin on her crimson lips more amused than usual.

Max's brows creased, lips curling in a bit of confusion as he looked to her expression. He wondered if any smile he'd ever seen on her prior to this was genuine at all.

A small breath left his parted lips, head tilting a bit. "No." He stammered a bit, shaking his head out of the gaze he seemed stuck inside. "I mean, I think…" He looked up to her, a hint of worry crossing through his eyes like a passing cloud in an otherwise clear blue sky. A sharp exhale left his lips, eyes stuck on hers again. "No, I think they're beautiful."

Her brows lifted, her grin magnifying as her chin lifted. "Maybe that's the vodka," she said, wrapping her hand around the bottle and topping him off again.

He chuckled. "Maybe it's you," he said.

"Maybe." She lifted her brows, watching him drink, noting the way he swayed when he tilted his head backward, the way he gripped the counter with his free hand as if he'd fall without its brace.

"You know," he started, stumbling when he moved to sit the glass down. Malum extended her arms, helping to steady him, but the heat rolling against the fabric of his shirt, dying to break through the knitting and kiss his skin, completed distracted him from the amount of strength within them.

After he steadied himself, with her aid, he chuckled.

"Easy." She laughed, using her grip on him to turn him around.

"Oh, man," he said, keeping one hand on her forearm and raising one to his head. "How does this happen all of a sudden like that?"

"You're just not seasoned enough to feel it coming on," she said, helping him to stand.

When he steadied, her hands still on his sides, she moved against him. Her fingers slipped across his sides, his back, pulling the fabric of his shirt gently into folds between her finger and thumb.

"So warm." He smiled. "How are you so warm?"

"Maybe you're just really cold," she said, taking a step closer.

He smiled, feeling the temperature rise with one small step. He remembered the street the previous night, the heat shielding him from the cold air of October. With so much happening to his mind now, so much influence his brain was drowning in, Max wondered if that hadn't all been an illusion too, if it weren't as cold as it seemed, if she weren't as warm. Maybe his mind found some way to justify being so near to her, so near the woman whose gazes caught his voice inside his throat, a woman who so obviously enjoyed all the things he'd never been.

He decided not to be a disappointment this time. This time, he could be who everyone expected him to be. He'd be who she wanted.

Hesitantly, he lifted his own arms, fingertips brushing against her arms, barely touching, but close enough that the nerve endings in his flesh had begun to fire. He licked his lips, his palms inching closer and closer to connection as his fingers and thumb spread out across the curve of her shoulder. He felt like he'd been numb, that nothing before her had ever existed. Her flesh felt hotter than anything else, softer at the same time, and comforting in its materialism. It was real. It existed. And here, somehow in this same realm of life, he existed with her. What could matter more than this connection to someone who spent his life desperately trying to discover what exactly it was that made humans feel connected to one another? Maybe it wasn't the emotion of a song, maybe it wasn't words or feelings or thoughts. Maybe it was the certainty of skin, the seeing and touching that proved it true. It wasn't invisible, it wasn't without color or scent or taste. The only thing he could know for certain between the physical and the spirit was the physical. The body could be proven. It was so undeniably true that no one needed to prove such a thing. But the idea that residing inside a body was a soul, well, no matter how many years he'd spent in Catholic school, no matter how many Saturday night masses he'd attended, no matter how many Sundays he spent praying, it could not be proven. So why hold back in fear of it?

He held onto her more tightly, moving his hands along her back. Using that grip, he began to urge her closer, and she complied all too eagerly.

He smiled. If the small breath that left his nose had passed through his lips, it might've sounded a bit like a laugh.

"What is it?" She said, smiling a bit.

"I like being close to you," he said without thinking through a small, somewhat sloppy grin.

"Wait," Malum said, feigning an amused confusion, "Max, are you drunk?"

"Nah. I mean, well, I don't really know." Max slurred a bit. "I've never been drunk before. I guess the only way to really know for sure is have a few more drinks. Like, enough that we know I have to be drunk. Then we'll compare me right now to me after a few more of these." He held his empty glass up and almost dropped it.

"Your logic is sound." Malum grinned, chilling him when she pulled away to grab the vodka. She poured a bit more than necessary into his glass. She watched Max as she did, noting in the silence, how very angelic his straight nose and creamy skin appeared. If she didn't have such a natural aversion to such products of perfections, she might actually be genuinely attracted to him.

When her golden eyes moved away from him, scanning the countertop of bottles and cans, she frowned. "No more Sprite?"

"Maybe in the fridge—."

"Ah, stop. You move from here to there and that mother hen friend of yours will surely be on our case. I'll go get it."

Max smiled, watching her contently as she moved around the counter and into the kitchen. When his eyes fell onto the drink, he wondered if he really was drunk. He wondered if he could have the typical drunken experience he'd seen happen so many times at so many of these parties. He shook his head.

His only opportunity here was Malum, and the typical drunken experience would require them never speaking again. That thought alone was heartbreaking, and then he chuckled to himself.

"What's so funny?" Malum had walked up to the bar without Max even realizing. "Let me in on the joke."

"It's, um, it's nothing." Max said, still smiling.

"It's not nothing, you can't even keep a straight face. I'd love to know what type of thoughts fly through a drunken Maxwell Lenett's mind." She poured Sierra Mist into the vodka. "Not Sprite, but I actually think this is better."

"I, uh, I was just thinking that, although I've witnessed plenty of drunken experiences, seen the aftermath of them, I've never really had one."

"You know, I want say that shocks me," she said as she twisted the cap back onto the soda. "But it doesn't." And it really didn't. Malum knew things about Max no one could know, not even himself. Well, no one except maybe Bonum. Even still, Malum had access to things Bonum didn't, things that Bonum's Higher Up didn't bother with, things too hidden inside recesses far too dark for anyone in her line of work to find. They wouldn't even know where to look. "Any reason you've never joined in on the fun?"

"I, uh—." I'm catholic, he thought, Doesn't sound like a justifiable answer. He knew plenty of Catholics, Philip included, who didn't use the faith as an excuse to deny all the basic coming-of-age experiences most people went through before their twenty-first birthday, especially well into their late twenties. "You know, I saw a lot of people do a lot of dumb things that I even felt embarrassed for them about. Then I saw them do even worse things, things that ended up hurting them a lot more than falling and getting a bruise. I just stopped coming to the parties. Focused on my work. It felt more important anyway."

"And yet, here you are," she said softly.

Max chuckled. "Yeah, well, here *you* are."

The alcohol allowed Max's emotions full range of motion, and he went from finding his current situation exciting to now feeling guilty over it.

Malum could tell a nerve was struck. She brushed her fingers over the back of his hand, the warmth of her touch and the coldness of the drink in his palm created an odd tingling sensation in his hand, one that felt like it'd been asleep and was waking up.

Max looked up at Malum like a lost puppy. He was vulnerable, confused, and feeling very uneasy. Sure, it could have been the booze, but Max worried that it was Malum. Malum, who had been giving him all these feelings. Malum, who made him as afraid as she did thrilled. Malum, whose beauty was topped by inhumanly fascinating eyes. Malum, who was standing so close to him in this hotel room.

She grinned. "And you like being here with me?"

"Yes," he whispered. He looked away briefly, clearing this throat a bit. "Do you, um, do you like being here with me?" He smiled fearfully.

"Hm," she tapped the first finger of her other hand against her lower lip, eyes rolling as if she were considering it. When she finally looked back to him, she smirked. Leaning forward, she whispered, "No."

"Oh," he said, looking down and lifting his glass, losing the connection to Malum's hand in the process.

The glass shook against his lip, his lips shaking on their own, they needed no help from his hand. He told himself it was the liquor, but he feared that it was Malum. Everything that had been happening to him was because of her. He felt his first attraction in years to her, visited his first party willingly in years for her. He took his first shot with Malum, got drunk for the first time with her. He wanted more firsts with her.

He thought about first kisses, first touches. He wondered what it would feel like to have another person's hands trail along his skin in that intimate way he never let himself truly consider. He wondered what it would feel like if those hands belonged to Malum, if her heat were caressing him while she did. Just as his mind was wandering into much more intimate firsts, he emptied his glass, forcing his focus to return to reality.

He looked to Malum shyly, the pain of all the rejection he feared now visible to her.

Her brow lifted, and she smirked. "You're not going to ask me why?"

"Um, okay" he said, brows knitting together as they lifting in the center. "Why don't you like being here with me?"

Malum looked over her shoulder, then turned her head to look over the other. She slid down the counter, leaning very close to him, and whispered, "I'd rather be somewhere with you alone."

Max's brows raised, genuinely surprised by what she said. If it were true, he thought, it's a good thing he didn't confess his lack of sins to her.

Still leaning into him, and edging closer, Malum lifted her chin slightly. Max lowered his own, following the instinctual pulls to meet her in the middle of the small space between them. He wondered how warm her lips would be as he stared to them, heart pounding in his chest as his own neared them, closer and closer until his hand slipped from its spot on the counter, sending his empty glass plummeting to the floor. His body slumped a bit on that same side, losing the balance of the counter, but Malum's hands were quickly on his sides.

He looked down to them, swallowing thickly at just how low they were. Their heat, snaking its way inside his T-shirt, kissed the tender flesh just above his hip bones.

She'd done it on purpose, sure, but she looked up to him after she looked at her hands. Smiling gently, she said, "I just didn't want you to fall."

"Thanks," Max said as he tried standing straight without swaying.

"I don't think the theory needs tested," she said, smiling as she removed only one of her hands.

"I'm really, I'm not that drunk. I'm fine," Max lied. He knew his was inebriated. He knew that he was struggling to even stand on his own. She knew it, too.

Worse, however, Max knew that he was not fine. He was attracted to his new friend, and in this state of easy confessions and less concerns, that was potentially dangerous for him.

"You're not fine," she said, no smile to her lips, no playful tone to her voice.

It made Max extremely nervous. Although Malum was only referring to his issue with standing, he assumed somehow she meant in general. He figured seeing him stumble was unattractive, especially in a room full of men standing tall and confident, and that being so affected by what was, to the other men, barely a sip, might seem like weakness. He didn't want her to leave him, and he worried her exit was coming.. He had to fix it somehow. "I…I'm fine."

Malum drew closer to him. She noticed the change in

Max's breathing; He was no longer breathing through his nose. His body had turned off, lungs frozen in their place, fear gripping the organs and halting their one function. Desperate for oxygen, he parted his lips in an effort to catch his breath.

Malum, taking note of this change, couldn't take her eyes off of his mouth.

She could feel, beneath the one hand still holding onto his body, Max's chest rise and fall as his lips remained parted. They were so inviting now, not just because of Malum's duty, but also because of the way they breathed. It represented to Malum the nervousness rushing Max; the fear, the worry inside him. He'd never been drunk, never been so vulnerable, and here, standing before her, he was the most timid man she'd ever been sent after.

Malum couldn't help but stare at them as she stepped closer. Such innocence was usually so abhorrent, but the potential of its corruption at her hands made it seem the most appealing thing in any world she'd experienced.

That appeal, that untouched territory, forced Malum's body into instinct. Nothing was as calculated as it had been. She didn't have to think about moving against him, touching him. She didn't have to tell herself to. She didn't even have to acknowledge the fact that she wanted to.

Max watched her as she moved against him, feeling the heat touch him gently. He closed his eyes, momentarily basking in the comfort of it, but they fluttered open again when Malum lifted her hand up to Max's face. Her palm rested on his jaw, she brushed her thumb along Max's lower lip. Max drew his head back slightly, the warmth of Malum's fingers feeling hotter against the delicate flesh of his lip, but he found that he was against the wall. He had nowhere to go.

With furrowed brows, he gazed at his friend with uncertainty, excitement, and fear. He thought he'd built a tolerance to Malum's heat, but the undeniable fact of just how hot her hands were was troublesome. She'd just been holding a glass, a glass full of ice and cold liquids, how could her hand feel this hot, and why only his lips now?

Then the realization of body part struck him. He thought he'd blown his chance when he knocked over his glass, but it would seem, in this moment, that Malum was picking up just where they'd paused for it. A quick exhale left him. His heart began to pump more quickly.

"Just need to get you adjusted to it." Malum's voice was almost a whisper. While it remained assertive, it was sultry and seductive.

"Adjusted——." His brows creased a bit, but her thumb fell from his lips. Using it to hold his chin, she urged him forward, closer and closer, their lips almost touching. He felt such heat, it surrounded him, brushing against his lips, his cheeks, and flowing around his neck and shoulders. Draped in comfort, lips almost touching hers, Max's eyes fell closed again, and, a moment later, he felt the gentle pressure of her lips on his.

Pinned between the wall and Malum's lips, Max thought for sure that he was dreaming. She was warm and soft, her hands caressing his jaw as she kissed him tenderly.

No one who had ever been this close—granted it wasn't a long list—had felt so undeniably good.

Her heated lips shot fire through his own, tingling his teeth as it moved inside his jaw, and wrapped around its joints.

Melting against her, Max groaned a bit in this throat, his lips parting slightly to consume more of hers.

Malum's hand moved gently from Max's jaw, caressing his cheek lightly as it brushed by, stopping in Max's hair. She kept her palm near Max's neck as her heated fingers, now lost in an untamed jungle of thick blond locks, traced circles along Max's skin.

While this massage elicited another slight moan from Max's throat, it also caused his hair to become wrapped around Malum's fingers. She began to close her hand, drawing Max's hair along with her fingers as they moved slowly into her palm. Now that Malum had a fist full of Max's hair, it was time to bring him even closer. With a sudden but deliberate tug, Malum moved her fist toward the floor causing Max's head to tilt backward slightly.

Shocked by the forceful tug, Max inhaled roughly as his eyes popped open. They were met by Malum's golden orbs as she pulled her lips away from Max's.

After a quick pant left his lip, Max smiled, leaning back into Malum. Although hair pulling had always been associated with bullies in his mind, Max somehow enjoyed the way the dominance of the tug blended with the softness of Malum's kiss to create something that he felt beyond his head or his lips.

As he tried to keep his thoughts straight, they all seemed to completely escape him, and his mind became very clear. It no longer needed to talk to him, and it no longer needed to talk to his body. His instincts had come back as quickly as they'd left. His lungs breathed. His heart beat. His blood flowed. His arms raised. His hands, which had found Malum's face, pulled her against him. The warmth of her body radiated from her like a great fire, spreading its heat throughout his body, but Max couldn't deny another heat coursing through him. This one, like a slippery serpent, started at his core and rushed through each appendage, encouraging his hands to grip her more tightly, and his lips to push at hers with greater urgency.

At first, he refused to acknowledge what this heated desire meant, what it was pressing him to do, but when her hips fell against his, the acceptance of what was occurring became too apparent to ignore.

The thought sent Max into a panic. He couldn't focus on Malum's lips, although he desperately wanted to. He had to focus on his own body, instead of hers, and ensure nothing was acting on its accord in pursuit of this connection.

What troubled him was not being certain whether or not he actually wanted it. He wanted Malum, he knew this to be true, and he wanted to be this close to her. He wanted to kiss her. But he felt, until this attempt at drinking, that he had only wanted these things in conjunction with getting to know her better, and eventually through that deeper understanding, develop an actual relationship.

As it presented itself now—Malum's tongue tracing his lips before it crossed their barrier into his mouth, her free hand running down his side while the other played with his hair—Max wasn't sure what Malum wanted.

He supposed anyone else at their age could begin something serious this way. But he wasn't anyone else at their age. He wasn't even anyone else at this party.

Still, the physicality of the embrace was pleasurable. He moaned slightly as his hands moved from Malum's face to her shoulders. He considered using his grip there to ease her away from him, but the feel of her skin was too enjoyable, too exciting to stop, and his hands ended up wandering further, down her arms, brushing at her sides, and falling away to her hips.

He wished he knew exactly how to proceed, how to touch Malum and exactly where. He wished he knew how to take Malum's clothes off as he imagined what bare flesh would feel like on his fingertips.

That thought crept up again, seizing him so suddenly his muscles tightened.

He didn't know how to continue such acts for a reason. He held a very specific reason, one so deeply tied to his beliefs that he felt guilty for even considering it. He thought of Jessie, the subject of his solemn song, and how easy it was to deny even this person whom he loved so dearly. What was it about Malum that made those temptations seem so much more appealing? Was it her, or was it just the booze?

Completely enveloped in the prospect of what may happen between them, nothing outside of Max seemed to exist to Malum. She felt his chest move against hers when he breathed, felt the pumping of his nervous heart.

She felt his hands stop their exploration, but felt his fingers tighten around her dress when the softness of her lips move against his jaw, the wet sensation of her tongue as it peaked out sporadically amongst the faint, teasing kisses to taste his flesh.

Everything about Max in that moment—his heavy breathing, his needy seize of her dress, the dulcet moans that would escape his lips—became overwhelming to Malum. She no longer cared about who he was or how gently she had to handle him. His morals were irrelevant to her. The taste of something so pure beneath her lips, something so hard to sully coming so close to such a fall, the high it provided was unmatched.

She moved her lips to Max's again, her fingers floating above his jeans to brush against the tender flesh of his hip bones, before they were lost into the cotton barrier between them. He felt heat, searing heat, dancing along his chest. It burned at first, but then, soft pets followed. Gentle pets, fingertips to flesh, as she led him into an even deeper kiss.

Max's frame was draped in porcelain flesh, and while Malum disliked the feel of its perfect ivory, she was excited by its sensitivity. The way that he would gasp and tremble at a brief kiss or fleeting touch was proof enough that these specific kisses, these touches to specifics spots, were brand new, each one bringing Max closer and closer to the greatest event he was never meant to have.

"Max," she whispered, ready to suggest they go elsewhere; ready to guide him—hurriedly, as she was growing impatient—through that act which stood before her kind as a righteous dam, and with each touch, each heavy breath, each push and pull of ecstasy, another chunk of that dam would break away. By the time they were finished, the floodgates would be broken, and sin would run as rampant through his veins as the blood did when she touched him. "Why don't we…" she whispered, kissing him between words.

"Why don't we take a little break," Philip's voice interrupted.

The pair looked over to him. Malum's lips curled, a great exhale left her nose.

"Philip," Max said, trying his best not to slur.

Philip's eyes narrowed. "We're drinking now?"

"You always drink," he retorted.

"Yes, but you never do."

"It's my fault," she said playfully.

Max smiled to Philip, awkwardly saying, "This is Malum."

"Hi," she said, unhooking her right hand from Max's

waist in order to shake Philip's.

"Hi." He smiled, trying to mask the immediate distaste he felt for her, but failing. "Well, it's nice to meet you, but I'm going to need to steal Max for just a moment."

"What? Why?" he protested.

"Just for a moment. Come on."

"What's your problem?" Max asked, looking to Philip upset, but he walked with him.

"My problem? Max, you just chugged three drinks handed to you by the woman you were avoiding so desperately the other night that you fell asleep on the toilet."

"The tub." He rolled his eyes. "But that was before I knew her."

"You don't know her now."

"You don't know half the men you hook up with, and Craig doesn't know any of the women."

"You don't hook up, Max. You don't drink. That's my point."

"It's only a couple of drinks," he said, pulling away from Philip and heading back into the kitchen.

"Hey," Max called to Malum as he approached her, taking her cheeks into his hands. After leaning down to offer her a chaste kiss, she pulled back. "Sorry about that."

"It's okay," she said. "I should be going, though." Her golden eyes glanced over to Philip. She knew she wasn't getting anywhere with him watching her so intently tonight.

His hands fell. He exhaled defeatedly. "Oh, right."

"No, no." She took his cheek in her hand now. "I have to be in North Carolina tomorrow for work. I need to get some sleep."

"Wait…" Max smiled, his brows knitting. "North Carolina?"

"Charlotte, specifically."

"Well, we're…" His brows furrowed completely, a small scoff leaving his parted lips. "We're going to be there tomorrow."

"You're kidding," she said, grinning.

"Nope." He smiled.

"Then I'll see you tomorrow, maybe."

"Maybe?" he asked. "If you're done with work you can come to the show, or if not, we can hang out after, right?"

"I mean, if your babysitter over there lets me." She raised a brow, glancing over Max's shoulder.

"He thinks he's watching out for me."

"How old does he think you are?" She curled her nose.

"No, it's not that. He just…"

"He just does whatever he wants. I mean, I watched him at that party in Ohio. He drank and went scurrying away with someone he just met. But you." She scoffed.

"Me, what?"

"Well, God forbid," she said, gritting her teeth, then she smiled through it briefly. She could hardly say the word. "God forbid you have any fun. I mean, you never come to parties, you never get to meet anyone, and you finally have, and—." She paused, exhaling. "No, I'm sorry," she said, acting sincere.

"No, go ahead." He smiled, taking her hand.

"Maybe I'm just upset because I…Well, I never meet guys like you." She masked the grin trying to spread across her lips. She was good at this. It wasn't a matter of ego. It was fact. "Guys like you are pretty rare. Maybe I'm just mad that he doesn't seem to think you deserve to relax a little. I don't know. It's just…Why can't you have fun? Why are you different?" She scoffed, looking down. She was selling it. She knew exactly why he was different, even if Max and Philip didn't.

"I don't know," he whispered softly, brows knitting a little as he considered it.

She rose to her tiptoes, placing a small kiss on his lips. "I'll maybe see you tomorrow, then?"

"Yeah, see you tomorrow." He smiled, watching her walk away.

Philip stood against the door frame, arms crossed over his chest as he watched her exit. When she opened the door, she looked over her shoulders, eyes narrowing as they met Philip's.

His brows creased when he caught her expression, head tilting as he stood away from the frame.

Her eyes, those golden rays inside her irises, seemed to burn red. His lips parted, he took a step closer instinctively, but she turned her head, and was gone.

He looked over to Max, who shook his head, taking a bottle from the array on the counter and disappearing into the next room. When he closed the door behind him, he locked it.

CHAPTER FOUR

"Dude!" Craig called to Max, his voice echoing inside the room, pounding into Max's ears. "Man, I am so sick of you locking us out of rooms and shit. Get up!"

Max winced as he sat up. His skin felt tight and dry and his head was killing him. He lifted his hand to his eyes to rub at them. They were dryer than they'd ever been. No, this was it, he decided, as each pound of Craig's fist to the door felt like a blow to Max's head. No more drinking.

"All right," he grumbled, flinging the blanket off of himself, and shuffling to the door.

"Damn." Craig scoffed, walking by him. "All my shit's in here."

"Sorry," he mumbled.

He moved out to the kitchen area of the first room, the one with a refrigerator full of food, and removed the coffee creamer. He hoped to make it back to their other room before he saw Philip, but his luck just didn't go that well.

"Morning," Philip said. "There's already coffee made over here."

"Yeah," Max said lowly. His lips frowned a bit, his head lowered. "Thanks," he said as he moved back into the kitchen.

Pouring himself a cup, Max saw visions of other pouring liquids, the fizzing clear Sprite and the smooth clear of the vodka. His free hand rushed to his mouth, an overwhelming lump rising in his throat.

"Best not to think about it," Philip said. "At least not until you're up and it's out of your system."

His head tilted toward Philip slightly, offering a small smile, but his eyes never looked up to his friend's.

After stirring some sugar into his coffee, Max took the cup, shoulders hunched around his face, and went back into the other room.

"Another thing, dude," Craig started when Max entered.

Max paused, eyes rolling as his head went back. He didn't know which room was worse.

"Don't stand out in the open like that. You know he's not gonna let that shit happen. Next time you see someone you like…" He stood, throwing his bag over his shoulder, then he put a hand on Max's shoulder. "You lock her in the room with you. Get it?"

There was so much wrong with what Craig was saying, but Max's entire being hurt too badly to form even a one-word response. He smiled.

"All right," Craig said, patting him. "Thirty minutes. Let's go."

Max moved through the hotel rooms slowly, seeing the array of bottles in, and piling around, the trash can.

He hadn't changed his clothes when he went to bed. He didn't feel like changing them now.

Anyway, they smelled like Malum, like the strange blend of vodka and Sprite, and some other indistinct scent he couldn't place.

Either way, it was all a marvelous blend he could curl up inside in the backseat of the van. He could close his eyes, inhale deeply, and relive the only time in his twenty-seven years he felt like he was normal.

Maybe the alcohol was to thank for that. Sure, it hadn't blocked all of his moral-code from seeping into the romance of the evening, but without it, he was certain he would've just pushed Malum away. He hoped Philip wouldn't aid him in that.

His eyes flashed over to Philip, who was leaning against the side of the elevator, a toothpick in one hand, his phone in the other.

Why hadn't he gotten Malum's number yet? Such a weird thing not to have after more than two minutes of knowing someone.

Then again, he considered, maybe the connection she desired wasn't manufactured. Maybe she desired something a bit more personal than that.

Too personal it almost seemed last night as Max considered it.

Sure, he was mad at Philip, but in this moment, Max, looking back on himself almost giving up one of his strongest convictions, felt a bit thankful for him, too.

Philip's emotions weren't so mixed. He was able to drive for about ten minutes before seeing Max, hungover and in last night's clothes, got the better of him.

"What was the plan, then?" He said pointedly.

Max's eyes shot over to the rear view mirror. "What?"

"What was the plan last night?"

"Nothing happened."

"No, but it sure looked like something was about to."

"Man, Phil." Craig scoffed.

"You stay out of this. Put your earphones in and watch some porn or whatever it is you do when you're not being a complete dick, but you." He looked back into the mirror at Max. "What were you thinking?"

"I'm twenty-seven," he muttered. "Three months older than you, you realize," he said more clearly.

"Yeah, three months older than me, but that behavior had nothing to do with your age."

"That behavior? It's the same behavior as yours. It was much milder than Craig's."

"Yeah, and I try my best to save those poor drunken girls from him. If they're sober, that's not my business, but *you* weren't sober."

"It was only a couple of drinks——."

"It was far more than you're used to."

"Dude, Craig's right," he snapped, his headache getting the better of him. Malum's words getting the better of him, if he were really honest.

"Excuse me?"

"That. That right there. You're not my mom."

"No, I'm not, but I know her pretty well. What would she think of——?"

"What would yours think? You forget I know yours, too. You forget we went to the same school. Maybe your sister approves of everything you do, but your parents wouldn't, so until you come to terms with that, don't lecture me about mine."

Philip shook his head, his nostrils flaring. "You're not

everyone else, Max. You can't do the stuff everyone else does."

"Why?" he asked, his voice growing louder. "Why not? Why can't I have fun? Why can't I relax a little? Why can't I meet a girl and get to know her the same way everyone else does, huh? Why?"

"I don't know," Philip said, and he truly didn't, but from the time they met, Philip's friendship always felt more like a brother checking on his younger sibling.

As they grew older, as Max's strong beliefs never faltered, that sense of protection couldn't fade, either. All Max was, all he'd ever been, was gentle, timid, kind-hearted. He was certain the things the nuns said were true, never swayed away from their teachings when it came to his own personal choices, and while he'd confided in Philip one night, many years ago, when they first started this band, that he felt his purpose had something to do with the way he was leading his life, Philip couldn't help but to agree. Maybe not because he believed in Max as some sort of modern prophet, not entirely anyway, but because it was a gimmick not many bands in their genre adopted.

As they got older, however, passing twenty-first birthdays, twenty-fifth ones, Philip started seeing Max in a light Max himself was now losing focus on. Max was purity in a time of corruptive forces being the most trendy. He was respect in a time when people seemed to disrespect themselves in the pursuit of trying to gain it.

To Philip, Max became the one soul on earth who was incapable of deceit, of untrustworthiness. Max was the only person Philip knew for certain put others' needs ahead of his own personal gain. That sense of protection, that big-brother bond since childhood, was only intensified by this. And now, seeing Max drunk and stumbling, seeing his hands on someone's hips, a body against his in such a way, it made Philip feel like *he* was failing. Of all people in this world, he didn't want to fail Max. "I just think people need a role model like you," he said softly.

"Yeah, well, stop inviting fans to the parties and they won't know what I am."

He looked out of the window. Strange for him to want to be so hidden only a few days after he'd decided to be so seen.

He put his own earbuds in, turning the volume as high as it would go. It wasn't in an effort to tune out Philip, however. He wanted to tune out himself.

When they arrived in the new city, they scoped out the club they'd be playing, and found a restaurant nearby. They wouldn't be staying in Charlotte tonight. Max couldn't remember if he'd told Malum that or not. Because of this, he hoped he'd see her at the show. It didn't matter what time they planned to leave. Max was making time for her.

When they exited the car, only Craig removed his earbuds from his ears. Only Craig and Philip would look at one another.

Max refused to have another uncomfortable conversation with Philip. He refused to be told what to do. He wasn't a child, and, as Malum so astutely pointed out, he should be allowed to relax every now and again.

When they entered the restaurant and the hostess greeted them, only Philip and Craig responded to her. When she led them to their table, Max watched Philip and Craig slip into their booth, then he removed one of his earbuds.

"Mind if I sit there?" He pointed to the table behind theirs.

Her head tilted a bit, eyes shifting to the two men in the booth before moving back to him. "No, that's fine," she said, setting his menu down on the empty table.

"Thanks." He smiled, replacing his earbud as he slipped inside the booth.

Craig craned his head so he could see around Philip, his brows creasing as he stared at Max's back.

He hunkered over his notebook, the new music he'd written and recorded before they left for the tour pouring so loudly into his ears he could feel its vibration in the buds themselves. He lifted his left hand to his lips, biting at the nails feverishly.

He hadn't written anything in days. He was starting to shake because of it.

He felt his waitress pound her notepad against the table, and he looked up to her wide-eyed. Somehow he'd forgotten where he was. All he could see were a blending of letters, some in black, some in blue, some smooth waves of words, others the product of trembling hands.

They were spinning around her round, cheerful face, and he had to blink a few times before they vanished.

"Sorry," he said, quickly pulling the wire to one his buds.

"No problem," she said, gum snapping as she smiled widely. "Whatcha having to drink?"

"Just water, please. Oh, and coffee. Two coffees, even. That way you won't have to come back right away."

"Okay." She chuckled, her own pen dancing across her notepad. The action itself seemed to calm Max. His shoulders loosened, chin rising as his chest fell forward. If anyone else in the restaurant had seen him, they would've assumed he'd fallen in love with the young woman standing before him. But it was that movement, the flicking of the wrist, bending of knuckles, that made empty pages full. God, how he wanted to look down to his notebook and fill it with such ease.

"Anything to eat, or are you too focused on work?" She winked. Another snap of her gum.

"Uh, yeah, just work right now," his brows creased as he looked down to his own paper. "Thank you."

She only smiled in response because his earbud was back in his ear before she could form even the first letter of a word.

She took three steps to her left, standing in front of Craig, whose eyes were now narrowing on the back of Max's head, and Philip, who was turned in his seat to eyeball the same man.

The waitress's brows lifted, a snap of her gum caught their attention, and they looked up to her.

"Friend of yours?" She chuckled.

"Colleague," Craig said.

Max's mind was in overdrive, Malum at the forefront, but behind her, his fight with Philip, his dislike for Craig, the agony not writing was stirring inside him, and, most importantly, the untimely questioning of all the fundamentals he'd built his life around.

His air shook out of his nostrils as he lifted the first cup of coffee to his lips. So focused on his unfortunate writings after the night of the time loop that he didn't notice he'd forgotten to add cream and sugar to it.

The bitter coffee seemed appropriate for his mood, so he elected, through the distasteful scrunching of his nose, to keep it.

Flipping page after page, nothingness after nothingness, finally he came to the entry made just after Bonum, when he'd sat down at the elevators and written.

Armed with such inspiration, filled with the ideas of her, the pages were whirlwinds of words, thoughts, feelings. Remarkable. Something about her was simply remarkable.

Even as he remembered her now, his memories were flushed with gentle clouds. They flowed around her in baby blue fogs and pastel pink smoke. Touched by the blues, her fair skin appeared to mirror the hues of the color, and her cheeks were brushed with the softer tones of pink and red. Everything seemed blurred, but in a comforting way, as if she were blending into the woodwork around them to create a place in time and space that wasn't just memory.

His lips parted as he looked around the coffee shop of that hotel, eyes blinking slowly as he tried to pinpoint where one object ended and the other began.

He smiled, eyes still open and fixated on the notebook pages before him. He wondered if Bonum were a guardian someone sent to provide lost artists with the inspiration to find their way back home.

"Not quite," she said.

Inside his memory, Max smiled to her, but then his brows knitted together here in reality.

That voice didn't sound imagined.

He looked up from his notebook, stunned to see her sitting before him.

"Not quite?" He said, as he pulled his earbuds from his ears. How had he heard her?

"Your writing," she said, extending her hand over his notebook, and slanting it toward herself. "You think I'm your guardian angel?" A wryly grin moved across her lips— the same pink hues as they were inside his memory, the blush of her cheeks matching exactly. She hadn't looked like that in actuality, not when they were at that hotel. His eyes narrowed.

"You couldn't have read this from…" He looked to the side, out into the restaurant. "Where did you come from?"

"I'm here for work," she said, pulling the notebook entirely in front of herself now, the grays of her eyes scanning over each line of messy letters and sloppy sentences.

Max made a mental note to ask Malum if she worked for the IRS, too. "Right, but I mean, you weren't just sitting there a few seconds ago."

"Eh, depends on your definition of a few seconds, I suppose," she said, her words slow, as she was more focused on what he was saying in his writing than what he was currently saying.

"A few seconds is one, two, three. That was a few seconds."

"Ah, we're using the standard method for measuring time. In that case, no. I've been here for much closer to fifteen minutes."

"Fifteen minutes." He breathed through his nose audibly.

"I think you were hallucinating," she said, breaking her gaze from his words. "What's that like?"

"What's hallucinating like?" His brows raised, a large smile spreading across his face. "I don't know. I think I was just daydreaming."

"Isn't that the same thing?"

"No, daydreaming is just being lost inside your mind. Hallucinating is like…" his lips pursed. Like seeing letters floating around the face of your waitress.

"Seeing something in reality that isn't actually real," she finished.

"Right."

She nodded, looking back down to the notebook.

He rested his chin in his hand as he studied her briefly. "You know, I don't normally let anyone read that."

"Well, I'm in it. It's only fair if I see what you've written about me."

"That's not how it works." He grinned.

"No?"

"No."

"Then how does it work?"

"It works the way it works with everyone. You get to know what I think about you the same way I get to know what you think about me."

She looked up, her left brow arching as a playful grin tugged at the corners of her lips. "You want to know what I think about you, huh?"

He exhaled a laugh, looking down shyly. He looked back up, and simply admitted to it.

"Okay," she said, closing the notebook in front of her. "I think you're a very talented musician, and that those musical abilities are challenged in greatness only by your skill for language. Lyrically, at least." She winked. "I think you're quite handsome. Your eyes are especially catching, but I think you know as well as I do that doesn't matter to me."

"Then why mention it?" He smirked.

"Because it matters to this," she brushed her hand reverently over the beaten-up notebook cover. "Wouldn't it be easier to get people to listen to what you have to say if they're already captivated by your appearance?"

"Logically, I suppose, but I'd hope that's not the case."

"Tragically, it is. That's why you were crafted the way you were."

"You sound certain."

"I am."

"Are you, like, one of those people who meditate a lot? You believe in fate and all that?"

"I believe in divine purpose," she said, eyeing the pendant on his chain. Her eyes flickered back up to his, "Don't you?"

"I used to," he said. "I mean, I do. Maybe just…not as certainly."

"You should. You have something to say to the people of the generations after yours. You should be careful with what you tell them. You wouldn't want to be a part of the overwhelmingly large amount of influences leading them down the wrong path."

He shook his head. "No, I wouldn't."

"It's okay." She extended her hand to his, patting it gently. "What you've written about me, these pieces on angels and heaven, they're really quite beautiful."

"Yeah?" he asked weakly.

"Yeah. I like your friend, Philip," she said, nodding toward him as she looked over Max's shoulder. "Maybe you should ask him what he thinks of it."

"You know Philip?"

"Almost as well as I know you." She winked.

His brows creased. She was so cryptic. Strange how he always found comfort in it.

"Well, I should let you get back to your writing. I just saw you across the way and thought I'd say, 'Hey.'"

"Hey." He smiled.

"Hey," she said, slipping out of the booth and making her way across the restaurant.

Max's eyes fixed on Bonum until she disappeared behind

a corner of the opposite end of the restaurant. She and Malum must know each other, he thought. He wondered if they traveled together.

"So," he heard Philip's voice from behind him.

His eyes closed, a sharp exhale leaving his nose.

"Am I allowed to ask who that one was?"

Max swallowed thickly, tilting his head over shoulder, but not actually turning around. "One you'd approve of."

"Oh, yeah? Why's that?"

"She gave me a saint charm instead of alcohol."

"Yeah, I like her already. Where'd she go?"

"I don't know."

"We don't have to leave tonight," Craig offered, but Philip shot him a glare.

"So, since we're talking again, Maxwell, would you like to join us over on this side of the booth?"

Max rolled his eyes. "I just want to get some writing done, okay?" He felt awful when he wasn't creating, but the hangover wasn't helping.

He put his earbuds back in. When he opened the notebook this time, he felt no need to revisit the old attempts from this week. He took three clean pages and filled them with his soul, with his choices, his decisions. He wrote about the desire to break free from his oppression, and how now, looking back on the bit of freedom he had, found it a product of coercion.

Maybe the choices he made looked like rules, maybe they were constant reminders of what he couldn't do, but after seeing Bonum, after being reminded of Gemma around his neck, of Christ there, Max wrote that his limitations only appeared as such. No drinking, no sex, no fun. It seemed so binding, but what bound him to this world was flesh alone, and he refused to spend an eternity in actual chains, paying for the few cheap thrills this body could actually experience.

When he finished, he felt reborn. He turned his body in the booth and smiled to his band mates. "I think I've got it."

"Okay, let's hear it," Craig said.

"You know he's gonna have to perfect it first." Philip reminded him.

"I'm gonna head over," Max said, tucking his notebook under his arm. "I'll see you guys there."

"Wait, why are you going this early?"

"To get set up. I don't know. I feel productive," he said.

Max approached the bar like a parishioner standing before a great cathedral. Standing in front of its door, Max gazed up at the architecture, noting the bright lights hearkening back to old Hollywood, and how they actually appeared more like stars. They were tiny, some of their bulbs dying out, some flickering sporadically.

It made him think of his own life, of how some nights on this tour felt tragic, as if he'd spent his life pursuing someone's destiny, but how others seemed to validate his reason for being in that specific place at that specific time.

Considering the concept of time itself, Max was all too aware of when this shift happened. After that loop of time, that slowed moment, every time Max stepped foot onto the stage, it felt like home. It was when the audience actually watched him, when their eyes saw him and not his image through their screens; their screens which only recorded him in some self-serving evidence that their own lives were busy and entertaining. It was that moment, that night when everything truly changed.

He moved to the door slowly, reverently touching the black bars that line its glass. If what he'd written today mattered as much as he felt it did, if Bonum's reaction to his poetry about muses and angels was any indicator of the mass's, then this building was so much more than just a building. This set was more than just a set.

He walked around the side of the building, his hand staying in constant contact with dirty brick that had been painted black. He noted the way the paint peeled away beneath his touch, how it flaked and chipped and fell away with the wind. There was something liberating in seeing the red bleed through the darkness, the way the reality of what the brick was still found a way to free itself from the surrounding forces.

He stopped in front of the back door to the bar. Running the nail of his thumb against the paint, Max smiled when he watched the paint fall away from his finger and the brick simultaneously. Then he knocked on the backdoor, and waited for the manager to let him in.

On the manager's heels, he carried his and Craig's guitars inside the area where the bands could set up, taking it upon himself to remove each instrument and tune it.

Each strum of each chord, each sound-- unamplified and without audience-- was more powerful than any other heard on tour thus far, and Max understood this increase of music required an increase of voice.

He took his notebook from his bag, opening it to the new pages, the pages written about Bonum. As his fingers moved across the strings of the guitar, he began to hum the melody of the words he'd written. He imagined which would be sung cleanly, which would be screamed. He could see himself performing them to masses larger than any the band had yet seen.

This message, the retelling of an ancient myth, would reignite interest in the outdated belief system Max was so confident in believing, but maybe he'd offer a new insight to it— this idea that angels weren't winged warriors, but simply people who showed up in one's life whenever they lost track of who they were.

Who he was. Max smiled thinly. He wasn't sure he ever really knew how to define himself. He knew the stage was a part of him, the music was, but what seemed to be the most clear now was the blurring question, "Why?"

Whatever message he had was always hidden deeply between the lines of his lyrics, and he was always sure that it had to be that way for the band's sake. Now it seemed that message, not of God, but of goodness, should be evident.

After setting the guitars aside, Max moved out into the main area of the bar. He stood side stage for a moment, seeing the venue from the same viewpoint he always had, but tonight his view didn't matter.

Tonight, what mattered were the people who were there for him, the people there to hear something they could carry with them through their own dark times, something that would feel significant in a world that praised manufactured importance and thrust it on whoever had the prettiest face.

Max was determined to make the message what mattered. He didn't want to be what they reached for. He wanted their shared experience, that emotion that each person simply by being a person felt, to be what they sought at his shows.

As he moved into the center area of the bar, he stood where they would be standing. He looked to the stage, trying to imagine shoulders against his, heads in front of him, hair and smoke and flickering lights obstructing his view. He closed his eyes. If everyone could hear, not see, maybe they'd make different choices.

Max considered his own. He thought about Malum, and how appealing she was. With his eyes closed, without the images of her golden eyes or delicate features, he could go only by what she felt like to him. In his sober state, he wasn't sure.

He felt a sudden determination not to drink, to go back to his typical show standard. But the idea of sharing more of himself within his music made the shy man nervous, so perhaps this should be put on reserve for the next night.

He took a few steps closer to the stage, still trying to gauge everyone's vantage points, before he stood against it. He let his fingers brush over the large wooden plank situated on the edge of the stage to create a strange sort of barrier. Looking upward, imagining himself as they would see him, Max realized the clear separation between him and the masses beneath him. It was the most obvious disconnect, and he'd been aware of it all along.

After a nap and few cups of coffee, Sacrifices Surrendered were   ready to set the stage.

Max stood aside as he watched Philip move to his drums, adjusting his seat, and taking his sticks in his hands.

He played with the pendants on his chain, rubbed his fingers against the crucifix. He wasn't sure if he should go on as he was, nervous and planning to be vulnerable, or if he should have one small taste of an easily attainable influencer to ease those nerves.

His hand rushed over his face, losing itself into his hair.

His other hand moved to his lips, and he chewed at the nails. Looking down to them, he saw more of the blue paint chipping away.

When the beating of Philip's drum was steady, signaling for Craig to return to his guitar on the stage, Max had run out of time. He pulled his shirt off, throwing it aside, and, determined to be as exposed spiritually as he was physically, Max joined his bandmates on stage.

When he sauntered onto the stage, lifting his guitar and wrapping it around him, he felt the vibrations from his initial strum surround him like a blanket of security. That slowing sensation, destiny revealing itself to him in the language of the spirit, encouraged him to embrace the strange comfort it provided.

Suddenly, caught inside the calming waves of his guitar, Max felt even more confident in his decisions. Each beat of the drum, each chord strummed beneath his fingers, beneath Craig's, filled him with further confidence— this was what he was meant to do. Finally, after years of feeling like his destiny was tied into his message, it'd come together. Everything made sense in that moment— the eyes on him, his eyes on them, the sense of relief washing over him when he considered how liberating it would be to speak out loud what he'd kept hidden for years.

His voice, more powerful than it ever had been, sent shivers down the spines of those at his feet. The sounds of music wrapped around them in the same warm, calming air. It was perceivable, and yet, entirely unknown to them.

It was shared. Max's greatest desire was the sharing of experience. He didn't want to watch the same videos as someone, to scroll through the same photos. He didn't want his connection to the people below him to be built on carefully edited images and the consumption of them.

When he removed his guitar for the next song, he spoke into the microphone. "This next song is about our phones," he licked his lips as he met eyes with a few of them. "And how we should find attachment in each other instead."

He heard Philip begin the beat, felt the trembling of the large speakers when Craig strummed through the strings of his guitar, then he removed the microphone from its stand. This time, when he circled around it, he didn't merely crouch down in front of the people. He didn't take hold of the hands that were reaching for him. Instead, he moved to the edge of the stage, setting down on it awkwardly. Looking at the faces, seeing the curiosity in their eyes, he smiled, pushing himself down from the stage and standing among them.

When he lifted the microphone to his lips, the words flowed more easily than they ever had. He felt an ease, his feet in line with their feet, his eyes level with theirs. He felt a shift in the energy, a closeness created by the heat of so many bodies in such a tight space.

He performed almost the entire song there, leaning against the stage, feeling hands touch his shoulders, his arms. But then, as the song came to its final chorus, he realized that there were only a few fleeting seconds separating him from the slow, somber story that tore out a piece of his soul.

Maybe it was a small piece; but he felt more comfortable giving it away than the specific piece Jessie desired. Maybe not. But if he could stop one person in this crowd from performing an act they simply weren't comfortable with, he felt convicted in the idea that his bad-boy reputation was worth it.

Still, standing before such a crowd, feeling all of those eyes on him, the idea of confession here, in front of all of them, had been much more appealing than the practice of it.

He climbed back onto the stage, taking the acoustic guitar and resting it on his leg. Swallowing thickly, his lips parting, Max moved his mouth against the microphone.

"This one is about…" his eyes moved from blue to green to brown. So many souls capable of so many feelings, so many minds capable of so many thoughts. Was destiny always meant to push a person to their limit, or was this nervousness some sign of a wrong choice? He cleared his throat, "This one is about leaving." He strummed the A minor chord, and the song began.

———

Guilt rushed through Max. It was beyond feeling like he had a message to give. He was disappointed in himself for not giving it, so when he left the stage, he rushed straight toward the bar, instead of his merch table.

"Excuse me," Philip said.

"Just one, Philip." He said, "Come on."

"You look sick."

"I feel sick," he said, rushing a hand over his forehead.

"I don't think a drink is going to help you. It's probably the source. Let's go."

He swallowed thickly as he followed Philip. This feeling raged about inside him, bouncing off of the walls of his stomach as a great pit swirled around within it. He felt his lungs expand differently, as if they wanted to expel more than just air, and a perceivable weight caused his vocal chords to thump.

He coughed in response to it, this immense pressure on

his throat, his chest, his lungs.

"Max," Philip said, "Are you okay?"

"Fine," he hacked a little, rubbing at his throat as his breath left his nostrils sharply.

"Are you sure?"

"Yes," he said, voice groggy, "Yeah, I'm sure."

He swallowed purposefully as he moved behind his table, picking up his sharpie with a shaking hand.

When he saw the first person step in front of him, that same slowing sensation washed over him. He stared at the young kid before him, feelings flooding him, suggesting to him that this kid looked up to Max for a purpose.

Max smiled lightly. When he reached to the shirt in the kid's hand, Max saw the color of his nails. Bright purple.

The kid smiled bashfully, looking up to Max and stammering, "Do you ever get picked on for it?"

A sad smile spread across Max's lips. "I get picked on for a lot," he said, signing his name across the image of his body on the black T-shirt. "Don't let anyone tell you who you are," he said, and then his brows creased slightly. With the small offering of advice, the lump inside his throat, though still very present, wasn't as hard. He cleared his throat. "Sorry. I think purple's a great color on you."

The boy's smile spread widely across his face. "Thank you."

"What's your name?"

"Paul," he said.

"It's nice to meet you, Paul." Max smiled.

"You, too." The kid's smile was wide and genuine. "Thanks."

When Max looked over to the next person in their line, his eyes wandered behind her in surprise. Each show they seemed to gain a bit more notice, a few extra faces in the crowd around them, and each time he took a moment to ask his fan's name, or offer them some cryptic advice that seemed entirely random to him, yet extremely powerful to the individual, his lungs pained him less and less.

By the time they worked through the entire mass around the table, Max felt he could breathe properly. He hadn't coughed once during the last five or six minutes.

When the soundcheck was done for Changing Nuances, Max, Philip, and Craig started making their way over to the bar. Normally, the latter two double-fisting a couple of drinks to the side-stage area, while Max followed with a glass of water.

Tonight, however, a familiar face intercepted Max on his way.

His brows raised excitedly. "Malum!"

"Hey." She smiled. It was a Herculean task considering all she sat through.

"You're here," he said as he wrapped his arms around her.

"Yes," she said, returning the embrace. "I never get to see you perform," her voice was bubbly behind her grating teeth.

"Well, what'd you think?" He smiled, somewhat nervous, as he pulled away from her gently.

"I think it's remarkable that your lyrics are paired with such heavy music."

"Yeah, it might be a little different," he said, looking down bashfully.

"No, it's good." She swallowed thickly, the pain of its goodness still fresh on her skin, "I mean, it's actually, genuinely *good*." She needed to change that.

"Thank you," he said.

"So, what do you say we sneak out of here." She grinned seductively.

"Well, I have to be back after their set," Max bit his lip.

"That gives us at least forty-five minutes, doesn't it?"

He smiled, "Yeah, it does."

"I can't imagine a drink or two taking that long," she said, turning her body in the direction of the door and taking his hand in hers. "This bar down the block has a special drink in honor of some convention in the city this weekend. It's super sweet. You'll like it."

He chuckled, looking over his shoulder to Philip who was handing the bartender a fifty as Craig began to trap a few glasses of something dark and fizzing between his forearm and his chest.

"Okay," Max said. "Let me just tell—."

"If you tell them you're leaving, you're not going anywhere." She raised her brows. Max knew she was right.

"Yeah," he said, looking back to his friends once more. "Okay, let's go."

———

"It's called the Death Omen," the bartender said.

Max's brows raised.

"I take it you don't watch the show," he said.

"No," Max answered.

"We're trying it," Malum said. "Bring us two."

When the bartender brought the glasses, Max noted the soft blue color of the drink. It looked like a slushie, and he chuckled at the image of that floppy-eared dog dressed in a grim reaper's cape.

"What?" Malum chuckled, taking the straw in her fingers and bringing it to her lips.

"I'm just hoping it's as sweet as you say," he mimicked her actions, and took a sip.

"I can't," she said, recoiling from the drink and sliding it over to him. "You take mine," she said, her hand falling away from the drink and to his leg. Then she flagged the bartender down and ordered a Manhattan.

"Okay," he said, smiling a bit. He tasted absolutely no alcohol in these drinks. He was certain they were extremely watered down, and with the name and appearance, the bar could definitely get away with that.

"The show was exceptional tonight," Malum said, the shiny black polish on her nails gleaming as she circled her drink around in its glass.

Max's brows lifted, the straw of the first Death Omen falling from his lips. He swallowed it smoothly, struck by the blur already hazing the edges of his vision. Okay, maybe this thing wasn't so watered down, after all.

"You were there for the show?"

"Did you think I just showed up after?"

"Isn't that what you usually do?" He grinned, taking another large pull of the straw.

"Oh, okay." She chuckled. "Yeah, maybe that is true. But I'm glad I got to see you tonight."

"You're starting to like the music, aren't you?" He attempted to flirt.

"Well," her voice sang playfully. In all honesty, the heavy riffs and screams made Sacrifices Surrendered's sound exactly her type of music, but it was Max that prevented her from enjoying it—Max and his angelic face and heavenly voice. Nevermind the secret meanings of those lyrics. She had to consciously stop herself from sneering. "I think I'm just really starting to like you."

Max chuckled shyly. "That so?" A slight hiccup escaped him unexpectedly, and he adjusted slightly to try to hide it.

"It is." She laughed, pushing the empty glass away from him and replacing it with her full too-sweet slushie drink. "You shirtless is definitely a plus."

She brushed her fingers softly against his chest where the jacket left it exposed.

"I feel so awkward without it in here," he said, then he exhaled a pant. "Why is it like that?" He slurred a bit.

"Why's what like what?" she asked, tilting her chin a bit as her eyes gazed into his.

He inhaled shakily, eyes fixating on her lips as she wetted them. His hand moved instinctively up to her, his fingers wrapping gently around her wrist. Inside his palm, her skin was soft, warm, comforting. Against his chest, it was searing,

"Why is it so hot at first?"

"Is it?" She said coyly, but the mixture of triple sec and vodka gave him a bold streak.

"You know it is. You said you had to get me adjusted last night."

"I run warm," she said, pursing her lips playfully while her brows lifted.

"No, come on," he said. "Tell me why you're so hot."

"If I tell you, you have to tell me something about you."

"Something like," he stammered, taking another drink. "Something like what?"

"Does that make you nervous?" Her brows raised.

"What?"

"Secrets."

"So, why you're so hot is a secret?"

"Well, you've already sensed my reluctance to tell you, haven't you?"

"Okay," he said, "What kind of secret, though?"

"Something deep," she said. She knew plenty of his secrets. "Something not even Philip knows."

"Philip knows everything." He looked aside as his eyes widened.

"He seems to think so," she muttered, picking up her Manhattan and taking a drink.

Max's forehead creased as he watched her. "You really don't like him, huh?"

"He doesn't like me."

"Okay, so, you don't like each other. You haven't said more than two words to each other, though. I don't get it."

"He sees me differently than you do."

"Obviously. He's gay." He hiccuped again, his hand rushing to his lips bashfully.

"That's not what I meant," she shook her head. "You're a bad drunk."

"What? I'm not even drunk," he said, rearing his head back at the end of his statement as if the word offended him. "Actually, I told myself today I wasn't going to drink at all tonight." His smile lessened, and he looked over to the half-gone second slushie.

"I'm a bad influence," she said, and when Max looked back up to her, her right brow lifted, and her lips everted into a coquettish pout.

His parted lips turned upward softy, eyes fixated on her lips, her fingertips now petting his chest in gentle waves of warmth.

"Can I kiss you?" He smiled nervously, forgetting entirely about the issues at hand.

"You don't have to ask," she said, hoping the influence of that statement would be lasting and extend beyond herself. High hopes.

He slipped down from his seat, practically stumbling into her lap, but she welcomed the unceremonious closeness. Her legs parted to accommodate him, her hands rushing across his shoulders, and onto his neck. Pulling him into her, Malum was forceful with her lips. She swiped her tongue across his lower lip, pulling it between her teeth and sinking them, somewhat pitilessly, into it.

Max groaned a bit at her, his lips pushing against her more vigorously. His hands moved to her immediately, the desire magnified by the violence which seemed, to him, misplaced.

Odd to Malum was the pleased reaction from Max, who was by design righteous, and to her, that made him quite boring. It was a pleasant surprise to her own desire, but in all honesty, the taste of someone so genuinely pure was too alarming to her body to allow her to enjoy any bit of pain she inflicted on him. At least it was proving he was easy enough to seduce with a little alcohol.

"Hey, guys," the bartender said, then he tapped the bar loudly. "Hey, guys!"

Malum tilted her head away from Max, his drunken state causing him to take a moment to catch up.

"His phone just vibrated off the bar."

Malum looked down, watching the screen, now cracked and splintered, illuminating with the name *Philip*.

"Oh, no," Max said, seeing the time when the call stopped.

"What's wrong?"

"Forty-five minutes was..." he shook his head, blinking

his foggy eyes as he stood up and away from the bar, "Like, two hours ago."

"Oh, your table," she said, lifting her brows in the center so that her golden eyes appeared like those of a lost puppy.

"I gotta get over there. They wanted to leave by… I think midnight."

"Well, I'd walk you, but I think it's best if I don't."

"Why?" He looked genuinely confused.

"I'm not gaining entrance to any party tomorrow night if Philip thinks this is my fault."

"Oh," he said, moving back against her and lifting his hands to her cheeks. "But will you be okay getting back to your room, or your car, or—?"

"You do not need to worry about me," she smirked.

"Okay." He smiled nervously, biting his lip. "Party tomorrow." His brows creased. "We'll be in Nashville."

She nodded.

"You knew that, huh?"

"It's where I'm assigned."

"You're assigned there tomorrow?" His lips collapsed into a small line beneath narrowing eyes.

"Yes, for work."

"Malum…" He exhaled, his shoulders falling a little as his lips curled. "What do you do?"

CHAPTER FIVE

Malum's features never shifted. Her golden eyes peered into Max's nervous blues, the curve of a cocky smile urging only one side of her pouting lips upward. Her brow arched. A grin began to form.

Max's phone vibrated against the floor again, Philip's name illuminating the darkness around their feet.

Her eyes glanced down to it, then she looked back to Max. "Better get that."

His nostrils widened in accommodation for the deep breath he inhaled. Licking his lips as his head shook slightly, Max looked away from her. His brows knitted together, rising in the center, as he bent down to pick up his now-broken phone.

The muscles beneath the flushed skin of his chin and upper lip trembled in an effort to contort his lips into a frown, but Max fought it, knowing that if he didn't hold the expression in, he would surely cry.

He felt the need to sniffle when he looked down to his phone, the drinks causing the white letters of Philip's name to extend in all directions into long, blurring lines.

He kept his head down, but his eyes went back to Malum's. Nothing about her stance changed, not the slightest shift.

"What do you do, Malum?" He asked in small bursts of breath.

"You tell me a secret," she whispered, leaning forward as her tongue swiped over her teeth, "And I'll tell you one."

He swallowed thickly, chin quivering beneath tightened lips.

She reached out to him, petting his arm gently. "Wait, are you upset?" She moved down from the bar stool. "Come here." She put her arms around his waist, pulling him against her.

His shoulders rose, head shying away, and his arms shook in the indecision to return the embrace or to pull away from it.

"Stop," she whispered, her voice calm and dulcet as her hands slipped down his arms and urged them around her. When he complied, his clammy palms hovering over her back, she ran her hand up his spine, the fingers of her other slipping into his thick hair. "I travel from city to city as a recruiter. I go to bars, clubs, coffee houses, hotels."

"A recruiter?" He stammered, his brows creasing.

"Uh-huh. I work for a major conglomerate. A lot of different groups with a lot of different specialties, so we take in a lot of different clientele. More people than you realize are willing to sign our dotted lines. It's not always a difficult task. Sometimes, though, people are already committed to our one real competitor, and that's where I come in. We figure out who those talented people are, and then I'm sent in to bring them over to our side."

"Your side?" He shook his head. "What kind of talented people?"

"People with a platform, usually. People, somewhat like you, actually," she feigned surprise as she pulled back enough to look at him. "You're talented. I haven't seen a manager around."

"He, uh…" Max's brows creased, his nose scrunching, "He was discovered drugging people during business deals. Horrible stuff. It was right before we left for the tour, so it's been just us right now."

"Well, see, perfect example of a talented group of guys in desperate need of new management. I just simply let people see that what we offer is so much better than our competitor."

"So you're a recruiter for, like, a talent agency?" He looked into her eyes, brows still tightened.

She pursed her lips, blinking away as her brows lifted. "Talent agency." She nodded. Lying didn't matter, but it wasn't entirely untrue, she supposed. "Yeah, something like that."

"Am I the person you were sent to recruit?" His lips closed tightly, the muscles beneath them shaking again. For the first time since Jessie, Max thought he found something genuine, something fervently real. Their connection was palpable. He was certain it was heartfelt and profound.

She inhaled deeply through her lips and then they closed. Tilting her head as she looked up to him, she saw sincere emotion trickling down from his glassy blue eyes and into the rest of his features. She smiled, lifting her hand to brush away a thin bit of moisture that escaped his eye, and said simply, "No."

"Don't lie," he said weakly, his eyes narrowing as he

frowned.

Her face, serene in expression, shook slightly. As she petted his cheek softly, she said, "I wouldn't lie to you."

"No?"

"No."

He smiled as much as he could through his worry, lifting a hand to his eye and rubbing at it.

"I'd have been talking business by now, right? Trust me, I cut right to the chase. Plus," she accented the word playfully, "It would've been the perfect excuse to see every single one of your shows."

He nodded, a small gesture, then he leaned back into her. Nestling his face into her neck as he wrapped his arms around her, Max inhaled deeply, attempting to summon the courage, even through the liquor, to confess his secrets to her. After all, he owed her one.

His lips parted, his tongue pressing against the roof of his mouth, but the phone in his hand started to vibrate again.

He pulled back from her, one arm still around her while the other moved his phone into his line of sight.

"I really," he said lowly, clearing his throat as he looked over to her. "I'm sorry. I have to go."

"I know you do. It's okay."

"Are we…?"

"I'll see you tomorrow night in Nashville," she said. "If I don't make it to the show, which hotel will you be in?"

"It's a small one. Um, something Sunsets, or Sunsets something." He shook his head.

She smiled. "I'll find you."

He smiled weakly, nodding. "Okay."

"Come here," she said, tilting her head upward.

He smiled, leaning into her, feeling the warmth of her

lips on his.

"Be safe," he said.

"You, too."

———

Max paused when he caught sight of the van. Craig was sitting in the back, and Philip, standing in front him and the open doors, had his phone to his ear.

Max's chest rose heavily as he watched Philip throw his hand up in exasperation. Then he walked across the road in their direction.

"I don't know where he—." Philip's lips parted when he saw Max heading toward them. "Max—."

"Please, don't," Max said, never lifting his head as he opened the side door of the van, and climbed in.

"Oh, no." Philip scoffed, looking at Craig as he tossed him the keys. "Let's go."

When they climbed in, Philip pushed Max's feet off of the bench in the back. "No, no sleeping. Not right now."

"Phil, come on," he groaned, tucking his head under the sleeve of his balled up jacket.

"No," he said, yanking the jacket out from under him. "Where were you?"

"I lost track of time—."

"Lost track of time?" He scoffed a laugh, shaking his head. "You weren't at the table. You left us hanging. You weren't there to meet people. You're the one always going on and on about the fans, about new fans, about connecting to people, and learning their names, and making sure they know that they matter. Well, did they matter to you tonight?"

"Of course they did," he mumbled. Guilt was already festering inside him, crashing into the pools of dejection left from the disagreement with Malum. Not to mention the way the booze exacerbated each emotion as it washed over him.

Philip shook his head. "I can't believe how irresponsible. This is your job. This is my job and Craig's job, too. If you want to have some mid-life crisis exploration of all the things you didn't get to experience, then that's fine. Obviously whatever I'm trying to do to stop you won't work. Good. I give up. Do whatever you want, but don't think I'll allow you to drag us down with you."

Max's hand rushed to his head, and he buried his face inside it. He felt so small, so weak, but he didn't want Philip to see his tears, mostly because he didn't want Philip to see how drunk he was.

He held his breath, hoping it would stifle his sniffling. When he finally let go and inhaled, Philip heard the shakiness of his breathing.

His brows creased as he leaned forward, trying to look at Max.

"Max," he said, voice still sharp through his concern. When another shaking sniffle came from his friend, he said more sternly, "Maxwell, are you crying?"

"Just stop, Phil," he whispered, another sniffle when he inhaled.

"Max, wait, what happened?"

"Nothing, I'm fine."

"You're drunk off your ass again, aren't you?" His voice was smaller, more disappointed than upset.

He rubbed at his eyes. "My head really hurts. I just want to go to sleep."

"Fine," Philip said, his jaw clenching as he moved into the passenger's seat. "Fine."

———

If the sun shining hotly into the window hadn't forced Max into waking up, he never would've realized he'd fall asleep.

He groaned a bit, eyes screwing more tightly closed, but his lids couldn't stop the sun from illuminating them into a heated red tone. Opening his eyes, Max found himself staring straight into the sky, and he winced as his head turned away from it.

Lifting his hands to his eyes, rubbing at them rather roughly, Max sat up blindly. His nose was scrunched, brows tightly creased, but his left dared to open.

Still in the van. Alone.

He discharged his breath in a bit of a grunt as he reached into his pocket and withdrew his phone.

Twelve o'clock. Great.

He tossed it onto the seat as he turned, swinging his feet onto the floor of the van, and then he leaned over himself, resting his elbows on his knees. Scrubbing his hands over his face, feeling the puffiness of his eyes, the dry scratching of his spit when he swallowed, Max promised himself no more drinking. He exhaled. Well, maybe no more drinking anything new.

He opened the door to the van, stepping out stiffly. He groaned when he stretched. Every organ, every muscle, every bone felt like it'd been run over and smashed, and worse than any physical pain, Max felt the discomfort of his spirit looming over him. He only wished he remembered why.

As he rounded the van, opening the back doors to remove his bag, Max typed a message to Philip.

Where are you guys? What's our room number?

His brows furrowed when he sent it. Something about Philip made him queasy.

He shook his head, tucking his phone into his back pocket, and then he grabbed his bag and threw it over his shoulder. When the skin of his shoulder felt the polymer pad, he paused and looked down.

A sudden bolt of embarrassment pulsed through him. His head shot up, eyes scanning the streets for any bystanders as he threw the bag down and rummaged through it hurriedly.

He withdrew the first shirt he found, quickly covering himself with it, but then, slowed and considerate as the fabric brushed against his chest, Max looked down, seeing the black nails of Malum's hand as her fingertips spread their smoldering heat through his upper body.

With the remembrance of her touches came a flood of unpleasant memories, cascading over him in waves of torment and distress.

He remembered the feel of Malum's lips, the comfort of her embrace, and the way it was all ripped to shreds when the fear of potentially losing trust in her replaced it all. He saw her face when she reassured him, felt the unease in leaving her still, the coldness of the air when it blew inside his open jacket, and the guilt that seized him when he saw Philip and Craig outside of the bar.

He ran his hand through his hair as he walked, eyes on the dirty sidewalks of another city. He wasn't sure who he was becoming, who he was meant to be inside this world of dark, smoky bars and endless opportunity, but he was certain he didn't like being the guy who let down the people who made his work possible, nor the kind of guy whose friends didn't reply to his text messages.

He exhaled as he looked up to the buildings near the van. He knew it was all his fault. Everything with Malum, everything with Philip, Max was the cause for it. He couldn't blame her if she didn't show up, and he didn't blame Philip for leaving him to fight his hangover off in the van.

When he found a hotel at the end of the block with Sun in the name, he went inside, relieved when he went to the front desk and found that his bandmates left a key aside for him.

As expected, when he opened the door to room 1315, it was empty.

"Yeah." He exhaled, wiping at his eye again. "Of course."

Slinging his bag onto one of the beds, Max dug out a clean shirt and yet another pair of black jeans. He looked down to them briefly, rubbing his thumb over the texture of the jeans, then looked up to the bathroom door.

There were so many moments in his life, on tour, with his friends, when he chose to be alone, when he chose the silence of a twenty-four-hour diner at two a.m. to the loud, fun, rambunctious energy of his own hotel rooms. Every night in each passing city, Philip and Craig brought these hollow, copy-of-a-copy-of-a-copy rooms to life, filling their walls to their absolute capacity and then some, causing the bland, cold walls to warm with the vibrations of being alive.

He'd never seen a room so devoid of them, so hollow, so empty. Being alone inside its cheaply papered walls and dirty carpets showed the room for what it was—a mirage of a home. He hadn't realized that when he was alone elsewhere the impact was far different than waking up alone in a van or sitting in an empty hotel room, not until he experienced it.

He looked over to his phone, now thrown onto the bed with the rest of his belongings. His jaw shifted, causing his lower lip to extend further than his upper one, unsure if the burning sensation behind his eyes was his hangover, or his heartbreak, but he wanted to call Philip. He wanted to tell him that he was sorry, not just for their fight, but also for missing a crucial part of their evening. He wanted to tell him that he wasn't sure, sitting in this room alone, if he could do the job at all without the guidance of his best and most trusted friend, that the safety he felt with Philip was something transcendental, something that even the most talented poet would struggle to describe.

He checked his messages, ensuring that he hadn't simply missed the notification of Philip's response, and he exhaled as he tossed the phone back onto the bed.

Standing, he stormed into the bathroom, forcibly flinging the door closed. He shook his head, gripping the sink on either side. He hunkered over its stained, once-white ceramic, allowing his palms to absorb, not merely notice, how cold it was. He felt like a spoiled child. No wonder Philip had always treated him as such.

His eyes moved slowly up from the sink to the mirror. This man staring back at Max, this man with a swollen face and sad eyes, was unrecognizable.

He looked away in disgust, quickly stripping himself of his miserable, smoke-scented clothing. Sniffling now in the after effects of such an atmosphere, not just the continuing explosions of emotions firing off at rapid speed inside him.

Maybe, he considered as he moved into the shower, pushing and pulling at its plastic curtain with just the tips of his thumb and forefinger, that this all had something to do with that great and powerful destiny he felt thrust upon him in Ohio those nights ago.

He snorted, turning the water handle almost entirely in the hot direction, which once was surely indicated as such by a piece of sculpted red plastic, long since fallen out and remedied by filling in the vacant slot with red nail polish.

After suffering through the great crisis of whether or not he'd meet his destiny on this path he took in search of it, Max was given that glimpse into fate. The slow, drawn out, comforting vision of witnessing his impact on each person standing at his feet, all of the eyes gazing to him, hands reaching for his touch, seemed to be confirmation of everything he'd desired. The knowledge of these people, hearing their names, and understanding them in some miraculous and unexplained way, only further proved the goodness of that moment.

But now, even the hot water felt cold. Now, he was more alone than he'd ever felt. Now, he worried that this spot in time, which paused only for his focus, was a signifier of something else entirely. Or maybe he was simply acting out in spite of every sign, in spite of the time loop's positive affect on him, in spite of meeting someone as spiritual and pure as Bonum, and maybe, even those chosen by the fates, still had consequence for their actions.

Max hadn't felt invincible at that bar with Malum, or at the party with her, but he did feel something he'd never experienced before. Whether or not it was some different form of a very familiar emotion, he wasn't sure, but whatever it was, it fueled his desire for her, and that desire was what proved him fallible.

In one night, the forgetfulness of absent minded

affection caused him to damage his relationship with two—
quite possibly, for Craig hadn't spoken a word last night,
three— people and his reputation as a man of connection.
The weight of this guilt, resting as heavily as the world on
Atlas' shoulders, was almost crippling.

Max imagined this night, as he rubbed his facial scrub
into foaming suds against his face, as a correction for all he'd
done wrong. When he spread the bubbling soap across his
shoulders, he saw himself cleansed of all that he'd sullied the
night prior. He let the water pool inside his cupped hands for
a moment, lifting them to his face as he closed his eyes. He
prayed to Gemma, still wrapped securely around his neck,
begging her for guidance through these tempting times. He
asked his holy spirit to bless the water, so often seen as
purifying, and make it such. When he splashed it over his face,
feeling it slip down his neck, chest, and abdomen, he felt he
could be forgiven.

All he had to do now was ask for it.

After hurrying into his clothes, Max ran his fingers
through his wet hair, flipping it to the side and letting the
droplets of water fall against his cheek where it settled.

He didn't want to look into the mirror again, didn't want
to see how little the bathtub baptism actually regenerated. He
simply wanted to find Philip and Craig. He wanted to get to
the venue, see the stage, touch the walls. He refused to make
being late a habit.

After throwing his leather jacket on over his gray tank
top, he threw his phone into his pocket, and left the room.

He approached the bar hesitantly, fearful of the reactions
his friends would have to seeing him. He didn't want to be
ignored, and didn't want to fight. A part of him hoped they'd

act like nothing happened, but an even greater part of him wanted to apologize.

He looked over his shoulder, remembering that they'd taken everything, including Max's guitar, into the venue already. He didn't like being so useless, and didn't expect it would help his case with Philip and Craig.

Walking around to the side entrance, Max merely looked at the wall. It was bare, clean. He didn't want to touch it.

When he entered, he saw Craig at the bar, chatting with Billy from the opening band. His eyes rounded the room, but he saw no trace of Philip, nor of a merch area for any of the three bands. He noted a back hallway, its walls as far as he could see plastered with old, punk-rock, 70's styled posters, all black and white and violent, and realized it was the connection between the front door and the area he was standing in now.

Walking up to Craig hesitantly, Max inhaled a breath of courage as he looked up to him, but Billy saw him first.

"Yo," he laughed when he saw Max, and Craig looked over his shoulder toward him.

"Hey," Max said timidly.

"Well, well, well." Craig laughed, too, slapping Max's shoulder. "Let me guess, you need a drink." Craig, still chuckling, flagged the bartender over to them. "Three more."

"No." Max exhaled. "I don't think I'm—."

"Ah, come on," Billy said. "A few nights of actual fun, that's just not enough."

"Well, it's…" Max offered, his words spaced between uncertain pauses. "Not tonight."

"Come on, man. Phil's in the other room with the merch. He ain't gonna know you had one drink," Craig said, rolling his eyes. "Just don't be a shit like last night."

Max shook his head, his eyes falling. "No, I'm…I don't know what happened."

"You found that girl again?" Craig asked, taking one of the drinks the bartender brought over and offering it to Max. "That one from the restaurant?"

"No," Max said, his arm lifting toward the drink, but his fingers recoiling into his palm. "No, not her, and, no, thanks, to the drink."

"I already ordered it. Don't let it go to waste. You'll be fine," he said, practically shoving the drink into Max's hand. Sure, he could've set it back down on the bar, and he considered it, but Max kept it. "And, not her?" Craig chuckled again, looking to Billy. "There was a girl, though?"

"Yeah," Max said, his forehead tightening.

"So, I see why you lost track of time."

"What? No, it wasn't—." He scoffed.

"So, you missed out on meeting people, the one thing you never stop bitching to me about how I gotta do more of, for what, then?"

His brows furrowed, lips curling downward. "Have you ever spent even two minutes with any of the multitude of women you've met just this year alone trying to get to know them?"

Craig snorted, "No," and he took a drink.

Max shook his head. "Here," he said, setting it down on the counter. "I really don't want it."

"Whatever, man," Craig said, watching Max walk toward the hallway. "I wouldn't bother him, dude."

Max glanced back over to Craig worriedly, but shook his head and continued.

Once inside the hall, Max paused. Both walls, as well as the ceiling, were covered entirely with a myriad of posters—large, uneven, white letters sprawled over sloppily cut rectangles of black, and bold, gray posters advertising shows from 1976 for only fifty pence.

Max looked at the men's faces, their mouths slightly open, but not posed to be attractive, their hair messy and perceptibly dirty even through the colorless snapshots. Everything about them, including their tight pants, chained necklaces, and blood-soaked faces screamed *rotten, vicious, sex.*

Max's head began to turn down, his eyes still fixated on the images of true rock kings, and when his eyes finally parted with them, he looked at his own appearance. What right did he have, with Christ on his neck instead of a lock and key, and dull gray clothes instead of a bare chest and torn up jeans, to stand on a stage and claim himself as rightful ruler there?

Maybe it was a sign of the changing times, he wasn't sure.

As he moved through the hall, Max saw the potential of many paths of his life in the faces of his predecessors. He wondered what they'd be like if they were born decades after their passing, if they'd be like Craig, or Philip. He doubted any of them would be like himself.

When he reached the end of the hallway, another potential stood before him. Philip, and the path their friendship either remained on, or had veered off onto.

As he approached him, Max watched Philip's eyes move to him. His lips were tight and he looked back to the CDs he was laying out.

"Hey," Max said.

"Finally crawl out of bed, huh?" Philip said, still focused on work.

"Out of the van, you mean?" Max lifted his brows as his lips pursed. "Yeah."

Philip feigned a smile in response. Pulling the stacks of

stickers out of box, he began to lay them across the table, still refusing to look at Max.

"Well, I wanted to help, but I saw you guys brought everything in, so——."

"Why don't you just go hang out with Craig?"

"Because I wanted to hang out with you——."

"Nah, it's fine."

Max's lips parted, inhaling through his mouth in an effort to find the words, but he just stared at his friend.

"Look, I get why you're mad——."

"I really don't need an apology right now, Maxwell. If you could just leave me alone for the night, that'd be cool."

"You're being a little dramatic," Max said, attempting to adorn the comment with a lighthearted laugh.

Philip sat the stack of stickers down, his hand moving to his hip. His jaw clenched, lips pulling together, and finally he looked at Max.

Max's eyes widened when they connected to Philip's, his anger all too clear.

"You know what, Max? I've spent a long time with you. I know everything about you. I know, despite what everyone might think when they find out we went to the same school together, that it was you who got bullied, you that everyone groaned about me bringing to the movies, or out to eat. I mean, until you hit puberty and got so pretty, but the point is that I remember the kid you used to be, and I remember how you stayed that kid even though you've had every opportunity to be someone different. When we were young, I used to wish you'd actually take shots with me at parties, and when we turned twenty-one, there was a part of me that wanted to see you go wild, but that's because I was always seeing you like you were one of us, like you were the same kind of person everyone else was. "Well…" He looked down, spreading out the stickers. His brows knitted together, lips pursing. "You're not."

"Yeah, thanks," Max whispered, his voice cracking even at the low volume.

"You don't get it, Max. You think it's your destiny to be some great messenger, well, you had me convinced. You had me convinced that you were something greater than society makes us, that you had something pure and artistic and smart to say. And I thought, for all the reasons we shouldn't be friends, that if it's your destiny to be someone important, then maybe it's my destiny to make sure you stay that way. Maybe the whole reason I feel so 'motherly'," the word's sourness was evident through his shaken voice, "toward you is because you're not meant to have the experiences necessary to keep a sweet, naive guy out of harm's way. But I do. I've had all those experiences and then some—thank you for reminding me every time I ask you not to make the same mistakes, by the way—."

"Philip—." Max breathed.

"No, it's fine. If it's me who has to understand the world to keep you safe from it while you're up there trying to save people from peer pressure and sin or whatever, then that's fine. That's fine if it's our fate. But…" He inhaled, the air trembling inside his lungs as if it would leave his body in tears. "I see now that's not true. You're not free from temptation, and I'm not able to save you from it. So, yeah, you had me convinced, Max."

"H-had." He nodded his understanding.

"Had." Philip said weakly, his cheek in his teeth, lips trembling.

"Well, I'm, um, I'm sorry I disappointed you, then."

Without looking back to Philip, he turned away from the table, rushing himself into the hallway of the ghosts of rock gods' past.

Max rushed through the hall, swiping the back of his hand across his right eye and sniffling. He stopped in front of the first photo that caught his attention, looking again at the image that must've spawned the most cliched description of what a rock god should be. Fine, Max thought, wiping at his nose and sniffling once more. Fine.

He stormed over to the bar, stopping just before Craig and Billy, and called for the bartender.

Max's nostrils flared, his heavy breath escaping them in quick, anxious bouts. Soft, but painful sighs sounded in his throat sporadically as he exhaled, almost as if the action were causing him pain, and his lips tightened into a small line.

"Dude," Craig said, peering around Billy to look at Max. "What happened? You good?"

He blinked a few times, eyes staring off to the side of the counter. He shook his head slightly in response to Craig, his teeth now firmly embedded into his lower lip.

"You…want a drink?" The bartender said, lowering her head to try to see Max's face and better gauge his state of being.

"Yeah," Craig said, and she looked over to him. "Get him… I don't know, man. Let's just get him a Crown and Coke or something."

Max's lip fell out of his teeth, the muscles beneath his jowls and chin attempting their solemn contortions once more. He shook his head, lips thinning in his effort to stop the emotion from bubbling up to the surface, and by the time the bartender set the drink down in front of him, it was blurring behind the obstruction of his watering eyes.

"Thanks," he said curtly, grabbing the glass and taking a significantly sized drink from it.

He coughed when he swallowed, the strength of the whiskey still a bit harsh for his newly acquired taste for alcohol, but in this moment, it didn't matter. All caution was to the wind. If this was what everyone thought a rock star should be, fine. If this was what Craig and Malum thought, fine. But Philip… If Philip had no faith in him, if Philip thought he was just another asshole with a guitar, then what did it matter what he thought of himself?

His trembling hand brought the glass back to his lips. No hesitation when he threw his head back and consumed what remained in it.

He gasped a bit when he swallowed, head falling forward as he set the glass back down.

Craig watched him with raised brows, eyes narrowing a bit when Max ordered a second drink, and after he chugged that one, Craig asked, "You feel better?"

"No," Max said, half mumbling. "I need another. Something else though, please."

"Something else like what, hun?" The bartender asked.

"I don't know——." He looked over to Craig and Billy, then back to her. "What are they having?"

"The one in the black shirt has what you just had. The other's got a Tom Collins."

"What's that one taste like? No, never mind——" he shook his head. "Just give me one of those, please."

She raised her brows at him, tongue rolling between her teeth and close lips. "Yeah."

"Act like we're not here," Billy said. "Could've asked me what I have."

Max shook his head again.

"I hope you don't get sick," Craig said, watching Max devour the drink.

This one tasted a bit like sugar. He decided before he was finished with it that he'd order another.

"Man, seriously," Craig said, "The doors don't even open for a few hours. Pace yourself."

Max replied with his go-to reaction for the night. When the bartender brought his second drink, he took it in his free hand. Looking over to the guys, he asked quietly, "Where do we get set up in here?"

"Over there," Billy pointed behind them, "See the doorway? Go through there to the right. If you need the bathroom, it's to the left."

Max stood up quickly, determined to make a beeline for the doorway, but he paused. The ice inside each drink clanged against the glasses, and Max blinked a few times. He exhaled through his mouth, brows lifting as he stared wide-eyed at his destination. Suddenly it felt so far away.

"Just sit, man." Craig said. "You're gonna fall if you try to take off."

"I'm fine," he grumbled, stumbling his way toward the doorway.

When he reached it, his shoulder hit against the frame, but when he checked his drink, confirming it hadn't spilled, a triumphant pull urged his lips into a sort of pout, and he nodded. Then, going right, he found the room with his guitar.

"Maxwell!" He heard the voice faintly at first, but each time it called to him, it became more clear. "Maxwell, I am not joking this time. Up!"

Max's eyes blinked open to see Philip standing before

him, shaking his head disapprovingly. "We've literally got twenty minutes, so if you want to try to have some water or something…" He closed his lips tightly, offering a bottle of water to him.

Max's brows creased as he sat up. Yet again, the memory of falling asleep escaped him.

"Thanks," he said, taking it, but when Philip just turned and walked away, Max tossed it onto the other side of the couch he was sitting on.

He leaned back into the soft cushions, running his fingers over his forehead.

He sat up jerking his arms out of his jacket and ripping his shirt over his head. He looked down at his jeans, so neat the way they formed to his body, and he dug the nails of his right hand over the same knee. He looked over to the table next to the couch, in search of his pen. When he located it, he took it from his open notebook, and brought it to his knee. He pulled at his jeans with his left hand, lifting it until there was enough space between his fingers and his leg, and he stabbed the pen through the fabric. The point went in fairly easily, the smooth surface of its funnel-like socket slipping in after, but the rubber grip refused to push inside the thick material. Seeing this, Max simply yanked it downward, forcing the fabric to rip open in a hurried, frantic motion that ended with the ballpoint jammed into his flesh.

He withdrew the pen immediately, his intoxicated state preventing any signal for alarm to reach his brain, as he released his jeans. He leaned forward a bit, looking over his work, pleased with himself when his fingers brushed over the fringes of the torn fabric. Catching sight of the tiny bit of blood caused by the pen, Max arched a brow. He remember the photo in the hallway, the gory images of rock gods.

He wondered if anyone had anything bigger and sharper than a pen.

Max felt differently when he took the stage. The anger he felt at himself coursed through his veins alongside the alcohol he drank to create a deadly cocktail of sadness and self destruction.

He stumbled through his singing, his screams punctuated with overly-accentuated gasps of air. Every movement of his body felt in time with a melody that played out at his funeral. Each word, carefully crafted inside its line for some profound statement that Max felt too embarrassed to share outright, sounded like a eulogy devised from his former-self and performed here by someone who only pretended to care.

Nothing mattered to him where he stood, not like it usually had. The people below him, he felt certain now, were only interested in the idea of him, not in the ideas he wanted to share. The Hall of Rock Gods confirmed it. Even Bonum agreed.

He scolded himself, which added anger to the words he screamed, chastising himself for thinking he, with his strict belief system and devotion to its deity, could be somehow appealing enough to a young crowd of technology and toxic behavior just because he had a handsome face.

Bonum seemed to think it was enough to get him by. Philip seemed to think his message was. But he dashed everyone's expectations of him into the dirt last night, including his own, by losing sight of the people who mattered most.

As he looked at them now, attempting to bend down and get nearer to them, Max couldn't recognize a single spirit behind their eyes.

He knew it wasn't them, that this disconnect was not their fault. They stood where they always stood, watching him as they always watched him. Even as his knees buckled and he fell forward, their hands reached up in search of him.

The collapse, while timed perfectly with a lyrical display of weakened emotion, probably seemed performative to them. But to Max, it was the weight of all he'd done somehow changing him into an entirely different person that forced his palms onto the ground.

His knee, without the protective layer of jean, scraped against the cold, hard surface of the stage. He felt the tiny fragments of rock and dirt pressing into the newly torn flesh like mountains of burning salt.

He gasped when he lifted his head, falling back onto the stage to sit before his followers.

A few of them looked worriedly to his knee, now colored in the violent red of his fall, and he looked back to them with a grin.

"It's okay," he breathed into the microphone, reaching out to one of them and pushing her hair behind her ear. Winking as he stood, he lifted the microphone back to his lips, expelling from his lungs, with all his might, the words necessary to close the song. Then he moved to his acoustic guitar, looked around as he sat on the stool behind the microphone stand and set the instrument on his lap.

What's punk rock? he thought. What's heavy metal?

His tongue swiped over his teeth, a smile painting his lip as his jaw shifted wryly.

He let his fingers strum over the chords unceremoniously, then he looked over his shoulder to Philip.

Philip's eyes were discernibly worried under his confused expression, and Max, deciding he liked the playful gesture, winked to him.

He turned his head back to the microphone, licking his lip as they formed the words, "This next song," he exhaled, a cough tickling in his throat causing him to look down, to see his knee, his ripped jeans, his blood darkening the pieces of fabric that touched it. Mortal. Not a rock god. As he was, sitting before the crowd with a saint on his chain and blood dripping from his leg, Max was undeniably human. He wondered briefly if that message did still matter. Maybe it did. Maybe through all of this, it still mattered. He cleared his throat, and instead of simply providing the title of the solemn song, he said, "This next song is about saying no…" he looked around to the crowd, eyes becoming more and more real, deeper and significant, as he stared at them. "It's about saying no, even when you want to say yes."

Philip's lips parted, brows lifting. He looked over to Craig who shot him a confused expression. Craig didn't know what Max meant by that, but Philip did. He also knew it was one of Max's biggest struggles with his faith because it was one that separated him so completely from most people in this time. At least, if it were a product of his intoxication, Max hadn't said enough to fully explain it. But Philip made a mental note to discuss this with him when he sobered up.

Max's energy shifted with that song. Something about the energy of the room seemed to change around him.

He felt the people below him as he'd always felt them—connected and close to him through the shared emotions of music, of words, and songs.

He inhaled differently while he sang its solemn words. His lungs expanded smoothly in the production of sound, and the vibration of his vocal chords released it beautifully.

Somehow, through his most weakened performance,

Max found a strength inside him he didn't know he had, one that urged him to present more of himself to the people devouring his voice. They were starving for him, he could feel it. His skin prickled under the shiver that rushed down his spine. His heart pumped heavily as he sang. Everything in that moment felt perfect. Like it had during the time loop, a silent confirmation was clear: *you are where you should be*. Even when nothing about who he was in that moment made sense.

When he left the stage, he let his hands brush against everything— the old rusty banister that lined the stage steps, the thick chunks of red paint on the checkered wall which seemed to be slapped onto its white background unprofessionally but on purpose. This room felt alive, even if he didn't.

He looked at the people at his merch table more closely, his shyness regained by his vague confession, but no one seemed any less thrilled to be meeting him.

He wondered, as he smiled for photos and signed CDs, if that tiny explanation could provide such a harmonious energy to his performance, what a full blown confession might do.

Philip and Craig resumed their after-show ritual, leaving Max to fend for himself in the clean up of their table.

He supposed he deserved it this time, but considered all the times prior that they hadn't lifted a finger to help him. How many sober nights did he spend packing up the boxes and loading the van while those two found release in booze and one night stands? Why, suddenly, did a punishment remind him of how things always were?

He looked down the Hallway of Rock Gods, unable to

even see Philip and Craig from this venue. It was absurd that he should have to pick up after them for years, and yet one screw up from him ends in a shunning.

It didn't matter. Maybe it was better this way.

His shoulder checked the door frame of the hotel when he pushed it open, but he didn't even pause. He hurried to the elevators, fingers pressing the button multiple times before the large metal doors of the car behind him opened.

Stumbling into the elevator, Max's hands rushed up to his temple. His body was swaying, even with all of his weight pressed against the wall. He knew this wasn't where he should be. He knew he should be writing, making music. All that he had to give was locked inside his mind, begging to be poured out onto paper, but in this state, he wasn't sure he could even hold a pen.

All Max could think of was his failure the previous night, of the way he disappointed everyone, and when the doors opened, Max exited a bit more cautiously. The movement, although almost entirely imperceptible, felt like a rocking boat to his foggy mind. He focused on the floor beneath his feet, on each and every step he took. He felt he was walking on some great path now, that every action he'd taken, no matter how wrong, led him here to this moment. He stood in front of room 1315 wondering if this was what God had planned.

"Hey," Craig said, ever the gracious host, when Max entered. "Max, my man, stellar job with the clean up. Only took you..." he grabbed the wrist of the girl tucked under his arm, tilting her watch up toward him as she chuckled. "I don't know, man. Like, not even a half hour."

"Yeah." Max tried to smile, but the comment wasn't as

much a compliment as Craig seemed to think it was. "I always usually do it by myself, you know?"

"Not last night. Last night you didn't help at all," Craig laughed, his beer-soaked mind causing him to forget the friction this memory caused.

Max had almost forgotten it himself.

"Yeah, well, one night in how many years?" He inhaled deeply, looking around. "Where's Philip?"

"I don't know," he said, wrapping his other arm around the girl.

Max shook his head, eyes jumping from person to person. As he scanned the room, his hands slipped into his pockets. He was still drunk, sure, but that didn't stop him from realizing that he was the only one in the room without a shirt on.

What would the Rock Gods do?

He straightened his shoulders as he continued, trying to embody their energy. He bit his lip nervously. He wasn't sure he could sell it.

Walking through the open door to the adjoining room, Max smiled when he saw Philip standing against the counter of the kitchenette.

"Hey," he said as he approached. "Philip, listen, I—"

"Max," he said, setting a can of soda on the counter and lifting the glass he'd just poured it into. "You'll find something to your liking here, I'm sure." He smiled tightly, trying to walk by him, but Max grabbed his arm.

"Wait, Philip, can I please just talk to you?"

"If you were sober, I'd say yes." He said, trying to turn again.

"Phil, come on. Don't be like this with me."

"Max, honestly, I just need a little space right now."

"Yeah, space. I didn't realize we were dating."

"No, but we've been friends for nineteen years which makes what you did somehow worse—."

"What I did. Okay, I know it was shitty, and I've tried to apologize—."

"Shitty?" Philip's brows raised.

"Lame, or whatever," Max exhaled, his shoulders falling. "I'm sorry—."

"I don't need an apology," he said. "I see you every day but there were people there last night dying to meet you, and it was their only opportunity."

"Yeah, I know," he said weakly. He already felt horrible about it. "Why do you think I had some drinks before I came up here? I can't handle this. I feel so terrible about everything—disappointing them, disappointing you. I—."

"I'm sure there's an open cathedral somewhere, Max. Go to a confessional if you feel bad. I'm not your priest."

"No, but you're my best friend."

"Max, let's just be colleagues tonight, okay?" He patted Max's shoulder and walked away.

Max's nostrils flared, mouth curling into itself. His scrubbed his hand over his face, not comprehending why he said what he'd said. He came up here with a purpose. He came here with confirmation of his and Philip's purpose. He felt it in that song. His intention was to rectify, to apologize. Instead, he felt he forced the divide between him and his best friend further apart.

He looked away, dejected, huffing as his eye raked over the endless supply of bottles of forgetting.

He didn't care anymore. He was over it. If it didn't matter to anyone what he did, what he said, if the message wasn't actually there, if Philip lost all faith in him, then nothing mattered. He certainly didn't matter, not if everything he thought he was doing for some divine purpose was just a random event of career lottery; of talent for no reason. If it didn't matter, if nihilism was a more plausible option for the world than spirituality, then maybe he should take an entire bottle, drink it until it's as empty as he felt, and find some sort relief from all this emotion in the arms of someone he didn't even care about.

His lips curled, quivering as he shook his head in the negative manner. No, none of that seemed to be the answer. Why, then, was it so appealing?

"Mix me one, bartender," a playful voice called from somewhere just to his left.

Max looked over to the familiar sound with a smile on his shaking lips, "Malum," he breathed, rushing over to her and wrapping his arms around her.

"Hey," she chuckled, returning his embrace.

He inhaled deeply, nestling his face into her, breathing in the musky hints of heated embers lost inside the scent of vanilla dipped strawberries.

He groaned slightly, the comfort of her scent embracing him as perceptibly as her soft skin against his, her heated fingers rushing up the back of his jacket, smoothing over his neck, and spreading through his hair. He felt the warmth emitting from her palm spread from the centralized point beneath it. As it branched out, following the trails set out for it by her fingers, it curled around his head, slipping inside his skin as it made its path, and warming him from the outside in.

"You feel so…" he exhaled, brows creasing.

"Good?" She chuckled.

"Yeah." He winced, scolding himself. "I, um, I wasn't sure I'd see you tonight."

"Why?" She pulled back, just enough that they could see each other.

"Last night, I—." His lips pursed. "I thought I messed up."

"No, you didn't."

"Well, you might be the only one who thinks so."

"Philip's mad about you being a little late, huh?"

He nodded, looking away to try to hide how heartbreaking that fact was.

"Okay, you need a drink," she said, moving around him to reach for the bottles. "What are you feeling like tonight?"

"Well," he said as he approached her, his hands in his pockets. "I heard you order a Manhattan before, but I don't know what's in it, so…"

"You don't want whiskey, do you?" She chuckled.

"I don't—I'm not totally sure, but I think I had some earlier."

"You're not sure?"

"Craig ordered me something." His brows creased. "It was harsher than anything you've ever ordered."

"So, you trust my judgement, then?"

"Yeah." He smiled, his lips parting as he bit his lower lip.

"Good," she said, pouring some cola from the same can Philip had used into a glass. When she reached for two separate bottles of clear liquor, Max closed one eye, trying to read the labels, but his vision was too blurred in his current state to decipher them.

She took a lemon slice, squeezed its juice into the mix, and then handed it to Max.

He smiled as he took it, lifting it to his lips, his eyes staying on hers as he sipped it. His brows lifted. A pleasant smile crossed his face, and then he took a larger drink.

"Good, huh?" She grinned, pouring herself a Manhattan.

Watching her, seeing the simple drink she made, Max's eyes looked around the room. Trying to gauge through his narrowing, foggy eyes which type of guest held which type of drink most often, he looked back to Malum.

A crooked smile crossed his lips when she looked to him.

"What?" She chuckled.

"Why do I feel like everything you make me is something guys like Craig refer to as 'girly drinks'?"

"Because you're sweet," she said, reaching her hand out to him, her fingertips dancing across his chest, slipping under his jacket to strum against his tattoo. "It only makes sense for you to drink accordingly." He inhaled the crisp smell of lemon lingering on her hand. It was fresh and natural, reminding him of the clean comfort of summer in a room filled with the thick smoke of cigarettes and drugs.

"Well, what does that say about you, then?" He attempted to punctuate the question with a flirtatious wriggle of his eyebrows, but he knew he failed. "I mean, you don't like anything sweet."

"That's not true."

"It's not?"

"Nope," she said, taking a drink and then setting it on the counter. She closed the small space between them, "I like you." Her heat rushed against Max's chest in slow pulls as her hands moved up the edges of his jacket. Occasionally on their journey, her knuckles brushed against his stomach, his chest, causing him to flinch in the soft connection.

"It doesn't bother you that…" he shook his head slightly, corners of lips turning upward through the sadness.

"That what?" she asked tenderly, hands slipping across his neck, fingers lacing behind it. He felt her thumbs tracing small circles just beneath his hair, and his eyes fluttered closed in the comfort of the warmth of such a gentle touch. "That what, love?"

A faint groan whined inside his throat, and he exhaled, "That I don't have a purpose."

Her brow arched, a smirk rolling over her lips. Continuing her ministrations with one hand, allowing her other to slip into his hair, she cooed, "Whatever would make you think that?"

He groaned again, leaning his head back into her touches. "I don't know." He whispered, brows creasing when he considered Philip, and how their connection was seeming to break right before his eyes.

Seeing his wincing lips, Malum moved against him, her heat brushing over his bare skin and igniting every nerve ending buried beneath it. Her hand moved around his neck, thumb brushing against his jawline tenderly.

"Not a very convincing argument," she said.

"No," he smiled, leaning into her hand as it caressed his cheek. "No real argument against it either, though."

"That's not true," she said. "I happen to know that you have a great purpose."

"Yeah, getting drunk and slurring through my songs," he almost scoffed, but, under the command of her pets, the grunt passed through his lips as a sort of moan.

"Drunk or not," she whispered, "your place is on that stage. Your purpose is the music. I know I'm not the only one who can feel your soul inside your songs..." she cooed, his head leaning forward, following the course of her hands as her thumb slipped over his lips. "Who can hear your heartbeat inside every rhythm..." their foreheads brushed together, her lips whispering against his. "Who sees you come to life beneath the lights."

He exhaled another soft moan, brows pulling together, lips trembling as they parted. Her heat embraced him everywhere, encapsulating his lips, his cheeks, his neck, brushing over his body, searing him in the places beneath his jacket that her fingers caressed for the first time.

When their lips finally touched, Max fell forward, shoulders collapsing as his body melted against hers. Gripping her tightly, Max's chest rose and fell heavily. He wanted to let his hands move up her sides, wanted to explore her body, but it felt wrong to do so. It felt wrong to even think of it. But she felt so right, so warm against his body. He let his hands pull at her dress, rolling the fabric nervously between his fingers. Her lips against his felt softer than the velvet of the garment, warmer than the friction made by his fingers. Parting his lips, Max deepened the kiss, worrying as he did so that he was wrong for it. He didn't want to pressure her, didn't want to push her, didn't want to push himself, but the softness of her hands kept moving lower, flowing across the curves of his shoulders and down his torso, allowing him to experience, not just the heat of her flesh, but the heat of his own passion; it ignited for the first time in undeniable pleasure, and the inescapable desire for more of it.

Feeling his tighten hold on her, and the tremble of his shy, needy body as it pressed tentatively against her, Malum grinned against his lips. A pleased sigh stayed in her throat, soft but triumphant, and she moved her lips away from his. He whined, brows creasing, practically pouting at the sudden absence, but she placated him quickly when her lips pressed delicately to his jaw. Trailing a few tender kisses along the prominent bone, Malum's hand brushed over his stomach, fingers slipping down against the hem of his jeans.

He grunted a bit, lips parting to expel a subtle gasp, as her lips lowered still and connected to the sensitive skin of his neck. Letting her other hand slip out of his hair, she used its placement on his neck to pull its opposite side more closely against her, lips parting, allowing her tongue to escape them rhythmically, as they delivered a line of delicate kisses to the flesh.

"Malum," he gasped, hands gripping her desperately as her fingers popped open the button of his jeans. "Wait. We—."

"Oh…" She pulled away gently, lifting her hands between them as she curled into his chest coyly. After glancing through the room briefly, she looked up to him and grinned. The scenery wasn't why he asked her to wait. They both knew that.

Taking his hand in hers, she turned, hurriedly pulling him away from the kitchen.

Philip caught their movement from the corner of his eye, head turning as he watched the pair push through a group of girls who were all struggling to remain upright as they stared at the illuminated screen of one of their phones, and then slip inside the bathroom door.

His lips parted, body shifting on the instinctual urge to chase after them, but he settled again quickly. He turned back to look at his date for the evening, eyes glancing over toward the door once more, before he turned his body away from it completely. If Max was who Philip thought he was, who he truly believed he was despite what he said in anger, then he wouldn't need Philip to save him. He'd be able to save himself.

Once inside the bathroom, Max heard the lock of the door click, then the light flickered on.

Malum's hands were on his jacket again, urging him toward her as she backed against the sink. Stumbling a bit as she pulled him against her, Max's hands gripped either side of the counter behind her. She giggled, lifting her hands to his cheeks and leaning her chin toward him. He exhaled shakily, heart racing in the fear of being left alone in such a tempting situation, but her lips were nearing his again, warmth radiating from them, the promise of connection, comfort, compassion filling the space between them.

He smiled, hesitant and small, but he didn't want to deny her. He didn't want to lose her. How many chances would he be given, after all, to find this connection, the bond he felt he was missing his entire life.

He gave in.

Leaning into her, Max brushed his lips gently against hers. Her hands slipped away from his cheeks, moving next to his on the counter to hoist herself onto it smoothly.

Without pause, her hands rushed back to him, taking no consideration this time to go slowly as they ran up his chest and inside his jacket. He felt her heated palms roll over his shoulders, pushing the jacket down his arms from within in. He let his arms fall enough for the jacket to slip away from him, his rationale reminding him that he performed shirtless more often than not, and that this wasn't some signifier of any event that she would inevitably expect.

Max trembled beneath her touches, her hands roaming freely over his newly exposed flesh, as her lips parted and her tongue brushed over his. His breath escaped his nose heavily, brows creasing as his eyes screwed tightly closed, but he obeyed her silent command, parting his own lips, and allowing her entrance.

A gentle moan left her lips, vibrating against his, and his

knees shook in the mixture of sound, touch, and taste. God, it was overwhelming. He couldn't tell if it was pleasurably so, or troubling. Before he could decide, he felt her hands against his back, nails brushing over the tender flesh softly before they scraped against it, leaving pink lines forming in their paths.

"You're such a good kisser," she panted between kisses, her hands urging his body more tightly against her.

Unwittingly he complied, too focused on her breathy praises to realize what was happening, and before he knew it, his hands were on her thighs, basking in the warmth pooling inside them as he gripped her flesh in wanton need.

She moaned again, tightening her legs around his waist as she slipped to the very edge of the counter. Her lips broke their embrace again, following their original path to his jaw, his neck, but this time, without the obstruction of his jacket, they continued downward, wrapping around his clavicle as her tongue slipped between them to taste it.

Groaning as she touched him, Max's hands rushed instinctively up her legs until they met the hem of her dress. His eyes popped open when he felt the fabric, blinking a few times as he gasped for air, the understanding of what was happening dawning on him as if he'd been asleep for most of it.

"Malum," he said, brows lifting over worried eyes, but her lips were so soft, her touches so warm and comforting, he couldn't find the words necessary to ask her to stop.

His lips parted. He panted, fingers digging into her legs, as his body began to roll against hers. He moaned in his throat, teeth gritting in the denial of it.

"Malum." He tried again, half invested in the pleasure, and half afraid of it, as her hands continuing their exploration of his flesh. When they fell away from his stomach, slipping over his open button to his zipper, his muscles tensed. "U-um," he stammered, feeling the opening zipper brush against his perfectly functioning physicality. "W-wait," he gasped as her palm replaced it, pressing against him with both a physical and emotional heat.

She masked her frustration, though it was difficult. "It's okay," she whispered, moving her free hand to his cheek.

His forehead pressed against her, brows furrowing, jaw clenching as he scolded himself, mind screaming for his mouth to form the word again, to say no, to protest, but the sensations rushing through his extremities weren't just pleasurable, they were new, and the idea of her hand wrapping around the uncharted territory was as thrilling as it felt.

"God," he panted, more of a prayer than an exclamation, for he wanted to stop but certain he was unable to on his own.

"Not quite," she hummed, pressing her lips against his, moaning in her throat as both hands, one on his neck, the other in his pants, pulled him against her.

She felt him following her urges, his lips mingling with hers the point of his focus. He couldn't think about her hand, where it was touching, how it was removing him from his pants, guiding him against her. She moved to the very edge of the counter, hand disappearing under her dress to slip aside a silky obstruction before it returned to him.

"Malum," he said weakly, inhaling sharply through his wincing mouth, the muscles of his face contorting in what could've released his body in tears as easily as moans.

"It's okay," she whispered, hands still moving in their pleasurable patterns. Brushing his cheek, their forehead connected, she breathed against his lips. "I can't get pregnant, and you can't catch anything from me."

He groaned in his throat, eyes closing tightly again. Neither thing was a concern for him because he expected to stop before an act allowing such things could take place. But instead of words leaving his lips as she guided him into her, only breathy gasps and groans rolled out of his mouth.

"Oh, God," he breathed again. This time a blaspheme. "Oh, my God," he whined, leaning his head against her, letting it fall to her cheek, and then into her neck. He felt his lips curling, trembling in the upset of what was happening, but his body moved on instinct, pushing gently, tentatively until he had nowhere else to go.

"There we go," she whispered, an arm wrapping around his neck almost protectively, the other slipping up from in between them and brushing along his side. Gripping him there, she used her hand to push him back, and when he followed, she led him toward her again. After a moment or two, slow drags revealing his reluctance to her as if she weren't already aware of it, his body began to find a pace. He never pulled away from her, his face burying into the crook of his arm when he lifted it to her shoulder, wrapping around her in the desperate need to keep them close.

He breathed heavily, body reacting to his movement as much as his turmoil. He felt tears stinging against his eyes as his pace quickened slightly; he wanted to stop, he didn't want this, but he couldn't.

He heard the words *sin, blasphemy, Hell!* breaking through the melodic moans that passed through Malum's lips.

He whimpered softly, quick to close his mouth to mask it, but she heard it. Her lips curled into a grin, nostrils flaring.

She swallowed thickly, gritting her teeth; the softness of his untouched skin felt like a baptism, searing at her flesh now in the holy water, and the angelic sound of every noise he made shook against her core like prayer. Her head was pounding. This was worse than hearing his music, the message of piety and purity, but she grinned, gripping him tightly as he moved steadily inside her, knowing that the dam was broken, and that the completion of this one sin was the first of a flood that would wash away Bonum's message and replace it with her own.

"O-oh." He shook, raising his head as she ran her fingers through his hair.

He moved his forehead against hers, lifting a hand to her cheek and brushing it tenderly.I

s this what love felt like, he wondered, Is this what it means to be in love?

His shaking lips pressed against hers, closed but not tight. He wanted to remind her, in case her thoughts roamed as his did, that this was more than what it seemed, that its importance wasn't lost on him, that even through the blurring of his vision and the fogging of his mind, he was aware of what was happening, even if that was only half true.

"I don't think I—."

"Shh," she cooed, reclaiming his lips.

"I have to—."

"Don't stop," she urged. "Go ahead."

"But don't you—."

"Just go," she whispered, growing impatient.

Max groaned, tears slipping from the corners of his eyes as his motions slowed.

She felt his heavy, shaken breath flow cooly over her, and when his body stopped moving all together, she heard the sharp breath his lips inhaled.

Lifting his eyes slowly, his forehead still against hers, Max smiled hesitantly.

When she returned the expression, he leaned into her, wrapping his arms around her gently and hugging her.

"Ah!" She gasped, jerking away from him.

"What—Are you okay?" He looked her over frantically.

"Yeah." She gritted her teeth, a hand rubbing at her chest.

"Are you sure?"

"Fine," she said, looking down before removing her hand, watching the bubbling flesh cool and calm and become smooth again. "I think," she looked up to him, eyes falling on his chain, "Your necklace stabbed me."

"Oh." He looked down to the crucifix, then up to her, "Oh, I'm sorry."

"It's fine," she said, then she reached for it. "Maybe you should consider, though, wearing it like this." She arched a brow as she inverted it between her fingers.

"Oh." He chuckled nervously, taking it from her hand and clasping his fist around it. "I don't know. I—."

"It's not like you'd mean it," she said playfully. "You have to think about your image."

His image. What an image it was. He gasped briefly, letting go of the chain, his hand resting against the sink for balance. His eyes fluttered closed. He was unable to keep them open. There, crouched over a dingy bathroom sink, between the legs of a woman he just met this week, bloodied knee exposed through ripped clothes, flickering light above them, the sounds of people just outside the door, Max felt a shaken, slurring shell of who he really was. Who he used to be.

"Are you okay?" she asked, watching him as his body began to sway. His shoulder fell against the wall.

Images were flashing inside his mind, memories of the past fifteen or so minutes. Was any of it real? Had he felt with

Malum that which should have been reserved for Holy Matrimony? Or at least for the love of his life? Or was he merely drunk, stumbling into this bathroom with no one to save him but her?

She jumped down from the sink, using her impressive strength to help him sit back on the toilet.

"Yeah," he whispered, his hand hurrying to his head. "I'm so sorry."

"You have nothing to be sorry about," she said, moving her hands to his and brushing them. She tried to look as concerned as possible it was hard not to bask in such an accomplishment— no demon had ever actually corrupted a prophet before. How could she contain the excitement? "You're okay, right?"

"A little wasted, I think," he said, scrunching his nose as he looked up to her. He bit his lip. If what happened was real, Max surely under-performed. "Malum," he asked, his voice small, eyes to the ground.

"Yes, dear?"

"What happened… I… It was okay?"

A wide smile slithered across her lips. "It was perfect," she said, sliding her hand up his arm until fingers found his jaw. "You're perfect."

He smiled, nervously at first, but encouraged by her praises and gentle kisses, his chest stopped heaving as badly, his heart rate calming.

No one accomplished what she did this night, and she was determined to make sure no one in the inferno would forget it.

CHAPTER SIX

Out of the nothingness of unconsciousness, Max started to feel cold. His brows furrowed, eyes tightening as he became more and more lucid. He didn't want to wake up. A part of him last night hoped he wouldn't, for the reality he feared had come to pass.

Rolling over, eyes still closed, his hands spread across the bed in search of Malum, but the lack of heat already proved to him that she was nowhere to be found.

For a moment, a bit of hope washed over him. Maybe Malum's absence didn't mean that she left him. Maybe it meant that she hadn't been there at all. Maybe this had all been a dream— nightmare even. Though an admittedly thrilling one. Maybe the only sin committed was the impure thoughts. Maybe it was the same unholy fantasy that struck him so deeply in the coffee shop the first night he met her. Maybe, just maybe, Max considered, a breath shaking his chest on intake, his soul remained intact.

Swallowing deeply, mustering the courage to face the morning, Max finally opened his eyes.

His bed was empty, but in the one next to him was Philip.

Max sat up, looking around the room to make sure Craig wasn't passed out on the floor instead of sleeping in one of the beds in the next room. After confirming that no one else was in the room, Max slipped out of his bed. He wanted to wake Philip— he needed Philip—but when he stood, he saw a body next to his friend.

Inhaling deeply, looking around the room, Max wasn't sure what to do. He didn't know if he should get a shower, if he should get coffee. He didn't know if Craig could offer any aid. No. He shook his head. What would Craig do but belittle him for being tormented about something so common that Max's rejection of it was odd.

When he heard movement in the bed behind him, Max turned toward it quickly.

"Philip," he whispered, watching his friend roll over in his direction. "Philip," he said again.

Philip's brows creased, his lips curling. He groaned a bit.

"Phil, please wake up," he said breathily.

Philip whined, pulling the covers over him, still more asleep than awake.

Max lifted a hand, ready to shake his friend, but then he recoiled. Memories flooded over him. He and Philip weren't friends right now, not the way they'd always been. He felt his lips curling, tears welling up inside him. He needed salvation and he wasn't sure anyone, even Philip, could help him attain it.

Still, he had to try.

He stood, hurriedly moving toward the bathroom. Pausing at the entrance, hands catching on the frame, Max looked inside the room. It was lit only by the sun shining in the small window, but the memory of Malum, her flesh against his, her soft moans in his ear, needed no illumination to be remembered clearly.

He inhaled shakily, hands reaching for the sink slowly. When he grabbed the handle, he turned the water on, staring at it, images of his body against the counter flashing in his mind, blinding him in their intensity.

He leaned over the sink, splashing the water onto his face. He rubbed it across his eyes and over his lips, his chest, his arms, cleansing himself without ever looking into the mirror. All he'd see is someone he didn't recognize, and the thought of becoming a stranger to himself was terrifying.

He took the towel from the ring in the wall, drying his face first, then the remainder of his body. Looking down as he pressed it against his chest, Max saw Gemma staring back at him. He hadn't resisted anything. Purity of heart was a joke, especially considering the breaking of Leviticus, as Bonum pointed out when she saw the "cut for the dead" filled with ink just above that sacred organ.

His lips quivered, but he threw the towel down, his hands rushing to the back of his neck, shaking as his fingers pulled at the clasp of the chain.

Tears slipped past his eyes as he removed it from him, eyes accidentally looking up to catch sight of himself. A deep inhale caught inside him, his lungs refusing to move in the shock of what he saw.

He turned away from it immediately, looking down to the ground and seeing his fallen leather jacket, a piece of his image cast aside in his defilement.

Sniffling, wiping the back of his hand across his nose, Max walked toward the door, throwing his chain onto the jacket as he exited.

Semi-collected and back from the hotel's coffee shop, Max entered the room in determination. He took large, progressive steps toward Philip's bed, bending down in front of him and waving the open bag of muffins in front of him.

"Philip," he said quietly, getting only a groan in response. "Philip, please. Get up."

"Maxwell," he groaned, eyes screwing closed before they opened. When he saw Max, his features dropped. Sitting up and throwing the cover off of himself, he stared at Max in annoyance. "What are you doing?"

"I got you breakfast," Max said, sitting on the edge of the bed opposite Philip and offering him the bag.

Philip eyed him, his brow arching as his head tilted, but after a moment, he took it.

As he looked in the bag, Max added, "Two chocolate chips—"

"And a regular?"

"I wasn't sure what your friend liked."

Philip raised a brow, turning his head to look at the body behind him. His lips pursed, "Hm," he said pleasantly as his eyes raked over the smooth ebony of an impressively toned back. He looked back to Max, "Guess I did pretty well."

"Yeah." Max exhaled a small breath.

"I suppose you had another fun-filled night," he said, taking a bite of one of the muffins.

Max averted his eyes from Philip's judgemental gaze. "I wouldn't call it fun."

"Yeah, sure. Drunk, out of it on stage, come up to the

party and drink more. I saw your friend with you. Sounds awful."

"It was just…I…" Max's words caught in his throat. He'd never felt so uncomfortable, especially with Philip. "Philip, I didn't mean to miss the rest of the show the other night, and I didn't mean to get so drunk. Last night… I don't know. When you said you didn't believe in me, that was worst thing I've ever felt. Not just because I knew it was my fault, but because I don't think I can do this without you." He glanced up to Philip before his eyes fell again, his head hanging in the shame he felt. "One of the girls I talked to at the table last night," Max's lip trembled, the muscles urging him to give into his body's desire to sob. The weight of what he said to these people through his lyrics, of what they said in return upon meeting him, pressed against him from both sides, pushing his ribs toward his back and his spine into his lungs. "I wouldn't have known what to say to her if it hadn't been something you said to me. You know, everyone else, Craig, Jessie, society at large, they make me feel like I'm crazy, like I'm the oddest person they've ever met just for believing the things I do. But you…you never tried to make me think differently. You never made me feel bad for my beliefs, even though you've never believed in them."

"I believed in you," he said lowly, waiting for Max's eyes to find his before he continued. "You're a good guy, Max. If some archaic moral code keeps you that way, then I really don't see the harm in it. I mean, what you say in your lyrics, maybe if you weren't so cryptic with them, or maybe if you're clearer about what they mean like you sort of were on stage last night, it could really do some good. It wouldn't hurt to have younger people who see so much of the sex, drugs, rock and roll thing to see you standing up there, all handsome and talented, telling them that it's okay if they don't want to do that, it's okay if they want to wait until they're married, or stay sober, or focus on their creative talents instead of partying. That's a beautiful thing for the kids who feel weird because they're more like you than they are me or Craig or whoever." He inhaled deeply, looking downward as his tongue rolled over his teeth. "I just can't support you doing that if you're going to be a hypocrite about it."

"I didn't——." Max's words left his lips in gulps, breaking his focus on holding his sorrowful breaths. "I didn't…mean…to be a hypocrite." He shook as he inhaled. "Everything just sort of happened, and I didn't stop it."

"You could've stopped, though. Life doesn't just happen to you, Max. You can choose to allow it to happen, sure, but you can also choose to stop it." His eyes were troubled as he looked at Max, brows contorting as if he were in a great deal of pain. "Instead of stopping what was happening, you went out to the bar yesterday, throwing a tantrum because I wouldn't talk to you. No one put those drinks in your hand. No one told you keep drinking last night. No one told you to lock yourself inside a room with a woman you haven't even known a week, but you did it."

Max's impending sob caused convulsions in his chest. He looked upward, brows gathering together as they lifted. He nodded, tears breaching the inner corners of his eyes, and he picked one of the coffee cups up from the floor. Extending it to Philip, he said, "It's…got vanilla in it." He smiled sadly, swiping his hand over his nose, as he stood up.

"Max," Philip exhaled.

"No, you're right," he said, his lips thinning into a shaken line as he attempted to smile. He grabbed his bag and threw it over his shoulder.

"Well, wait. Where are you going?" He looked at the clock on the nightstand. "It's not even nine o'clock."

A shallow inhale entered his lungs. "The, uh, new album won't write itself."

Philip watched him as he left the room. Still conflicted, he stood from the bed, considering following him. Instead, he decided to shower. If Max wanted to write, Philip didn't want to interfere.

He went into the bathroom, his left foot catching on something. He looked down, saw Max's leather jacket on the floor. His lips pursed, head shaking. Disappointedly, he picked it up, hearing the sound of metal fall against ceramic as he stood. When his eyes followed the sound, his brows furrowed. The light of the sun shone in the window, illuminating the silver Saint Gemma, next to her on the ground was the crucifix Max had worn every day since they were fifteen.

———

Philip's continued silence was deafening. Max's mind was a relentless downpour of conflicting emotions, wreaking havoc on his mental state as pleasure dueled with pain. The memories of Malum pumped a blend of chemicals into his brain that made them feel as fond as fantasy. She was beautiful and mysterious, sure, but she held Max in her hands delicately while she helped him explore the world he'd been inside, but refused to experience, for almost his entire life. He smiled as he wrote the way he felt when he looked into her eyes, they way her warmth spread through him as if it'd been injected into his veins. *She's burning gold,* he wrote, *while I simmer in blues. Her heat lingering in my soul after each rendezvous. When will she return? If she'll stay, if she goes, it's something I can't even guess. Something only she knows.*

He looked down to the paper, the flashing memories following the evening hours. He wasn't just seeing her standing against a counter; she was no longer only black nail polish and dark drinks. She was open-mouthed kisses. She was moaning and touching. She was the realized desire every shameful fantasy longed for.

Each shaken breath becomes louder, my body out of my control. Every muscle is crying to move faster, harder, give in to every urge. The relief just the first few seconds of my lifelong deathly— No. He didn't like that one. He knew before he finished it.

He scrubbed his hands over his eyes, wishing he could confide in Philip. Talking to the paper wasn't as freeing as it used to be. Now, when he looked down to all he'd written, the poorly executed dialogue inside his mind, he saw the words as shackles, wrapping around his wrists and disintegrating into his skin. His binds weren't physical, not anymore. He'd traded them in for spiritual ones the moment he met Malum, the first time their lips touched. He didn't want to admit it, but he wanted her as fiercely as he didn't, and the only impulse urging him away from her was a belief almost no one believed.

"Hey," Philip said as he entered the room just off of the side of the stage. "Billy's almost about to start."

"Okay," Max smiled thinly, "I'm ready. Just have to give Craig my guitar to check when it's time."

"All right." Philip paused, exhaling shallowly. "Look, I don't know what happened in that bathroom last night, but I found this on the floor." He opened his palm, extending

Max's necklace to him. "Is there anything you want to talk about?"

"No." Max shook his head, avoiding direct eye contact.

"Well, I know I wasn't in the mood for listening this morning, but I didn't think you really had anything you needed to discuss. Obviously, if you took this off, something's wrong."

"I'm fine," he swallowed thickly, mouth dry. If he told Philip what happened, it would only confirm Max's hypocrisy. If he didn't, he'd have to face it alone, but it was his consequence after all. It was his choice, his action.

"Well, I think maybe you should put them back on."

"Yeah," he nodded as he took them. "Thanks."

He looked at the pendants briefly, lifting them to his neck, but he didn't lock them there. He bit his lip, exhaling through his nose rather sharply, then he set them down on the table.

He stared at them, seeing their reflective brightness in even the dimmest light shine so purely through the cigarette butts and crushed beer cans.

He wondered if he took a photo of it if people would see goodness blazing through the bleakness of sin, or if they'd see the saint's position next to such anomalies as a sign that even the righteous fall. Max wasn't sure which way he saw it. Not at this moment, at least.

A year ago, he would've said the former. A year ago he believed all that mattered in his life was staying true to the moral code so ingrained inside him from his youth. Now, seeing the success of those who bask in sin, witnessing the unending number of people who lie, who cheat, who fill the emptiness inside their bodies with chemicals and smoke, now Max, having succumbed himself to all things he once denounce, wondered if there was any such thing as righteousness to begin with. He couldn't very well protect something that didn't exist.

He frowned, his eyes falling to his hands wrung together. He needed a drink.

As he moved to the bar, a sweat began to form across his forehead. He looked around the crowds of people watching Billy, feeling his anonymity fade away. Eyes were on him. He could feel their intensity. His heart began to race against his ribcage, each pump of blood thudding inside his ears as it grew faster and faster. His breath was shallow, hurried. His lungs gasped for air as he grew hotter and hotter. He thought he was going to faint.

Suddenly, hands were on him, warm hands, hands that made his rising temperature feel cold in comparison.

"Malum," he gasped, "Oh, God." He threw his arms around her.

"You know, you keep calling me that and I'm going to stop correcting you."

"I didn't think I was going to see you. I was—." He stopped himself as he pulled back from her. If he said afraid, he'd sound desperate. Maybe he was.

"I had to leave before your babysitter came in and found me." She grinned. In truth, she wanted to stay, and in his intoxicated state, she probably could've influenced Philip the way she could influence most people, but he wasn't most people, and she couldn't take the risk. Besides, wanting to reward Max for helping her achieve her promotion wasn't a good enough excuse to remain so close to him. Sure, the transition had started with their fifteen minutes of fun—that wasn't truly fun for either of them—but it wasn't complete.

She saw inside Max's eyes, watched the turmoil spin around within the deep pools of blue, and even if she hadn't, she could simply touch him and feel how pure he remained.

She was growing impatient, however. When the fall was a shot in the dark, the chase itself was fun. Now that it'd begun, now that it was more possible than it ever had been, she wanted to see it manifested immediately. She congratulated herself for figuring out such a plan.

"Are you okay? You look sick."

"I'm okay," he lied. Oh, she liked that.

"Good, because I have a surprise for you."

"A surprise?"

"Yes. Did you come from this way?" She started to walk in the direction he just left. "I need a bathroom. Let's go."

"I was just going to get a drink," he said, meaning water, but taking the glass of vodka she offered him instead.

"Can we go now, please? We have very little time before you play."

As soon as they entered the back room, she pushed the door closed behind her and locked it.

"Wait, Philip and Craig will need to—."

"I'm sure they'll knock." She grinned, moving against him and pressing their lips together.

His body loosened at the embrace, falling against her as he lifted his hand to her cheek.

As she deepened their connection, her hands moved to the hem of his shirt, and he pulled away to look down to it.

"This has to go," she said, and he allowed her the action, but only because he went on stage without it, and would be going on shortly anyway. "Oh…" She brushed her hands across chest, starting at one collarbone and ending on the other. "This looks much better already. Now…" She set the bag down on the table in the center of the room, "This next." Her hands moved to his button and zipper, and he moved his quickly to stop their motions.

"Wait, Malum, we can't—."

"Calm down, tiger. Get your mind out of the gutter."

"What?"

She winked as she opened the bag, removing a sleek pair of black pants.

"What are these?" A small smile tugged at the corner of his lips when he reached for the pants.

"I thought you wanted to be a rock god," she said.

Max's forehead creased for a moment. He didn't realize he'd told her about that. Still, the gift was amazing. They looked exactly like the ones worn by the gods in the photos. What was even better than the pants themselves was the fact that Malum gave them to him.

"You were thinking of me?" He asked shyly, dipping his head when he looked to her.

"Of course," she said, her fingers dancing along his torso before they fell back to his jeans. "I'm always thinking about you."

His body stiffened when he felt his pants drop from his hips, but then he breathed a sharp laugh. A smile started to form across his lips, but his shoulders still curled inward.

Unaffected, Malum took a step back, her hands moving to her hips as her golden eyes raked across them. Max shook, his breath sounding in his throat as the heat trickled down his body like droplets of a fiery rain. He smiled again, swallowing thickly as he hurried into the leather pants.

When he got them on, she hummed in her throat, a satisfied grin on her crimson lips.

She closed the space between them, her fingertips

brushing against his hip bones before her hands spread out enough for them to slip inside the pants, just at the hem. His body tensed, tiny muscle convulsions causing him to shake. She was so warm, so soft. The way she touched him, in even the slightest form, ignited something deep within him, something that had been so dormant for so long that it gnawed at him whenever she drew near, desperate to break free. His hands brushed over her cheeks, down her neck, and across her shoulders, fingers curling in desperation, longing to wrap around her, hold her, touch her.

She grinned, tilting her head toward his. Panting as her left hand slipped further into the garment of the gods, sliding gently up and down, slow and steady and smooth, Max practically fell against her. His lips parting as soon as they crashed into hers. He groaned, gripping her more tightly, feeling her free hand tangle in his hair to pull his lips more harshly into hers.

"Oh, God," he panted, her pace increasing, her nails digging into his flesh as they slipped down his neck. "Malum," he exhaled, "I have to…God…"

He moaned against her lips as her nails scraped across his chest, half in pleasure, half in pain. That pain, the feel of his flesh ripping beneath her fingers, allowed him to get lost inside the pleasure her other hand provided. After all, the sins of flesh surely warranted punishment of the same tender organ, and feeling his atonement before the relief was even achieved let him get lost inside it.

When he shook against her, arms wrapping around her, pulling her into him, he buried his face into her chest, gasping and moaning and crying out to God as his release took hold of him.

His chest rose and fell harshly, heavy breaths falling from

his lips as he held onto her.

When his breathing slowed, he pulled back from her just enough that he could kiss her. He felt her grin against his lips and he pulled back, smiling in return.

He noticed something smudged across her chest, then he wiped at it. His brows creased and he looked down to himself, seeing four jagged lines opposite his tattoo, black leather pants beneath them.

She brushed her fingers over the skin around the wounds, arching a brow as she looked up to him. "So," she grinned, "Do you feel vicious yet?"

His lips parted, looking up to her wide-eyed. "I don't know," he chuckled nervously, looking down at himself. "Do I look like I am?"

"Yes," she bit her lip, eyes narrowing as she stared at his porcelain flesh now bloodied and broken. "You should go clean up, though. I mean," her brow lifted when she looked down.

"Right," he said.

When he went into the bathroom, the door knob to the main room twisted. Malum sauntered over to it, opening it just a crack.

Philip peered into the small opening while Malum slipped through it.

"What are you doing here?"

"Max wants me here." She leaned against the door, brushing her hand over it.

"Well, I don't."

"Feeling's mutual," she smirked.

"Yeah. I need in there," he said, reaching for the doorknob again. His hand recoiled. He looked down at it quickly, expecting to see the shine of burnt skin. His brows creased and he looked up to her.

"You should probably let it cool down." She smirked.

"What? Who are you, really? You don't care about Max. Not like you say you do."

"That makes two of us, doesn't it?" She chuckled. "I mean, that's why this all worked out so well for me. You're the reason. I should thank you," she lifted her hand to his cheek. Jerking away quickly, he rushed his hand to his face where her fingers seared his flesh.

"What— What are you?" He said, taking a step back from her.

"I'm someone who's helping Max become who he needs to be. Not who you think he is, not even who he's destined to be." She took a step closer, and Philip recoiled further, but every time he moved away, she closed the space between them.

"Who he's—" Philip's eyes narrowed, his lips curling in defiance. "What do you mean who he's supposed to be?"

Flickers of hot, white light ignited   inside her golden irises. "And we no longer care about who you're destined to be."

"We? Who's we?"

"See, Philip, your kind is really only a concern when we're manifesting, infesting, all that." Her brows lifted, lips pursed.

"My kind?"

"You don't have to run away from me," she said, watching his body stiffen when his back hit the wall. "I don't want to hurt you." She exhaled a small laugh, "Well, not anymore. I mean, for a minute there, I really thought I was going to have to, and I would've, but it would've been an awful task getting him back on stage at all, much less get inside his mind, but then you…" She smiled warmly, tilting her head as she looked at him. "You lost faith in him, didn't you?" She lifted her hand to his cheek, pinching it as she smiled.

"What?" He breathed, his head shaking a bit. "No, I didn't—"

"Yes, you did. You did, and I really should thank you."

His head shook, "Malum." He scoffed at the name. "Who are you really?"

"I'm someone you do not want to cross, Philip. He's mine now. You get in my way," she looked at the defiance in his face, her eyes narrowing. "And I will make sure Max never lays eyes on you again." Her features shifted all at once, and a bubbly voice said, "Be a doll and let us know when it's time for Max to go on," she smiled. "Thanks, Phil," then she turned and slipped back into the room.

Instead of Philip, Craig came to the room to collect Max.

"Whoa, what's all this?" Craig said when Max exited, looking at the tight leather pants clinging to his body. "What happened there?" He referenced Max's wounds.

"Nothing," he practically mumbled. "Trying something new," he laughed nervously.

"Yeah, well, Phil's real pissed. Your little girlfriend had some words with him, I guess."

"What? When?"

"Like, five minutes ago. He tried coming to get you, and she told him no."

His brows creased. He was in that room with her. Even if she'd left the room when he was in the bathroom, he figured he would've heard it.

Regardless, Max had a show to put on, and in the new garments, he needed a few shots to find the bravery necessary to walk on stage.

He didn't stumble, not like he used to. Maybe he was building a tolerance, he wasn't sure.

He found it disturbing, however, that the calming sensation usually brought on by the stage didn't take effect tonight as it had been. He watched the eyes below him, saw the faces as focused as they'd been, no phones, no obstructions. Something was off. Even the sounds of guitar seemed wrong. His voice felt weakened. Nothing mattered tonight as it should have.

His cross was gone, his saint tossed aside. He wore wounds, atonement for his worldly sins, and the garments of the gods felt more like the robes of a dark mass.

Still, he couldn't deny the way the people reached for him, how many mouths were moving in time with his. Maybe this new image was necessary for the message. Maybe all that mattered was what he said, not how he looked. Just look interesting enough, he thought, Just get their attention. But the fact remained, although lost upon his blurry mind, that he had their attention anyway.

When it was time to lift his acoustic guitar, time to bare his soul, a worse guilt washed over Max than any he'd experienced these past few nights. He'd given in to the one thing he held in such high disdain. The temptations he renounced, the fleeting memories of saying no, repeatedly, over and over again. A lifetime of lost love and inexperience dashed aside for his need to drown his troubles in booze instead of music. When was the last time he'd written anything even remotely good?

The guitar wailed as he pulled it over his pants, a sound that prickled at his skin.

"This song…" he exhaled, the words now meaning more than ever they ever had. "Is about saying no…" His voice cracked, he looked away. How dare he perform these words? "When you want to say yes."

———

Malum was gone by the time he left the stage, and when Changing Nuances' set was over, so were Philip and Craig. Max didn't know what to make of any of it anymore— his life, his message, his choices. He supposed it didn't matter.

Everyone at his feet still stared at him. Everyone sang. Everyone wanted to meet him, just for a moment, they wanted to see themselves reflected in his blue eyes, wanted to hear their names spoken in the melodic tone of his gentle voice. No one ever paid much attention to the crucifix. No one seemed to notice it was gone. What benefit was there in feeling guilty for something which seemed to have no great consequence?

Maybe it wasn't just that the message didn't matter, but that there was no message. At this point, Max wasn't sure he believed in anything, especially not himself.

Hurriedly, he ripped the remainder of the T-shirts from the wall, throwing them into the box, and shoving all of the CDs and stickers down with them. He wasn't concerned with folding. They'd taken advantage of that for far too long. If they wanted to punish him for his actions, that was fine, but they shouldn't have made how little they'd appreciated him all of this time so evident in doing it.

He picked up two of the boxes, kicking the third along

the floor in front of him, out the front door.

A few girls stood beside it, one of them freezing when she saw him.

"Oh, God." He heard one of them scoff, but he didn't look up.

"H-hey," the frozen one said.

He looked over, smiling to her. "Hey."

"Do you…need some help?"

"Oh, no. It's okay." He nodded. "Thank you."

"I mean, I don't mind," she said, taking a step toward him. She paused, looking to her friends and lifting a finger to them before she turned around and took the box from the ground.

"Oh, you really don't have to——."

"I don't mind helping," she said.

"Thanks." He nodded, and she followed him to their van.

"What's your name?" he asked as he opened the back doors.

"Casey."

"Well, Casey, it's nice to meet you. I appreciate the help." He pushed the boxes into the back of the van.

"It's no trouble. I actually, um, wanted to ask you something, but…" she inhaled, a bit nervous, eyes darting around when he turned to take the box from her hands. "I didn't wanna ask in front of my friends."

"Okay," he said, a bit hesitant. "What's…What's the the question?"

"I just…Your song, when she says she can't wait…You said tonight that it was about saying no even when you wanna say yes…" she rang the corner of her hoodie in her hands, looking down as her orange hair fell over her rounded cheeks.

"Yes," he said, taking a step closer.

"I just—I mean, it's stupid, but…" she said, looking up to him, but he could see something heartfelt inside her troubled eyes.

"I'm sure it's not stupid. What is it?" He places a hand on her shoulder.

"I told my boyfriend a few months ago that he'd have to wait, and I…Well, he doesn't want to wait anymore, and I guess I feel like I want to say yes to him when he tries to—I want to say yes because he wants me to. But that's not the same as actually wanting to say yes, is it?"

His lips parted, brows lifting as they creased together. "No," he shook his head. "No, that's not the same."

"It's probably so lame for me to still be a…" her shoulders shrugged.

"I've probably got ten years on you, and, uh, I'm…" his lips closed, the air thudding around his throat until it left his nostrils. His hand reached up for his pendant, but his savior was lost. Maybe if he didn't say the words aloud, it wouldn't count as a lie. Anyway, aren't white lies, at the very least, acceptable? Bad, but for the sake of good. "I think you knew that already, right?"

"I wasn't sure," she said lowly, "that's why I didn't wanna ask in front of anyone. I didn't figure you'd tell me, but I thought if I told you, you'd maybe understand."

"I do," he nodded. "It sucks when someone wants to walk away from you for something you're doing, or not doing, because you feel like if they leave, it's your fault, right? Like you had the power to stop them?"

"Yeah," she smiled sadly, the water in her eyes causing her lips to tremble.

"Well, you don't. Someone like that, they're going to find a reason to leave whether you give them what they want or not," he said weakly, voice cracking. The words weren't his. They were Philip's. They were Philip's words to Max after Jessie left him. "Someone who cares for you, Casey, they won't threaten you. They won't make you feel guilty. And they won't leave you. If your boyfriend is willing to do any of that, it's best for you if you let him go. Honestly, the more time you spend with him, if he isn't the right one for you, is more time taken away from whoever is."

She smiled widely, spreading her hands out nervously. "Can I—?"

He nodded, wrapping his arms around her.

Suddenly it all made sense to him— his message, his beliefs, what Bonum had been saying about his followers needing his commitments—his commitments, and he'd broken them all.

CHAPTER SEVEN

Max sat back in the large soft chair comfortably. His head was tilted, heavy, and pulling at the muscles in his neck.

He looked over to Philip, laughing as he poured a shot into some guy named Aaron's mouth. Philip already lost faith in him. He didn't want him to know what a failure he was, too.

Tears threatened the brim of his eyes, their blue shimmering behind the glistening pools of nothingness he felt. Maybe if Malum were here with him, maybe if she hadn't left that night, things would feel better.

It'd been two days since he saw her for more than a minute at a time. Two days he couldn't even remember. It was better that way— better when it didn't matter, better when he couldn't see the memories of what he'd done so clearly.

He lifted the clear bottle of memory eraser to his lips, swallowing as big a pull as he could. He didn't even need to mix it at this point.

All he could think about was Malum, where she'd gone,

why she left. He thought what they experienced would bring them closer, it certainly made him feel more connected to her, but all he'd really seen of her was flashes. He knew they weren't fantasies. He knew they were real, for each swift appearance brought with it a gift, some physical object he could grip and touch and feel.

He still wore his pleather pants. He felt rotten, felt his soul festering, a trend started by someone with such a name only fit. But now, added yesterday before his show, he also wore a thick chain around his neck.

"My pet," Malum had whispered when she put it around his neck, brushing her fiery hands across his collarbones.

"Don't leave," he'd implored weakened voice as pleading as his watery eyes. "Not again. Not tonight."

"I have business," her reply the same as it was today as it always was.

Today, she brought something else. Today she brought eyeliner.

"Just smudge it around your eyes," she'd said. "No need to make it precise. That's not the image we're going for, now is it?"

"Malum," his voice as fragile as he felt. "What is all this?"

"You wanted to look like your predecessors," she'd said, taking the eyeliner and drawing one long vertical line, crossing through it a smaller horizontal one.

Max had looked down to it, inverted with the symbol, he felt his beliefs as they oozed out of him, seeping out of every pore on his body, as if Malum's heat absorbed into his flesh and expelled anything that ran against it.

"Why can't you stay? Why are you away so much?"

"I've been promoted," the explanation made no sense to him.

"But you're still here. You're still with me—."

"Here, love," she'd said, lifting a glass to his lips and brushing his hair as he leaned his head back and let her baptize him in this unholy water. "Don't you stress. You're always my number one focus. It's just that, right now, there are a lot of behind the scenes things for me to handle. Paperwork, if you will."

"Can't you do that here? Can't we go get food after the show and I'll be quiet while you work?"

"And what would be the point in that?"

"Just wanna be near you," he said shyly.

She brought her hand to his cheek, smiling gently as she gazed at him.

He seemed broken, puffy eyes now adorned in smoky black, their purple crescent moons making his lack of sleep apparent. His lip was busted on the left side, a brief run in with the corner of the tub during a sloppy shower, and it appeared, for lack of care, to be infected.

"I've never seen you look so beautiful," she smiled, and she meant it.

He brushed his fingers across the cold metal of the chain, taking another drink as his eyes moved to the door. Everything inside him focused on that door, hoping beyond all reason, he'd seen Malum walk through it. When he didn't, he took another swig. Empty.

Standing up from the chair, his limp fingers released the bottle unwittingly, and he took slow, lagging steps toward the kitchen area of this hotel room.

Room 2121.

"Hey, man," Craig said, his arm around a blonde girl, a red head standing next to her. "Wanna do some shots with us?"

"Sure," he said lethargically, eyes staring off beyond them, but never actually fixating on anything.

Craig poured tequila into four glasses, handed them around, and then counted. After Max threw his head back, it fell forward in a dizzying motion that made his already off kilter body sway into the counter.

"You good?" Craig chuckled.

"No," he said, digging the heel of his hand into his eye and smearing the black around his cheekbone and off to his temple.

He sniffled a bit, shaken handles fumbling through the bottles, their glass clanging together. The sounds beat against his head as if they were the blunt end of a hammer, ripping into his flesh, breaking the bone beneath. What has he done?

"Dude, what are you looking for? I'll get it."

"Cherry vodka."

"Man, you drank all that. Stop worrying about this girl. I saw her today, right? It's fine."

Max shook his head. It wasn't fine. Nothing would ever be fine.

Max continued his search and Craig grabbed his wrist, trying to prevent more bottles from falling.

Max looked over to him, lips curling.

"I'll get it, man. It's okay."

"It's not okay," Max snorted. "Nothing is okay, Craig. Not with you, not with me, not with these girls. You two," he slurred, his hip falling into the counter, "Get away from him. He's gonna use you. You'll never hear from him again. And if that's something that doesn't bother you then…" he shook his head, chuckling a bit. "Then it doesn't bother you. Nothing bothers anyone anymore. What am I even doing?"

He grabbed a blue bottle, never stopping to look at what was printed on its label, and he turned away from the counter. Popping the lid as he scanned the room for Philip, Max watched him slip into the connected room.

As he followed him, he drank, and when he watched him go into the bathroom of the adjoining room, Max yanked the handle before the door was entirely closed and forced it open.

"What the—?" Philip stopped when he saw Max. "What are you doing?"

"We're gonna talk," Max said, pushing into the door and closing it behind him.

"I told you days ago, if you wanna talk, you need to be sober."

"I can't be sober, Phil," he said, tears already slipping from the corners of his eyes. "I cant."

"Why, because that girl isn't around so much? Well, I'd say count your blessings."

"How can you say that—."

"Because she's not good, Max. There's something wrong with her, and you know it. You said it the first night you met."

"I was just thrown off. It was before a show, and her eyes were—Her hands felt so—."

"Hot? Yeah, I know. I practically burned myself on a doorknob after she touched it."

"What?"

"Couple weeks ago, when you first took on this lovely new look. She backed me into a wall, Max, and you know I'm no weakling but—."

"No, but you weren't gonna do some MMA moves on her. You're a gentleman," Max slurred.

"Right, but I wouldn't let her just throw me around

either, and I'm telling you she's got strength."

"Yeah," Max's brows furrowed. He thought about the way she was able to hold him up, how easily she moved him into seats, and helped him walk.

"She told me my kind was only a threat to her when she's manifesting and infesting."

"Infesting—what does that mean?"

"I don't know. I mean, I didn't. It sounded so weird, like it rhymed and it was things people don't do, but it sounded so familiar, and then I looked it up. Max, do you remember reading about demons?"

"Demons? Philip, what are you talking about? I'm talking about a girl I met—."

"Yeah, a girl that met you. A girl who showed up at every venue we've played, always looking for you, always tempting you—."

"Tempting—."

"Tempting with booze, with her sexuality, making you late for shows, changing the way you look. Max, the three steps in demonic possession—."

"Possession?"

"Just listen, please. The first step is manifestation and infestation. That's the first step. That's what she said to me."

"You think Malum is a demon?" He blinked a few times. "You don't even believe in demons."

"Max, her name literally means evil. Don't you remember anything from school? Don't you remember Latin?"

"You remember Latin?"

"You're not getting it. You're not getting it because you're tired, and you're weak, and you're drunk, and it's not your fault. It's not. Max, during this phase, the demon is seeking your approval. It's invited itself into your life, it can possess places, objects, bars and shot glasses, but it needs your permission to stay. When I…when I lost faith in you, she said that's what happened, and now I know what that means. It means you didn't have anyone else, you felt alone, and she was the only one there for you, so you let her become that. You let her in."

Images of Malum on the sink flashed inside his mind. His lip quivered, heading shaking. This was crazy, even for someone who's been drunk for three days straight.

"Now, you're not sleeping, barely eating. I can see in your eyes your will to live is even dwindling. It's oppression. It's the second phase. It's attacks on the spirit, the body, the mind. Max, people report bite marks and they…they report scratches—."

"Scratches? No, this was…We were—."

"You were what?"

"Philip, I don't think I can sing 'Waiting' anymore. I can't. This girl came up to me, and she said it helped her knowing that I don't do that, but I did, and I mean, I do—I don't know what I am anymore."

A gentle knock on the door pulled their attention toward it. A soft, melodic voice said, "Hey Rock Star, are you in there?"

"Oh, God," Max breathed, "It's Bonum."

"Bonum?"

"The one from the restaurant, remember?"

"With Saint Gemma?"

"Yeah."

"Do want me to let her in?" Philip asked, seeing something akin to hope radiating within Max's forlorn blues.

He nodded.

Philip stood before the door, opening it slowly, just a

sliver at first. His lips parted when he saw her face this close, so similar to Malum's, but something surrounding her felt nothing like the ravenous energy that rolled off of Malum.

"Good?" He whispered, stopping himself from rolling his eyes. "Really?"

"Hi, Philip," she smiled gently. "Your skepticism has always been amusing. May I come in, please?"

"Yeah," he said, brows creasing a bit as he opened the door and let her in.

Through the small crack, she could already feel the weight of Max's soul, the heaviness inside his body.

"Oh, Max," she said, heartbreak cascading down her features as she moved against him. Brushing his face, the cooling sensations of her hands nestling against his cheeks, his head, his neck, she studied his features. Her thumb rolled under his eye, taking a bit of the smudged eyeliner with it, and her head shook as her frowning lips began to part. "What is this?" She said, her hand falling, smearing the top of the inverted cross painted in his chest.

"For the image," he choked out, tears falling from his eyes, pulling the liner down his cheeks. "It's just for the image, I swear."

She shook her head. "No," she gasped, but the word was stern, her expression was absolute. "No," she said again, reaching around him to take the towel from its hook above the sink. "Here," She said, applying a gentle pressure to his shoulders as she urged him to lean against the sink. His legs shook a bit, and she said, "Just sit." Looking over her shoulder, she said, "Would you mind helping me, Philip? Please."

"Yeah," he said, approaching them.

"Let's get him on the counter."

"Okay." He steadied Max, watching solemnly as the intoxicated body of a stranger who used to be his best friend struggled to move his limp legs. With Philip's help, however, Max was finally sitting on the edge of the counter.

"Thank you," she said to Philip, and he smiled as he moved out from in front of Max.

Bonum stepped in his place, standing directly in front of Max. "Go ahead," she said, "You can lean against the wall if you need to."

His body relaxed, a great exhale escaping his nose as if it had taken all of his energy to remain upright. His shoulder fell against the wall, and his head followed.

"What are we doing?" Max asked slowly, watching Bonum as she centered herself between his legs.
"We're taking care of you," she said, eyes on the water pouring from the faucet, as she damped the towel beneath it.

Bringing it to her chest, Bonum closed her eyes. Her lips moved as if forming words, but no sound left them. Then she opened her eyes, and brought the towel to Max's chest.

He flinched when it touched him, but she brought her opposite hand to the area, too, allowing it to cool, almost heal, the sharp pains the blessed water of the towel jammed inside him as it passed over the inverted cross.

"No more of this," she said, smiling up to him.

Max watched her intently as she pushed the towel across his chest, felt it stinging as its water passed into the scabby wounds of Malum's nails. It hurt him, but at the same time, it felt good, pure, something like forgiveness.

His eyes struggled to remain open, but he fought for vision. He wanted to see Bonum, her serene face, the smoky gray of her glistening eyes.

He lifted a hand to her wrist when her hand rose to his

face, clinging onto to her in desperation as she wiped the towel across his cheek. With the blackness surrounding his eyes, the towel removed his tears, each one falling into the material and absorbing into its wetness.

"Bonum," he whispered.

"Yes?"

"Why are you doing this? Why are you… Why do you care?"

Her eyes flicked to his, feeling as much as seeing the despair within them. She inhaled deeply through her lips, then let it escape her nose.

"Because, Max, I know who you really are." She wiped the towel under his other eye, the coolness of her hand soothing him in its pursuit. He nestled into the touch, eyes closing gently before he looked up to her from his slumping head. She smiled, "I know who you are underneath all of this."

"I don't," he whispered.

"Max, your message is important. What you say matters. People will listen to you. It's important that you don't stray away from who you are, who you're meant to be—."

"Who he's meant to be," Philip said. His brows creased.

Bonum looked over her shoulder to him, "Yes."

"That's what she said about him."

"Who?"

"Malum."

"Malum?" She asked, looking back to Max. Her eyes raked over his flesh, his tired eyes, the missing crucifix. "Max, you've been in contact with someone named Malum?"

"Philip thinks she's a demon," he muttered, eyes closing as the alcohol took hold.

"We need to get him to bed," she said, looking at Philip.

"And then you and I need to talk."

———

As they lowered Max into a third room, newly booked under Bonum's instructions, Philip watched her intently.

"Why are we hiding him here?" He asked.

"Just help me get him into bed. Under the covers. He needs warmth, comfort. He doesn't need to be around so much inequity right now, not in this weakened state."

"Weakened?"

"Philip, you want to know who Malum is? You need to help me with him first."

"Okay," he said, pulling Max's shoes from his feet and lifting his legs into the bed. He took the binding pleather pants away from Max's body, watching Bonum shy away from their direction until Philip covered Max.

She moved over him, brushing his hair from his eyes. Leaving her hand on his forehead, she lifted her other toward Philip. "Please, your hand," she said, and when he grasped it, Bonum closed her eyes, lips moving again as if in prayer, but silent.

Then she stood, nodding toward the door. When they exited, Philip immediately questioned her.

"Who are you? Who is she? What is all of this? What's going on with Max?"

"Philip," she exhaled, lifting her hand to the door. "Max is a prophet."

His face fell. "A prophet?"

"Yes. I know you struggle with faith, but if you believe

Malum is a demon, why is this so unreasonable?"

"Because evil, that stuff is so obvious. It's everywhere. I imagine most things in the Bible aren't meant to be taken so literally, so maybe a demonic force—."

"Maybe a demonic force is simply that," she said. "Max is a prophet. He has a message of purity to give to those who will follow him. It's why he's been given the body he has, the talents, the voice. Everything that would make someone here in this physical realm open up to his message, it was all part of the Divine plan."

"The Divine plan that Max is a prophet and…and what? Has a career in a band because of it?"

"Has a platform, yes. I'm here to check in with him, as I do all prophets, to make sure he's on the correct path. Each time I've visited since the time loop—."

"Time loop? You mean Virginia?"

"I do. That was Max reaching his full potential, that was the time of prophecy beginning. No one else in the room felt it. Not Craig, not your fans—."

"Max did?"

"Yes, and you."

"Why me?" Philip said, his skepticism reignited. If Max was part of some Divine plan, he could buy that. But not himself.

"You've had it figured out," she smiled.

"No, I—." his lips parted, his words to Max resounding in his mind. If it's me who has to understand the world to keep you safe from it while you're up there trying to save people from peer pressure and sin or whatever, then that's fine. That's fine if it's our fate. "You don't mean that I have some connection to…"

"Max wrote a song about guardians, these radiant human

beings who are assigned to those who need them. Mistakenly, he referenced me. But, Philip, that song is about you. You're his guardian. You were sent here with a purpose, too. A purpose that's linked directly to his."

"So when I…" he looked to the door, Malum's "thank you" in his mind. He licked his lips, head falling forward. "Bonum, if I stopped caring, if I stopped trying to chase away everything I perceived as wrong, then is it… is it my fault that he—?"

"No. It's not your fault. You're human, Philip. A human can only try so far. Max's is human, too, and sometimes temptations prove too tempting."

"But without me, if I turned my back—."

"You provide him with a certain strength, Philip, a remembrance of all that's moral—."

"And if I stop reminding him—."

"You can't blame yourself. This demon is quite tricky."

"She is a demon?" His eyes widened, brows raised in bewilderment.

"She is. I hadn't sensed her anywhere when I checked in, and each time, his writing, the advice he was giving the people, it all seemed as if his path was still correct. I don't know how she wormed her way inside."

"It started with drinks," Philip said.

"Well, we'll let him sleep now. I'll try and figure out how the inferno caught wind of who he was—."

"The inferno?"

"Hell," She said. "Someone in Hell was given the identity of the prophet. I intend to find out how."

She turned, but Philip took hold of her arm.

"Wait, you're not leaving him, are you?"

"He's sleeping. He needs it. I've prayed over him."

"But Malum isn't going anywhere. Every day she keeps slipping something else on him, in him, whatever. How am I supposed to fight her? She's strong and she has the ability to burn me—."

"I'll return. Max is more important to me than you realize. I'm not abandoning him."

"Okay, but we won't be here tomorrow."

"Philip, I know where you'll be," she smiled. "And I have the ability to arrive there whenever necessary."

"Right," he said, his hand falling away from her. She turned again, but he spoke, "Bonum, wait. Your name…Good?"

"Yes."

"If Malum is a demon…are you a—are you an angel?"

She smiled. "Something like that," she smiled, then she turned and walked away.

Philip went back into the room, watching his friend's sleeping body. Max appeared almost lifeless where he laid, but even when he walked, when he stood on stage, there was no light inside his eyes, no passion. She'd taken it all.

"I'm sorry, Max," Philip whispered, watching Max's chest rise and fall, however shallow. He petted his hair, lips frowning as he studied his sunken features, his broken skin. The bruises forming where Malum's hands gripped him, strength she couldn't reign in now that his soul was was breaking, his mind weakened, spirit practically dying.

It took no time, literally a flicker of time in the amount of someone's life, to create a sinner from a saint. Philip hoped that with Bonum's help they could return him to himself again as quickly.

Moving to the empty bed, Philip lifted the covers slowly. He told himself he would not fall asleep, that whatever part he played in Max's fall, whatever he'd done to fail Max, stopped tonight. It was finished. But the truth was that Malum's presence hadn't only weakened Max. It weakened Philip, too. They were all cosmically bound by the same spiritual force, and when Max felt low, Philip felt low. When Max was angry, so was Philip. Max's body needed rest. Philip's did too.

CHAPTER EIGHT

The pink of the sunrise doesn't shine through the window
It burns red through the glass
The blaze of the fire, the burning heat too powerful for the clarity
It buckles under the pressure making everything less and less visible
I can't see through the window
The glass is broken
I am broken

"What are you writing?" Malum said, sitting in the bed next to Max and looking at his notebook.

"Doesn't matter," he said as she took it from his hand, exchanging the book of his soul for a cup of coffee and bourbon.

"No, I like it."

"Yeah?"

"Yeah, it's darker than your usual stuff." She smiled. "Feels more personal."

"Maybe." He took another drink, then he turned his body to face hers.

"I think you should write some music and play this stuff," she said,

brushing her hand over the words. "People need to hear this."
"It's too dark," he mumbled, leaning his face into her shoulder.
"No," she said. "It's perfect."

The memory faded as his eyes blinked open. Six days ago. Six days ago they locked themselves in a room just their own. He'd written like never before—Not for the way it poured out of him. That was usually what happened when he sat before a blank sheet of paper, but for the subject matter. It was a strange feeling that washed over him in the time it took him to create the poetry for three new songs. It was comforting, for the first time since he met Malum, he was able to write what he was thinking clearly again, but entirely uncomfortable for what it was that he was thinking.

He thought about his convictions—a common subject for his writing—but now he questioned them. He looked at his life as if it were a painting set before him; a painting that depicted bright blue eyes lost in the creamy porcelain of perfect skin. No cuts. No bruises. But full of hopeful motivation for what was to come.

Here, sitting before the painting, Max saw himself, a ghost of who he used to be. Scratches, bruises, his body's temple now shared with someone who sought relief in it. A much more vivid story, a story of words written on a paper, not just a smiling image. And through all the experienced sensations of the physical realm, inside he felt so empty.

Maybe this what was it was to be an adult. Not in the sense of years, but in the sense of spirit.

With no practical knowledge on the questionable calls that threatened to leave track marks on a tarnished soul, Max wondered how he ever thought he could have spoken to such matters. All he knew was what he saw, what he heard, what he was told.

He'd watched plenty of people partaking, engaging, experiencing. He'd been told countless times how it all had felt.

The only pain he ever knew was heartbreak, and even that seemed laughable now that he experienced so much he swore he'd never do.

His body was weakened. His skin felt tight. His eyes were as dry as his throat, and blinking hurt as badly as swallowing.

He felt for a moment that he should pray, but like the efforts taken to soak the parched body parts, prayer seemed to do more harm than good to his wilting soul.

He sat up in his bed, both hands gripping the sides of his dizzied head. When he looked around the room, he saw only emptiness. He supposed it made sense, but he wasn't just alone. He remembered sitting on the counter. He remembered Bonum. And for some odd reason, he seemed to remember Philip and his disposition feeling more frantic than angry.

What had happened between them? Max wished he could remember what they said.

He exhaled, his body still tired, still aching, but he stood up. He was hungry, but for whatever reason, food looked unappealing. At least if his body was shutting down, the circuitry of his brain was functioning enough to leave a legacy of new music.

He walked to the bathroom, gently closing the door behind him, and looked at himself in the mirror. He really should write some music to go along with at least one of the new poems.

Philip's eyes fluttered opened. His brows creased a bit as he yawned, then he rolled to his back and attempted a stretch. Suddenly, his eyes popped open. He was becoming awake enough to remember every piece of insanity he learned, or believed, or even just hallucinated from the previous night.

He sat up quickly, looking for Max, but seeing the disheveled sheets calmed him. He put a hand on his heart, looking at the light pouring out from beneath the bathroom door, and then he sat back.

Demons and angels. Prophets. It wasn't real. Philip spent his entire life choosing logic over belief, and now, at almost twenty-eight, was he expected to alter his entire paradigm? Maybe if he'd seen something miraculous, even something demonic. But then again, hadn't he felt the burning intensity of Malum's flesh? Hadn't he seen her strength? And Bonum, with such a radiant energy of calm and wholesome vibrations that filled a room as easily as oxygen, hadn't she lessened the wounds of Max's open flesh? Were these things miracles? He wasn't sure.

All he could think of was Max. Max was right. And everything Philip thought Max missed out on in pursuit of that perfect spiritual plane was comprised of experiences that corroded Philip's soul. But maybe by design. If Philip decided to believe Bonum, to believe that angels exist and that they trounce around seedy hotel rooms in pink sundresses, looking for some tattooed band guy, well, then he'd have to believe that Max was a prophet, and that he was his guardian. His spiritual guardian. He chuckled. Atheist and homosexual,

Philip wished he had solid enough proof of his divine purpose to show the world, but then again, maybe it's all a matter of freewill. After this, Philip guessed he'd become agnostic at the very least.

He sat up, eyes on the sliver of light again. The room was silent. Eerily so. And the light never shifted or became obstructed by the occupant's footsteps. He never moved. Didn't speak.

Philip stood up from the bed, walking slowly toward the bathroom door, carefully listening for signs of struggle.

He was worried when he reached the door, terrified as he locked his hand around the knob. What if he opened this thin, cheap hunk of looks-just-like-wood plastic and found only his friend's body? What if Max succumbed to all that he hadn't been prepared for? What if a body lay on the floor with Max no longer inside it?

Taking a deep breath, Philip turned the knob and quickly opened the door. No body. Just nothing. Nothing but a light left on, but by whom? Philip and Bonum hadn't used this bathroom, and if Max got up and stumbled into it, where was he now?

———

The memories were blurring together. Standing in front of the mirror, trying now to see beyond himself, Max could visualize perfectly the curvature of Bonum's face, her serenity even when she was so obviously upset. She wiped away the grime of a week's worth of binging. She cared for Max. It was something so beyond the moment, so beyond the time and place. But every memory of Bonum, her smile, the coolness of her hands, as she stood between his legs was tarnished with flashes of Malum, Max between her legs, her smirk, searing flesh.

He wasn't sure which one was better— while both were enjoyable, both came with guilt. Malum was his connection, this figure of a partner he'd always envisioned. She was strong when he wasn't, certain when he felt unsure. She saw no problem in teaching him the ways of the lifestyle he'd rejected, which sounded bad when he thought of it in that way, but to the best of his knowledge, Malum had no knowledge of that rejection. Could that make her bad? Could she be blamed? Not if she didn't realize what she was doing, and she didn't, did she?

Still, the guilt of finding someone so ideal was every circumstance surrounding them. Max blamed himself. Who would meet someone like him, in his line of work, in his offices of intoxication and intercourse, and expect that he'd desire something far away from these things? Maybe it wasn't even like Malum to drink. Maybe she did those things for him. He told himself he was making excuses, but chose to ignore this, for as bad as things sometimes felt with Malum, they felt worse with Bonum.

It was nothing of Bonum, nothing about her, nothing of the circumstances the two of them experienced together. It was the aftermath of what he'd done elsewhere, everything he'd been doing with Malum, with Craig, the shots, the drinking, the sex, and the lost Saint. He hoped those things wouldn't tarnish his soul— a part of him now questioning if such a thing even existed— but there was something about Bonum, about the way her humdrum gray seemed to become silver in her excitement, something that made him feel the weight of his choices in their entirety. He felt embarrassed in her presence, shame filling his body to the brim when she saw him in his desperate state. It was the same piece of her, of whatever she was, that made him feel like his body was inconsequential, and maybe it was. But believing in that meant believing that everything he'd done with Malum was wrong.

A knock sounded at the door, and Max turned to face it. He narrowed his eyes as he looked at it, studying its elegant carvings, and then the ornate fixtures surrounding it. He looked up at the ceiling, perfectly clean, and then he looked over his shoulder.

He tensed. Throwing his back against the door, Max turned to face a sink and counter at which he had not just been standing. It was deep green counters, lavish bowls beneath two grand mirrors, not the dingy, one-white small sink and its tiny mirror. A panic seized him as his lungs shook in their intake of air. How did this happen?

"Max," he heard Malum's voice call gently from the other side. "Max, I heard a noise. Are you all right?"

He opened the door in a panicked swing, eyes widening when they fell on her.

"Are you okay?" She smiled.

He looked around at the scenery behind her, seeing Victorian styled wallpaper lining a much larger area than the one he'd woken up inside.

"Where are we?" He asked, lips passing short, sharp bursts of air through their separation, his eyes frantic.

"Where are we?" She feigned confusion. "We're…We're in Houston. You're playing here tonight—."

"How did we get here?"

"I brought you. You don't remember?" Of course he

didn't. It was by her design.

"No, I…I remember…" He wasn't sure what he remembered. What was real these days? What wasn't? "Why did we come here? I mean, what time is it? It was still dark out when I came in here, and you…Where did you come from? I was alone and it wasn't this room——."

"Oh, Max, come here. Come on." Her heat encompassed his arm as she wrapped her hands around him, ushering him to the edge of the bed. "It's six a.m. You were really partying last night, so I told Philip I was going to drive you here. We thought it'd be best for you to get your mind clear before the show."

"You told Philip…" his brows creased, his hand rushing to his head. "No," he said, images of Philip, Philip in the room with Bonum, Bonum between his legs, cleansing him. "No, Philip thinks you're a——." he held the word inside his mind.

"Yeah, he doesn't like me much, but we can at least agree on what's best for you."

"I must've been hallucinating." Again, he thought. "I don't even remember you being at the party last night."

"Yeah, like I said, you were really partying." She coaxed him back, her heat brushing over his chest. "Get at least a few more hours of sleep. Then, we have all day waiting for Philip and Craig, maybe you can figure out which music you want to play with that new song."

"New song," his brows creased, then he looked up to her. Four days ago. Another night alone with Malum. A night of writing, of touching, of heavy breathing, and blurry vision.

He remembered, as she petted his hair gently, the way his hands moved up her thighs, and as his eyes closed, he could see them brushing against her hips. He remembered how she felt beneath him, surrounded by opulent pillows and plush sheets, her heat encompassing him as her body encompassed his. Burying his face against her, clinging onto her with his hands, his arms, he whispered in her ear every thought—good or bad, right or wrong, guilt and shame, pleasure and release. She hummed in reaction to his words, encouraging, not the expected commands, *harder, faster,* but commands nonetheless, *write it down, don't forget it.*

How terrible it all made him feel. How divine was the pleasure, how sinful. He heard himself begging her, pleading with her for the pain, scratches, biting, hair pulling, any atonement his body might be able to endure for the indulgence he was taking.

As he laid in the bed now, Malum's hands petting him to sleep, he felt like crying. He couldn't make sense of anything anymore. Memories faded into reality. Reality blurred into visions. He didn't want to figure it out. He was tired, and for the first time in days, Malum was coaxing him to sleep. He didn't have the strength to fight it.

———

"Max!" Philip shouted into his voicemail, then he tossed the phone onto the bed.

He didn't know what to do. Max was nowhere to be found, not in the room with Craig, not the adjoining room, not the separate room on an entirely different floor that Bonum suggested.

He rushed to the front desk, asking everyone in attendance if they'd seen anyone matching Max's description. No one could verify that he had left. No one saw anyone with blonde hair all night. The only people they'd seen so far this morning were two women and a man with red hair.

Texts went unread, no replies. Calls went straight to voicemail. He didn't have Bonum's number. He wasn't even sure she used a phone.

"Dude, he's probably with Malum," Craig groaned, hangover fresh on his tongue.

"Yeah, that's a problem." Philip's eyes lowered, the frustration, worry, concern burning them with the desire to cry. But Philip refused. Max was a prophet, sure, he accepted it, and Philip was designed to protect him from the cruelty of the world. Fine, he could buy it. But what mattered, what kept him collected in this time of panic, was the fact that Max was his best friend. Max was his brother. He'd be damned if he was going to allow some demonic piece of plague to harm Max. Absolutely not.

"We could be getting another hour or so of sleep, man."

Philip's mind raced as fast as his heart. He was just in the room with Max. He spent all night in there. How hadn't he heard him get up and leave?

He stood from the chair opposite Craig's bed. "I'm gonna get our stuff from the other room."

"You need help?"

"No, it's fine."

He moved to the elevator quickly, eyes looking around at the strangers in the hallway, the ones awaiting elevators.

The two women standing next to him boarded the first car that stopped on this floor. Going down. Philip would have to wait.

When the second car stopped, Philip was pleased to find it empty. He hurried the doors closed with the continued pressing of the button which did so, then he pressed the number 18.

Eighteen eighteen. Philip wondered if the numbers had any significance beyond their floor and room.

"Okay," he exhaled, too impatient to wait until he got to the room. He rubbed his hands together, tried remembering the last time he'd done this.

Memory told him this wasn't how prayer works, that you don't pray to anyone but God, but Philip wasn't inclined to believe anything other than what he had seen at this point.

"So," he said, shaking his head at himself. He felt silly. But he'd rather be a crazy person trying to save his friend than a sane person who didn't care. "Bonum, I, uh, I need you." His body trembled against the cold metal of the wall behind him. Though his anxieties were fluctuating, expressing themselves in such a physical manner, Philip tried to tell himself it was merely a reaction to the icy temperature of the wall. Max needed him. He needed him to be strong. Philip swallowed his weakness, and continued, "We've got a problem here. I can't find Max. His stuff is still with me, the bed was obviously slept in, so I don't know when he left—."

The doors of the elevator opened, its ding interrupting his prayers, but only for a moment. When he exited the car, he looked around. No one was in evidence. He continued his spoken plea as he walked toward his room. "I don't know how I missed it. I don't know how it happened. Please, Bonum, if she is what you say she is…" He swallowed harshly, looking up the hallways on either side of him as he removed his key card from his pocket and swiped it over the handle. "If he is who you say he is…" He gripped the handle, pushed it downward. "I have to find him. Please help me find him."

When he opened the door and stepped through, Bonum was standing against the window. Her head turned over her shoulder to meet his gaze.

"Bonum," he gasped, rushing toward her.

"You don't know where he is?" She said, crossing her arms over her chest as she turned to face him.

He shook his head. "He was here when I fell asleep. I mean, my eyes were on him until I couldn't hold them open anymore."

"You didn't hear anything? See anything?"

"No, and I'm really not a heavy sleeper—."

"The oppression is worse than I realized."

"What?"

"The oppression. You've researched it, haven't you?"

"A little, but I…That's real? The three stages?"

"They're very real," Bonum said, taking Philip's hand. "I was hoping she was still just infesting, that she was showing up at bars and hotels, and that she could only enter a new room with the host's approval."

"The host as in Max?"

"Yes, but you didn't hear him speaking. She must've been able to enter without his consent."

"How is that possible if she needed consent?"

"When demons first manifest, during the first stages, they can linger around their target, possess the buildings he works in, the places he sleeps, but in the phase the demon is still seeking approval of sorts. It can't reveal its true self without permission to stay. She was clever in manifesting herself as a human. I assume that's how she gained access to him, by having him approve of this form. They developed a friendship, I take it?"

"Yeah, you could say that. I mean, she—I think he thinks they're dating, or something."

Her eyes widened, back straightened. "How far did this

dating rouse go?"

"They…Max tried to talk to me about this night, they shared some alone time in a bathroom during a party. I found his jacket after, his pendants. He didn't say anything happened, but he did try to talk to me after, and I didn't want to hear it. I was angry with him." He shook his head, exhaling loudly. "Stupid of me, but then last week, it was the next day, she was in the prep room with him. I don't know what was happening, but she wouldn't let me in, and he ended up with scratches, and I—."

"Yes, that's to be expected. Scratches, bites, these are common amongst the second phase, but sometimes sexual assaults will occur. If you're saying he believes they're together…Are you saying this happened?"

"I'm saying I assumed it did, but I don't know for sure. I mean, Max hasn't ever…"

"Yes, I'm aware."

"Aren't you able to pick up on this kind of thing? Like, can't you tell when there's a demon around? Or where it might've taken him?"

"Usually, yes, I can perceive purity of the spirit, the body, chastity, humility, compassion. Every time I checked in, these things were all intact."

"Well, Max saw you at restaurants, that one morning in the hotel, why weren't you at the shows watching him?"

"It's not my job to sit on his shoulder and act as a conscience, Philip," her voice grew stern. "Bars, parties, these are breeding grounds of sin, and the few moments I spent within them made me want to shed this skin and exit the physical realm. It's quite uncomfortable for me, for my kind. Besides, there are precautions taken. Preordained precautions. You're one of them."

"Me? The guardians?"

"Yes, you're meant to be a reminder of who he is, of the purity of his spirit, in situations that make angelic entities vastly uncomfortable."

"So, I failed. That's what you're saying. This is my fault." Philip's teeth pressed into his shaking lower lip.

"No, Philip. Not at all. Precautions aren't foolproof. That's why there are a number of them. You see, as a prophetic messenger, Max's voice should be too pure for the demon to hear, his words too pure for the demon to absorb. She's either quite powerful, or she—."

"I don't think she listened to us play," Philip said, his brows creasing. "She'd show up after, sometimes before for just a few minutes, or to the parties, but I don't know if she ever stayed for an actual set."

"That's why I never sensed her in the bars."

"Why, if you were in the bars, didn't you stay with him?"

"I told you, he was still on the correct path each time I checked in, and that is all my assignment consists of until someone drops the ball and gives in. From where I'm standing, Philip, you're the only one of the two of us who turned their back to Max. Let's not forget this the next time you question me."

"Yeah," he frowned. He scrubbed his hand across his head. "I'm sorry. I'm just worried about him, especially if—if I'm not still wasted, and this is real…"

"You can denounce reality all you want," she said, "but no matter how fantastical it is, that doesn't make it fantasy."

"Pretty fantastical," he muttered. "So how do we find him?"

"Well…" She exhaled. "Sometimes oppression can lead to increased paranormal activity. If she's successfully completed these other occurrences, especially the deflowering of the prophet, then I'm sure she was able to use her abilities to remove him from the room without your knowledge. She wouldn't even need to use a door at this point in the oppression. The physical realm is hers to bend."

"Great. So does that stop you from finding her too?"

"It makes it more difficult, yes." She said.

Leaning against the window again, her eyes began to roam over Philip. She studied his dark hair, gleaming brown irises, turning her chin every now and again as her eyes narrowed on his arms, his T-shirt.

His brows creased when he noticed this, and he lowered his head to try and gauge her line of sight.

"What?" He asked nervously.

Moving away from the wall, she approached him, eyes never leaving his T-shirt until she stood so close to him their bodies were practically connected.

He leaned his head back a bit, and when she looked up to him, he gasped. A flicker of silver shot through her gray eyes, then a spark, and then another, until her irises were swirling pools of the shimmering liquid. Philip's lips parted at the sight, and he could feel the tingling energy of her new, truer state of being.

"Oh, my—."

"Please don't blaspheme in my presence if you can help it."

"Sorry," he said, swallowing harshly.

"It's okay," she said, eye narrowing.

"Wh—what is it?" He breathed, an extraordinary feeling overtaking him.

Waves of calm spread through his body, absorbing the cool radiation from her palm as it swept over his chest, just above his heart. Her head tilted slightly, narrow eyes still fixed on his, and her lips parted briefly before she said, "You haven't followed Leviticus either, have you?"

CHAPTER NINE

Max's phone vibrated across the table on the left side of the bed. Malum's heated hand was quick to ignore the nagging Philip every time his name lit up the screen, but the last call buzzed long enough to cause the sleeping man to wake.

He groaned, rubbing at his eyes, marveling over how little sleep actually helped when his body felt so desperate for it. Maybe it just wasn't enough. Max's brows lifted as his eyes opened. Maybe if he could sleep for a month it would be enough.

Immobile still, Max's blue eyes, now adorned with the thin red rivers of congested vessels, scanned the wallpaper for signs of the previous place. He considered that everything with Malum in the ornate room had been a dream. But it wasn't.

His eyes traced the patterns of deep green on a metallic background of the same color, just lighter in shade. He imagined, as they curled and twisted, that they were great, hunter-green serpents, and that at any moment they might peel themselves away from the wall, inflating as they scurried down from their flattened prison, and wrap themselves around his neck.

His hand rushed to his neck immediately in the thought of it, fingers connecting to the thick, cold metal of the chains Malum had locked there. "Your collar," she'd said, grinning as she added, "My little pet." It was the trappings of the Rock Gods in the hallway, so it filled Max with a sense of accomplishment in that moment. Now he worried it was the chains of actual imprisonment. Even that didn't seem bad if Malum hadn't been so infrequent with her visits. His fingers pressed against the gold metal of the lock. He didn't know where she'd put the key. When she gave it to him, she'd been wearing her usual long, velvet dress, a picturesque portrait of the nineties gothic fantasy, but it left no room for practicality. No pockets. No place to store the key to her soulmate's soul, assuming either of them had one anyway. Knowing Malum, he scoffed a laugh, she probably just threw it away.

"Funny dream?" Her silver tongue spoke through the silence.

He felt the heat circle his arm, suggesting that the pressure of her touch would follow. When it did, he replied, "I don't think I dream anymore."

"Then what's so funny?" She asked, nestling her body against his, her lips kissing, tenderly, the back of his neck, his shoulder.

"Would you let me go?" he asked, feeling her body stiffen. He was quick to take her hand in his, quick to pull her shifting arm back around his waist, for he feared the anger that she might expel if he didn't clarify. "It's not that I want you to," he said, wanting to look over his shoulder to see her face, but too afraid to see the expression it wore. "I don't want you to," his words were soft, but not fearful, for they were true. Regardless of what Malum did, she'd taken from Max a connection he hadn't given to anyone else, and the emotional weight of this physical bond blended all too easily with the intoxicating influences that prevented Max from seeing Malum as clearly as anyone else might have. "I don't know," he whispered, remembering the pain of Jessie's absence, and imagining the feeling of Malum's, with their deeper experience, being far worse. "I don't know what I'd have to do to be all right," he said, and finally the tension of her potential anger lessened. Her arm slipped further around him, tightening its hold, feeling as heavy and unbreakable as the metal around his neck. "But…" He swallowed harshly. "If I wanted you to…would you?"

"No," she said. Max was hers now. If he were any other person, someone without the prophetic ability, her presence wouldn't need a manifested body. If possession were possible, she'd be within him, much further than just the psychological connection their intimacy provided. But the heavens were smart, weren't they? And a prophet's body wouldn't allow such an invasion. The very feel of his body against hers was uncomfortable, to be within it would be unbearable.

"Oh," he said, his brows creasing a bit. In the constant state of duality he felt around Malum, it made sense. If she'd have said yes, Max felt a part of him would've hurt. After all, he wouldn't want to lose Malum, it only seemed fair if she didn't want to lose him. He didn't want her to be so willing to let him go. The issue, however, felt far graver than that of a normal relationship. Max felt something powerful within Malum, something unexplainable. It glistened in her golden eyes, radiated from her heated skin, and now it seemed she had either a way of wiping his memory clean, or of moving him through space and time in a strangely inhuman way. But he felt her. He touched her skin and felt her fingertips on his. He felt her lips, her hair. He looked into her eyes. Whatever she was, if she wasn't just a person, Max commended her for such a perfected guise, then he scoffed. He's either still drunk, or genuinely losing his mind.

"Don't get me wrong," she exhaled, her fingers tracing the skin around his naval into circles of warmth, "I want you to be comfortable and to be happy," she tightened her muscles, hiding the need to shudder, but most of what she said now in love was genuine. Prophets weren't easily corrupted. Temptations were easily denied by those who have this sacred position. But here he was, Maxwell Lenett, prophetic would-be Rock God, in her fiery grip, half naked with chains around his neck. No one had ever given in to a demon before. She didn't know how to thank him for the advancement he'd unwittingly given her. The only thing her malicious mind could conceive of as kind was continuing the manipulation which led them here, for that would be the only way she could ever express any actual consideration for him. Nothing of love, of kindness or compassion would ever grow organically within her. But didn't he need some reward for what he'd done? "But I can't imagine losing our connection. Max, there is truly no way for you to realize how important you are to me." Sincerity felt strange in the gentle words produced by her wicked tongue. The fact that he wasn't able to understand their true meaning was the only solace.

He smiled, tightening his hold on their interlaced fingers. It didn't matter what Philip thought about her. Max felt he knew her. Everything about her in that moment, the way she cradled his body, holding onto him with her arms, the things that seemed so binding when applied with Philip's fearful lens, actually felt quite safe to Max. Maybe, before he attempted to pair music with his new, dark, rock god lyrics, a few more moments of her heated embrace would be all right.

———

"Now, you're going to give me shit about my tattoos?" Philip asked. "Seriously? With everything that's going on—."

"Remove your garment, please," she said.

His eyebrow quirked. "Take my shirt off?"

"I'd like to see your markings."

He exhaled, eyeing her suspiciously, but complied. As the fabric rose, revealing taut muscles draped in elegant flesh, Bonum's eyes narrowed each time her eyes connected to the injected ink with which he'd sullied it. A few lines of poetry rippled as his abdominal muscles rolled, a symbol on his ribcage waved as he inhaled, then, just above his heart, in the exact same location and in the same size as Max's single marking, was the same bold font that sat upon Max's chest—the same font, but different characters.

"What's this?" Bonum asked, her icy touches penetrating Philip's chest as her fingers traced along the letters DCCXXX.

"Roman numerals." He smiled hesitantly to her, fearing the wrath of the one of God's warriors as she chastised his self-injured flesh: if a warrior of God was, indeed, what Bonum was.

Philip didn't necessarily believe in all the biblical passages he'd been forced into studying, but his impressive memory withheld almost all of it, and Thessalonians stood out amongst the others. "You're not—you're not going to take your vengeance through flaming fire on me, are you?"

He looked up to her nervously and she grinned, "You don't follow the gospel, it's true." Her lips pursed in consideration as she stared to the markings, the clear, bold, unapologetic disobeying of Leviticus, then her eyes met his again. "Smiting the prophet's guardian might not go over so well with management, though."

He smiled, nervously at first, but then her calming energy caressed him.

"You really aren't just a person, are you?"

"I'm not a person at all," she said gently.

He nodded, eyes glistening as he beheld her— the soft hints of blue along her flesh, the pink hues of her creamy cheeks, and the swirling silver rivers inside her irises. The air around them became fresh, crisp and clean, caressing his shoulders as a plush blanket might, but one with the familiar scents of the fabric softener his mother used to wash his childhood comforters.

"Right," he whispered, eyes still absorbing the figure of a concept he'd seen merely as myth until this night.

"Why these numerals, though?" She asked.

"They're…" he hesitated, lips thinning as he considered it. "It's just personal, you know? Max has one to match and no one knows what they mean but us."

"So Max's numerals do correlate with yours?" Her excitement forced the pools in her eyes to course more quickly.

"Yes," he said, wincing away from her when he noticed the increase of movement within her fearsome eyes. "It wasn't my idea. I mean, I wasn't the one who suggested he break Leviticus—."

"I didn't assume that," she chuckled, "But it does create

a direct link to the prophet from his guardian."

"So we can use a cheap tattoo I got at eighteen years old to find Max because he also got a cheap tattoo at eighteen years old *with* me?"

"I believe so," she said thoughtfully, eyes narrowing a bit as she looked up to him. "You're still not entirely convinced, are you?"

"I'm not sure what I am," he smiled nervously. "Convinced enough to be afraid for Max right now. Convinced enough to let you try whatever you want to try."

"Let me just…" her finger tips spread out across the tattoo, palm open and covering it.

The cooling sensation that usually rolled off of her body grew stronger, the waves heavier and far more tangible. They begin to take shape against his chest, penetrating his skin in the tiny pricks of sewing needles, which grew increasingly painful as they continued until it felt as if a large icicle had fallen from a rooftop and impaled him.

"Seven hundred thirty." He blurted.

Bonum looked up to him suddenly, watching her hand jerk with his body as his chest rose and fell in pained, heaving pants.

"Right," she chuckled. "I've seen."

"You," he inhaled sharply, the pain of the icy stabs still enduring as she held her palm against him with greater pressure. "You asked about the numbers."

"Yes. Why seven hundred thirty, and why one hundred twenty two?"

"Oh, right."

"If it's too personal——."

"No, it's——I can feel your…energy in my muscles right now."

"It's a power more than an energy, and not in every muscle. Just the one that matters most," she looked up to him, a wryly smile slipping over her lips. Philip shook, looking down to her hand on his chest, feeling the beating of his heart skip momentarily. His lips parted and a slight smile formed on them, then he swallowed harshly through the pain, and looked up to her.

"I'm just saying we're a little beyond personal right now."

"A little." She grinned.

He looked away, trying to focus on steadying his breathing, and then he looked back to her. "Cain and Abel," he said.

Her brows lifted as her curious eyes met his. "The biblical brothers."

"Max and I always felt like brothers. He's an only child. I only have a sister, and we've got a pretty large age gap. Max and I were closer than most real brothers we knew. Always together, always watching out for each other."

"Doesn't sound quite like the story it's referencing."

"Yeah, well, Max was always the perfect student. He followed every rule, always did his homework, and most importantly to the nuns, he believed in the faith. Seemed easy to compare him to the righteous son who had God's favor during sacrifice. Me, though, I always acted out, I guess. I never bought into any of the teachings, and school came so easy for me, memorizing shit—ah, stuff—." He smiled shakily, "It was all so easy that homework was just a boring waste of time. All that, and one of the nuns finding me and Billy Mackey skipping class to make out in the bathroom meant I was no one's favorite student. So it was easy to see me as bad, as evil. But Max…Max was always so deep, so quick to see something no one else did. He said if I'm evil, it's only because we don't understand what evil really is. He said maybe every single evil person in the Bible just looked that way to the people around him. I looked that way because I didn't do what I was told. I didn't do a worksheet. Well, everyone in the Bible made a choice, and what if everyone in the Bible made a different one. What if, instead of killing Abel, Cain watched out for him? Would he still be evil? Maybe not. But would everyone still find a way to make him that way? He thought they would. He thought it was inevitable. He thinks we're all just looking for excuses, ways of demonizing our brothers so we don't have to face our own sins. I thought he was right. I still do, and I still see us as our own version of those brothers—he's still Abel because he still believes in all that's righteous, and I'm still Cain because I don't."

"That's actually reassuring," she said gently. "It proves that your connection is real and spiritual. And very powerful."

He felt her hand withdrawing, pulling with it the invisible force that left his chest as a knife.

"Did it work?"

"I'm going to need a map," she said.

"Angels need maps?"

"I can give you the coordinates if you'd like to find it yourself."

He smiled thinly, removing his phone from his pocket. "Digital map okay?"

"Yes." She took it from him, pinching her fingers across the screen as she studied it.

"Can I, uh, I can put my shirt back on then?"

"Yes," she said shortly, her focus on the phone.

"Starting to feel like Max over here." He chuckled as he slipped the shirt over his head. When he stood next to her, she looked up to him, and he asked. "Why do the singers always wanna take their clothes off?"

She blinked, brows tightening for a moment, and then she looked down to Philip's phone. "Here you are," She said. "You have a show there tonight."

"She just took him to Houston?" Philip looked at the blue line running through the map of his GPS. "What's the point in stealing him if she's only taking him to the venue?"

"I'm sure there is a reason. Get Craig and head out. I'll meet you there."

"Wait…" Philip said, but Bonum's skin began to glisten, bright lights seemed to flow out of her in heated, white beams that spread in all directions. He put his hand up, trying to block the brightness enough to see her.

"We haven't a lot of time."

"I know. I'm just wondering how I'll find you."

"Just call out to me exactly as you'd done here."

"Well, are you going to him right now, or——?"

"I have to find him. I'll check the venue first, your hotel, but I have doubts that this demon would have him somewhere so obvious."

"Okay, I'll get Craig and we'll——." The light filled the room, rendering Philip unable to see, speak, or focus. When it subsided, he lowered his arm from before his eyes and blinked them open. Bonum was gone. He hurried out the door to follow.

———

Max sat on the edge of the hotel bed, his acoustic guitar in his lap. Time seemed dull. Everything was slower, more perceptible. Even the vibrations of his strings as his fingers strummed over them were visible. They created a ripple through the air, invisible yet somehow seen, as they passed over Max's black pants in waves. He thought he could feel them pressing against him, pushing their way into his flesh. He wondered if they'd shake Malum's heat loose, if they'd penetrate even the marrow of his bones and release his body from the newly coded DNA inside him.

The sound of the doorknob echoed and caught his attention as it turned. He blinked up toward its slow cries of metal twisting inside metal, and his lips parted in anticipation.

The door drew open, gentle and without haste. The small sliver brought a hint of light into the room, and as it grew larger, the light grew brighter.

Instinctively, Max's eyes tried to close, but he focused on keeping them open, watching the dark silhouette as it slipped in through the small crack of bright light and then closed the door behind it.

As the figure moved closer, Max tried to see its features clearly; tried to confirm its ruby lips and long dark hair. Instead, the bits of sun that passed through the thinning fabric of the curtains illuminated only the figure's eyes—bright, inhumanly colored, and gold.

"Malum," he whispered.

"What are you doing in the dark?" She chuckled as she sat down beside him.

"Setting the mood," he said, looking back down to his guitar.

"You've picked the music?" Her brows raised in excitement.

"Yeah. It fits with the lyrics almost perfectly. Just had to make some minor adjustments to the syllable count."

"Play it for me?"

"Okay." He smiled.

She ran her hand through her hair, inhaling a deep breath as he checked his guitar for proper tune. Her nostrils flared when his fingers caressed the steel plates of brass or bronze. She hadn't gotten close enough to accursed instrument to take much note of it, and sitting so near it now, now that it threatened her sanity with its sound, made her jaw clench.

Her task was nearing completion. The corruption had begun. But how could she know what the free-will of a human man decided. Perhaps the music was fearsome enough, even with the single sound of one guitar, that her head wouldn't ache at its noise, but perhaps not. Maybe, through all the broken commandments, the hedonism, the lust, a great prophetic message would still spring forth through his narrative. What if he sang of events shared with her through the lens of his guilt? She knew it still pulsated within him. She felt it— the purity of the spirit threaten her manifested flesh with the simple touches bred in sin. It was irritating, for the acts of her coercion dulled it within his intoxicated mind, his mind high on the ecstasy of her human-esque physique, but if the would-be Rock God opened his lungs and revealed to her the same spiritually sound poetics told through in same heavenly growls of his harsh vocals, Malum was doomed for boiling blood and bursting eardrums. She had to make sure, however, that whatever song with which she sent him onto his alter contained the messages of her own will, not God's. Max's voice, his words, the strumming of his strings, all had to act as a sermon to a black mass no one in the crowd even knew they were attending. This was the entire reason for stealing him away. This was why she had to have hours of Max all alone without influence of Philip or the Bible or God, or even that pesky angel prancing about her prophet. This song; Malum needed it to be finished. She couldn't wait another day, another show. She was ready to gain her praises from the Lightbringer herself, to prove her worthiness above all others of the fallen legion. Max needed to complete his transformation tonight. But the holy man, his purity of mind, body, and soul, worried her. Sure, she'd corrupted the mind with alcoholic influences that made her manipulation quite easy, and used it to corrupt the body as well. But that spirit. Anyone could look into Max's glistening blue eyes and see the depth of the soul within their perspicacious skies.

She readied herself. Taking in a large breath, digging her nails into her arm, she watched his hand now strum the chords with a timed precision. Her muscles tightened. Her chin turned away from the music as she waited for the blisters and bubbling flesh. Nothing.

She exhaled loudly, stopping Max's movement.

"Oh, no," she said, placing her hand on his shoulder. "No, don't stop. I didn't mean to interrupt you."

"You're okay?" He asked, eyes raking over as much of her features as he could perceive.

"Yes. I like it so far," she said, and genuinely she meant it. Morphing the prophetic abilities to this degree, as long as it withheld when he sang, was not an accomplishment she took lightly. No one expected her to be successful in even the tiniest hint of his corruption, for no other demon had ever accomplished such a task, so when it happened, no one anticipated the message being moved so quickly.

"You heard three seconds, maybe," he smiled up to her.

"Best three seconds I've experienced so far." It was true. That music meant more to her than it did to Max, for it would set in motion a chain of events that would lead to humanity's downfall, if she could keep her claws embedded deeply enough. She surely intended to, and with her new accomplishments, she was certain she could.

He exhaled a tiny laugh, and then he looked back to the guitar. "Okay, I'll—I'll start again."

She inhaled, still preparing for the painful sonnet, but after twenty seconds of music, Max began to sing. There weren't any screams, no raspy anger as he bellowed out his lyrics, but the words, so draped in the darkness of her own presence, caused nothing more than a slight irritation to her ears. Her lips trembled slightly when his lips would curl over his teeth to produce higher notes, the purity of his soul still within him, but hidden in the deepest tissues of his lungs.

Shredded lungs can't breathe the air you live in
Drowning in the heated sinning of your skin
Melted muscles can't pull my weight out of the tidal wave
My tired soul, both salted and burned, is yours inside the grave
Oh, isn't it cryptic? But isn't that the way?
I know I should run but it feels so good to stay.
Oh, isn't it cryptic? But isn't that the way?
Please don't leave me here broken. Please.

"Oh," she whispered when he lowered his hand from his instrument. Feeling her jaw loosen a bit, she swallowed thickly.

He kept his head down, but his eyes rose to hers slowly. His brows lifted a bit, lips quivering as they tried to roll into a nervous smile.

"That was beautiful. Amazing how quickly you were able to create it, too." She smiled warmly to him, and the expression brought life into his sullen eyes. "I think you need to play this," she said, placing her hand on his. His chest fell heavily when her heat caressed him, fire warming the flesh of the icy room. "You are so cold," she said as she stood, moving to the top of the bed to collect the balled up wad of comforter and sheet.

"Yeah," he said, feeling the pressure of the blanket's weight as its softness brushed across his shoulders. They slumped forward, and he winced a bit, lifting a hand to the edge of the blanket to pull it over his chest. Everything ached. He thought he was tired, but the sleep he'd been allowed last night hadn't helped. Maybe his hunger was catching up to him. Maybe it was his clammy skin. He wasn't sure. What he knew with certainty was Malum's presence; her tiny acts of compassion, her praises, were the only pieces of experience that were positive, and he was desperate to keep her here enacting them.

"I brought you something," she said as she sat down next to him, retrieving a bag from the floor. "A present."

"A present?"

"Yes." She smirked, opening the bag in her lap. She lifted a hand to his cheek, warming his flesh as she brushed her fingers through his hair. "A reward."

"What's the occasion?" he asked, nestling the icy skin of his cheek into her palm.

"You completed the song. It's absolutely perfect."

"You really like it?" His eyes lit up, brows lifting.

"Love it." It was a bit of an exaggeration, but it would do. After all, this song is just a starting point—the new message, the darker one, the better one—and he had an entire album to create.

As Malum opened the black Styrofoam container she withdrew from the bag, Max's nose was teased with the delicious heat of sweet sustenance's scent.

"Chocolate batter. Chocolate chip," she said, wrapping

the end of Max's blanket around her hand like an oven mitt before she took the plastic fork in her hand to cut the pancakes. "I'm told they're the best ones from the little diner across the road."

She pushed the fork into a small triangle of dark mocha batter, and lifted it to Max's lips.

The corner's of his mouth trembled, confusion knitting his brows as a smile began to form. "I…"

"Don't say you aren't hungry."

"I have been, but it feels like I can't—."

"I know, pet." She grinned. "But now you can."

His brows creased, chin moving hesitantly toward the offering, and he smiled when his lips were able to wrap around the fork and take the food from it. A small groan sounded in his throat, the taste encompassing each bud of his tongue as the least nutritious food imaginable filled him with the hope of long forgotten nourishment.

"Good?" She smiled.

He nodded, and she brought another piece to his lips. He was quick to swallow it, his stomach demanding more as hurriedly as possible, and he chuckled, "You don't have to feed me."

"I know." She brought another triangle to his lips. "I like taking care of you," she added.

His brows creased as he swallowed, "You do? Why?"

Her golden eyes moved up from the Styrofoam to his curious blues. Explaining why she had to feed him wouldn't go over well. Another lie never hurt. "You've been working very hard. It's only fair for you to be pampered every now and again."

Being pampered now meant being allowed to eat and sleep. Max's brows lifted as he considered it. What happened to his life in the past few weeks? How did he end up here? His eyes moved to Malum's as she offered him another bite. As its creamy chocolate layers crumbled against his teeth, spreading their delicious flavor over his tongue and down his throat, Max realized his decent started with the woman sitting so near to him. The woman who was feeding him. The woman who said she loved him.

He didn't want to think about it too completely. He worried about the conclusion he'd come to. As he took another bite, he decided, therefore, to consider the benefits of this new state of being. He felt love for another person after years of thinking he might not ever open himself to the emotion again. He felt she loved him in return, but hadn't looked at the sentiment with any logic. Another fear of the outcome.

He took another bite into his lips, the first piece of pancake he'd eaten tonight that contained a few of the promised chocolate chips. He was too hungry to consider it at first, too worried about his body's rejection of food no matter how appetizing it looked, smelled, and surely tasted, but now, as the pressure of his teeth collapsed the fragile chocolate, Max thought of Philip. Philip, who loved chocolate chips in his muffins. Philip, who loved Max like a brother. Max's eyes lifted cautiously to the beautiful face before him. Philip, who hated Malum.

"You okay?" She smiled as their eyes met.

"Yeah, I…I just—." A sharp gasp interrupted him, and his hand shot up to his chest. "Oh, my God," he exhaled as an intensity spread through his chest, gripping his heart tightly. It began to pump more fiercely, as if it were trying to pump itself out of the grasp of a large, freezing hand, and Max's lungs began to heave in response to the increase of adrenaline pulsating through him.

"Max, are you okay?" Malum asked, moving in front of him.

"Yeah, I…It just—." It felt strangely familiar. Behind the pain, there was a tingle, something small and dainty that felt too playful and bright to actually hurt, but it did, and behind the coldness of the clutching hand were cool fingertips that caressed him in a calming temperature. Still, the effect was nothing he'd ever experienced before, too intense maybe to survive, but he grit his teeth to try to bear it better. He needed to focus on it, on its familiarity. He wanted to figure out what it was, and where he'd originally felt it, because hidden inside the overtly painful pressure of the grip was something peaceful. It was something that felt *good*.

"Here, let me see," Malum insisted, pulling his hand away from the tattoo on his chest. She gasped, recoiling from it when she placed only her first two fingers on it, and falling back away from him onto the floor. It was something powerful, something painful. It was something angelic. "Shit," she hissed.

"What?" He asked breathily, eyes scanning her features. "What is it?"

"I…don't know," she lied, standing up and pushing her hand against her temple.

"Malum," he gasped, the word almost too painful to speak in the moment. "You know. Tell me. Tell me what it is!"

She shook her head, her lips curling, flared nostrils expelling harsh breaths. "What time is it?"

"Time?" he stammered, his hand moving back to his chest, feeling the tingling cool sensation radiating from his tattoo into his palm. "Why does it matter what time it is?"

"It's almost eleven," she said. "We can't go to that venue yet. We have to wait."

"What do you mean?" He said, feeling the sensation start to leave him.

"If they find you…" she pursed her lips, brows creasing. "How specific is that radar?"

"Radar? If who finds me?" He gasped loudly, the pain leaving him in a swift pull that felt like something physical had been withdrawn. After removing his palm, shakily and slowly, away from his chest, he looked down to it, spreading his fingers, scanning it for evidence that he'd been stabbed. Nothing. No blood. "Felt like a knife was being pulled out of me," he said, then he looked up to her as she closed her eyes and began to mutter to herself. "What do you know?" He stood when she ignored him. "Malum, please. Tell me what this is."

"It's nothing," she said.

"Malum," he took her hand, and she jerked it away quickly, her eyes popping open and casting onto Max the same golden light that swirled within them.

His breath shook at the inhumanity of such a sight, but then he leaned forward. "Malum?" He whispered, more in awe than in fear, as his curious eyes narrowed in their inspection. "What…What is all of this? Your eyes, your heat. What…" He licked his lips until they pursed.

"Go on," she said, a brow raising over her stern eyes, eyes that calmed now that her focus had been broken. "Ask me. Ask me the question."

His head shook, but only slightly. He couldn't take his eyes away from hers, away from the way her skin seemed golden, the way the light inside her irises seemed to be embedded within her, escaping from the pores of her flesh and the sockets of her eyes. It was absurd, though. The words wouldn't rise from his throat, wouldn't form in his mind. It was such a ridiculous thought. She was a person. She was human.

"Ask me," she said again, this time moving against him. Stronger than ever before, her heat rolled off of her body in heavy gusts, pushing against his body like wind, and blowing the thick blond locks that hung in eyes away from his face.

"How are you doing this?" He stammered a bit, his head drawing back from the heat.

"That's not the question," she grinned, taking a step closer, the gold inside her irises now curling around itself like steam. "Ask me the question. We both know what you were thinking. Ask me."

He swallowed, his mouth drying in the heat emitting from her. The bright lights surrounded her flesh, outlining her frame in the glow of lamp lights, or of the sun, or of fire.

His head shook in the negative manner again.

"Come on," she said, lifting a hand to the delicate bit of flesh between his collarbones. "You believe in so much of that mythology. Ask me."

"You…you're just—." The words wouldn't form. His tongue felt too heavy to roll against the roof of his mouth, his lips too skeptical to push together.

Her fingers danced freely, uninhibited by the crucifix which used to lie in the spot indefinitely. "You can't believe in him without believing in me."

His head turned, and he looked to her from the corner of his eye. "You can't be…you can't be the devil."

Her brows lifted as she blinked, her curling lips softening into the most beautiful pout he'd ever seen. Was she really the bringer of light? It shone through her eyes, her skin, her heated, tantalizing skin.

A satisfied chuckle rose from her throat, and suddenly the light was snuffed. She stood before him, a mere woman, regular flesh—still porcelain and pretty—but regular nonetheless, and eyes that only looked odd because of their unnatural golden hue.

"You think I'm the devil?" She smirked as she leaned into him, brushing her hands over the blue polish on his nails, just as she'd done the first night they met. "I thought that was your line."

He shook his head, eyes scanning the room for evidence of what he'd just seen.

"Sit," she said, taking his arm gently in her hand as her other wrapped around his waist. She ushered him back to the bed, urged him to sit down, and draped the comforter back around his shoulders. "I just have to go to the restroom. Don't go too insane while I'm gone, okay?" She smiled warmly, kissing his cheek tenderly, and then moved into the room as if he'd experienced that fiery light all by himself.

He didn't watch her walk into the other room. He was too focused on his thoughts to hear her steps, but he felt it when she closed the door. That heat she radiated, Max felt it leave his skin. He always felt her before he saw her, always felt her leave without having to watch her walk away.

He knew he wasn't drunk in this moment. He wasn't sure anymore if he was crazy. He knew what he saw in her eyes, in her skin. He knew how it felt. It was as if a fire had been burning in the house of her body, and her eyes were windows, her skin like sheer curtains. And weren't her comments some proof of this? She insisted he ask her what he wasn't able to say. He wasn't able to speak the insanity he thought, but, as he considered it now, maybe everything about his beliefs seemed more plausible when kept inside his mind. The stuff of imagination really had no place in reality. Or did it?

He opened the Styrofoam container which still sat on the bedside, and took a small fragment of pancake into his fingers. Its fluffy batter felt to them as pleasing as it had tasted, and Max was still hungry, still starving, after what felt like days of not eating. Something stopped him, though, as he lifted it to his lips. Something inside him, or around him, something gripping him in a way that couldn't be seen or touched, but was still quite perceivable.

He struggled. Staring at the morsel of food between his shaking fingers, his lips parted, tongue desperate, not to taste the chocolate delight, but to simply feel the pressure of its presence against the nerve endings.

His stomach growled. Cramps had become common.

His fatigue now an obvious sign of lack of nutrition, Max almost wished he hadn't been granted those few hours of a good night's sleep, which, when compared to the amount of time he'd spent awake, might as well have been minutes after a normal day. His hunger felt so much worse without the daunting begging and pleading of his mind with his body to just sleep, and his body with his mind to just shut off.

Go quiet. How pleasant a black line of sight with no sound in its backdrop seemed.

Now, with one competent of his physical torment somewhat satiated, the others were magnified. Most specifically his hunger, and how little a few bites of pancake did to remedy two, or four, or five days—he'd lost all ability to gauge—of nothing.

In those days, those brief moments of diners with Philip and Craig, those seconds of desperation wherein he'd order a "whatever that drink is that comes with a toothpick and olives", were flooding his memory now as playing out almost exactly as this one.

"What is wrong with you, Max?" Philip chastised, "You have to eat. You're gonna pass out on stage."

"Oh, the stage is all you're worried about now?" Craig scoffed.

"What is that supposed to mean?"

"It means all this time, Mr. I-care-about-you-more-than-me is suddenly just thinking about our performance?" Craig's fork clanged against his plate when he stabbed it into a piece of sausage, causing Max's eyes to screw closed in the agony such a noise resounded inside his sleep-deprived, starving body. "Just think it's funny."

"There's nothing funny about this. But Max has made it clear he's his own person. No help from me will be considered, much less accepted, so..." Philip looked over to his friend, his shoulders slouched and closing in around himself as he rested his head between his hands. Philip frowned. Worry, empathy, guilt, heartbreak; all a blurry experience of one strangely complex emotion that triggered from his biological fight, flight, or freeze instinct only the ability to stand immobile and watch Max's decent. He licked his lips, pulling the lower one into his teeth. Looking down to his plate, Philip gently cut the white of his two eggs to separate them, and pushed one onto a small plate assigned for his coffee cup. Silently, he pushed it in front of Max, setting his own fork alongside it.

Max's eyes blinked over to it—it's delicious scent wafting gently under his nostrils causing his mouth to salivate. He swallowed the newly produced spit quickly, seeking relief for his burning, ever-dry throat, but it caused him as much pain as swallowing sandpaper might.

Still, the yoke of the offered food was the bright color of happiness, its softness a simple reliever.

He lowered his right hand from his temple and, without looking to Philip, used his middle finger to pull the plate in front of him. Shakily, he lifted the fork to the white of the egg, cutting the tiniest sliver and and lifting it to his lips. He swallowed thickly as he stared to it, gasping a bit in the absolute need to feel it slip inside his mouth, but nothing he did could move the fork against him. Even when he leaned forward, his lips, not sealed physically, seemed to have an invisible shield within them that refused the food any entry.

Philip watched in worried amazement, not understanding the debate occurring between Max and this unknown force. Why didn't he eat when he obviously wanted to? Was this a hunger strike? Was he concerned of his physicality? He didn't know, but nothing made sense.

"Max," Philip whispered and Max dropped the fork to the table with a clang.

He exhaled exasperatedly, moving his head back into his hands to hide the tears brimming in his eyes, and when he successfully held them back, he lifted his head, stood from the table, and left.

The next night while ordering a beverage from the bar—the only bit of food or drink his body allowed him to consume—he asked for a martini simply to try to eat the alcohol-soaked olives. Even that was a failure, resulting in him throwing the olive, and then the entire drink, against the wall behind the bar.

If it hadn't been for Philip's excellently persuasive verbal skills, Sacrifices Surrendered would've had to miss their own show.

Max knew, as he stared at the pancake, his own behaviors were the reason Philip's distance grew longer and wider spread. He knew it was because of him and the actions he'd been performing. But he couldn't help but feel like there was something else inside, some puppet master pulling the strings of his hands, his mouth, refusing him food, forcing his eyes open, denying him any sort of comfort or contentment.

Maybe it was God, he considered, dropping his arm defeatedly. Maybe he was being punished. Didn't he deserve it?

His free hand reached up to his throat, but missed and landed on his clavicle. He spread his fingers wide enough to connect to the targeted area, but he was despaired in finding nothing beneath them but his own flesh and a cold, heavy lock.

His crucifix, that holy savior that he pressed between his fingers for years, was still lying in an ashtray next to broken beer bottles and bent needles in a basement venue in some city he couldn't even remember from the previous two weeks.

You wanted to be that Rock God, he thought to himself, Well, here you are. Visions of those posters, bloody violence, vicious sex, imagery of anarchy, weakness masked in what punk rock teens of the seventies considered power. All he had to do now was stab Malum, and he'd be that modern god. Be careful what you wish for.

A soft wave of heat began to lurk around him. He shivered in response to it.

"Oh," she said as she approached him.

He looked up to her, wanting to beg her for answers. He knew she had them. She'd been there for the time loop, she reacted to the ice within his chest. She held plastic inside of sheets for fear of melting it with her hands. She knew something Max didn't. But asking her meant confirming something so illogical, regardless of what her answers were, that he wasn't sure he could handle it. Not in his present state anyway.

"Honey, are you still hungry?" She cooed, brushing her hand against his cheek tenderly. "Of course you can have more." She wrapped her hand in the same method, lifting the fork to his lips, and smiling when he leaned forward completely and was able to eat from it.

His brows creased. Nothing made sense. Was this all Malum's doing? Did she know something? Or was he doing this to himself? How often did insane people consider their insanity? It was all too much to comprehend. All he wanted was to eat.

CHAPTER TEN

"I can't even believe we left without Max," Craig said, watching the scenery swipe by his window. "You're driving too damn fast. Getting a ticket isn't gonna get us there any quicker."

"Max is already there, I told you. We won't get a ticket."

"Man, Phil, how do you know he's there? He isn't answering my calls or texts, whatever, but you not showing me proof that he answered yours——."

"He's there. Since when are you so concerned?"

"Since you haven't been, I guess. I don't know, man. I mean, I don't think I'm being too concerned to say we shouldn't leave a member of our band behind, alone, in another state."

"He's not left behind, and he's not alone."

"Oh, he's with that Malum chick? Is she an artist or something?"

"An artist?" Philip's brows creased.

"I mean, gotta be a fake name. Who uses fake names but, like, artists, or writers, or musicians. Actors, I guess, too, but—."

"She's not an artist," Philip snapped.

Craig's brows raised as he looked over to Philip, and he caught the way his fists wrapped so tightly around the wheel that his knuckles were turning white.

"Dude," Craig said.

"What?"

"Oh, my god," he laughed, rubbing his hand against his forehead. "I can't believe I didn't realize this sooner."

"Realize what?" Philip's lips curled, brows furrowing aggressively as he looked over to Craig.

"I didn't even think that's what this was about, but, hey, listen, man, Max is a pansy, I get it—."

"A pansy—?"

"He's sensitive," Craig mocked. "Fine, whatever, but he's into chicks."

Philip's eyes narrowed.

"No matter which one he picks to settle down and do that whole godly marriage, be fruitful thing with, you're gonna have to accept it."

"You're not actually suggesting what I think you're suggesting," Philip said, knowing clearly what was stated, but offering a space for retraction.

"Dude, it makes sense. I get it."

"Craig, if Max's life didn't depend on us getting there as soon as humanly possible, I would pull this van over and beat the shit out of you."

"His life depends on it?" Craig looked unaffected. "Okay, bro. Whatever you wanna make this about."

Philip's jaw clenched, teeth gritting together. Of course someone like Craig wouldn't be able to understand the complexities of human emotion, the variations of relationships, of love. To people like Craig, men and women couldn't be friends. To people like him, men couldn't be friends with anyone of the gender to which they were attracted. Craig didn't think he could ever have a female friend because he'd be too busy trying to sleep with her, so he projected that onto Max as well, and onto Philip, the same concept but with straight men. Of course, he wouldn't understand what loving someone looked like, how differently it felt from just being their friend, and how differently that love felt from actually falling in love with someone. And without the ability to even understand the most basic parts of being human, how could Philip ever expect Craig to understand paradigm-altering facts about angels and demons and Max's place between them?

Craig should be thankful such powerful, platonic forms of love existed, otherwise, he'd be a mess of bruises and busted skin along the highway. But if Philip was in control of anything, he decided it'd be his emotions. There was no way he was going to let his anger, his fear, or his worry prevent him from finding Max and helping Bonum save him.

———

"So," Malum said, separating another small piece from the pancake. "What do you think about playing your new song tonight?"

"Playing it? Not tonight," Max said, brows creasing tightly.

She withdrew the fork from him. "Why not?"

"A change to the set list the day of the show? Malum,

come on." He smiled weakly.

"So, what? Just cut out one of the others. It's not like you need the guys for it. They don't have parts in it."

"Yeah, but we're a band. I can't make those decisions myself."

"You write all the lyrics, and almost all of the music. I've watched you clean up merch tables, load the van, multiple times without them——."

"You watched me multiple times?"

"Max," she sat the fork down entirely. "You're distrusting me and I don't know why. I've done nothing but offer you a look into a future that isn't just basement shows and small venues."

"I like the small venues," he said lowly. "What do you mean a look into a different future anyway? I don't think new clothes are going to suddenly make my band more popular."

"Forget the band. That's what I'm saying. You can be your own rock star. You can travel the world, play stadiums. I can make that happen for you."

"How?"

"You don't need to worry about the how." She smiled, brushing his cheek, warming him with the heat of her hand. "Isn't that something you want? Don't you want more people to hear you? To see you?"

"Well, yeah, I guess," he said, watching her hand move to the fork.

"Good boy," she grinned, and let him eat another bite.

His brows furrowed, but he wasn't complaining. Whatever got him food at this point was fine by him. He just wished he understood the method. Why couldn't she just tell him what she wanted? What she knew.

"So that's why we've gotta play this new song," she said.

He opened his mouth to attempt to explain again why this couldn't happen, but his eyes glanced down to the pancake, the impending bite that seemed to come with agreeable answers.

"Right," he breathed the word.

Her brows lifted, a pleasant expression in her eyes, and she lifted the fork to his lips again.

"Just do as I tell you, pet. Dress how I dress you, sing what I tell you, do what I say, and I'll make all that happened for you."

"How, though?"

"It's how deals work. You give me something, I give you something in return," she smiled, lifting the fork again.

"But forget the band," he started, but her hand began to withdraw. "I mean, it's what you say, of course, but…is that negotiable?"

Her lips pursed together, golden eyes still horrifically gleaming even when they narrowed. Then all at once, her features softened, and she lifted the fork to his lips again.

"I don't mind Craig," she said, moving her leg across Max's lap until her body was positioned in it. She cut another piece from the pancake, brought it to Max's lips, and let him take it. "It would hurt you to lose Philip, wouldn't it?" She asked, watching him intently as he chewed.

He nodded, bringing a hand to his mouth as he said, "He's not just my best friend. He's basically the only real friend I have. We're like brothers."

Malum's lips curled in contemplation, her eyes shifting away from Max as her warmth caressed his cheeks, flooded over his shoulders, soothes his aching muscles. She considered her kindness a reward for Max's role in her promotion, but maybe she needed to remain kind as much as he needed her to. Maybe allowing him his band, his guardian, was the real way she could say thank you.

"If I let you keep him," she said, a parental tone to her voice, "You have to make sure he leaves me alone. No snotty remarks, no pulling you away——."

"Wait, if you let me keep him?"

"I told you, Max, you say what I want you to say and I'll give you a bigger platform to say it on. Keeping Philip around would make this more uncomfortable for me, but——."

"Uncomfortable how?"

"Max." She grinned, her annoyance evident. "Keeping Philip around you is something you want. Keeping him away from me is something I want. Now, if I don't get what I want, it will be bad for Philip, not me. Do you understand that?"

His brows creased again. "You're not…threatening…" He shook his head.

Malum chuckled. "Of course not." Not now anyway. Now Max wasn't fully converted, not yet. But if she could get him onto that stage, singing messages of lost morals, if she could get enough influence cast into enough of the youth who followed him, well, that would solidify his slot in to the inferno. It would solidify his corruption. It would solidify her triumph.

She couldn't let her desires get the better of her now, not when she was so close. All she wanted since the great fall was to be the right hand to the ruler of the inferno, the most beautiful and the most tragic of the angels, the Lightbringer herself. Malum followed her on her descent from heaven. Malum became Malum because she followed her. After so many centuries, so much corruption, this man, this beautiful, devout, prophetic man, was her ticket to sit, not beneath the inferno's ruler, but beside her.

"Listen to me," she said, trying to make her voice as gentle as possible, as slow to hide her haste as she could. "He doesn't like me. We both know that. So if I use my connections to improve the band, you understand why it might be a little irritating to see him gain some of the success from it, right?"

"I know, but Philip's…He's just very protective. We haven't known each other that long. When he sees that you genuinely care about me, he'll come around."

"Right," she began to force a smile, but then she considered it: Max, a legendary rock star, preaching to the masses the exact opposite of his holy-mission-message, Malum standing somewhere high above the crowd in a luxury box, the Lightbringer clicking the heels of her red shoes to the beat of Max's malicious music. A genuine smile formed in the visualization of that future. If attaining it meant sparing Philip, fine. If he got in her way, as she asked Max to prevent, then it would be easy enough to get rid of him. But who knows? Maybe at that point in Max's conversion, he wouldn't even want the holiness of the prophet's guardian near him. It was all uncharted territory. No point in getting her panties in a twist. And speaking of…

"I don't want to fight," she whispered, slow and seductive.

"I don't either," Max said, and, God, how he meant it. Fighting with Philip was bad enough on its own.

"Good," she said, leaning forward and pressing her lips to his. "A little stress relief before you play couldn't hurt," she grinned, nibbling at his jaw, and then his neck. "Could it?"

———

"Max?" Philip said as he rushed into the venue green's room. "Holy shit!" He ran over to Max and threw his arms around him.

"Hey, Philip," Max chuckled a little, returning the hug hesitantly. "What's, um, what's this about?"

"Oh," Philip pulled away. "I was worried about you."

"What? Why?"

"Bonum said you were here already, but I wasn't sure."

"Bonum? You talked to her?"

"Yeah," Philip looked over his shoulder as the door opened and Bonum slipped through.

"Hey, Rock Star." She smiled sadly as she pushed the door closed.

"Hey," he stammered a bit, looking down to himself. The inverted cross drawn by Malum, thick and bold against his pale skin, and the locks and chains were still secured around his neck. "I, um…I just…"

"Max," she said gently, bringing her hand to his cheek.

"Oh, God," he exhaled, his eyes fluttering closed. He lifted both his hands to hers, one settling on top of hers, the other wrapping tenderly around her wrist, as he leaned into the cooling touch. His forehead began to crease, the gravity of every emotion suddenly flooding him, and he closed his eyes tightly to try to stop himself from crying.

Everything about the icy breezes that slipped away from Bonum's hands usually felt so good, so relieving, so calm. Now the coolness seemed blocked off from him, pressing against his flesh but unable to be absorbed entirely. It filled Max with an overwhelming sense of dread, one that threatened to force upon his spirit every possible atonement for each trespass he'd committed.

"It's okay," she said lovingly, lifting her other hand to pet his head. "Just breathe through it. It'll get better." And it did. After a few moments of discomfort, Bonum's cooling energy began to regulate his heated temperature. It still felt jarring, but it wasn't as harsh.. "It must feel strange to be near me so sober after the oppression," she sympathized.

"The——." He inhaled sharply, the production of words somehow difficult when his body felt finally so at ease. Still, he urged his eyes open, and when he looked into Bonum's eyes, they weren't their usual tone of gray. They were glistening silver oceans, swirling around like smoke inside her irises, and he gasped. "Bonum, your eyes."

"We've reached a point where masking them from you is not only unnecessary, but also potentially dangerous."

"Dangerous?" Max swallowed, lifting his head. Her hand stayed with his flesh, falling to his neck in his movement, and he kept his hands on hers. "I feel like I'm not in control of myself anymore, Bonum," he said weakly, a tearful exhale passing through his shaking lips. The words were filling his insides, rising up his throat, and pushing past his teeth. He couldn't stop them "I feel like there's something happening to mess I can't pinpoint exactly when it started, but I know who I am right now is not who I was a few weeks ago." He winced, hating the idea of appearing so helpless, but her eyes pulled the his thoughts from him. "It has something to do with that slowing down of time, which felt so real, but now, I'm starting to question it. I'm starting to question everything, even my own sanity. I don't know if it happened or if I imagined it, or if I imagine you, or Malum, or even Philip right now. Probably drinking doesn't help it—I know that—but sometimes I feel so parched that any liquid looks like heaven, and I can't just drink water. I can't drink whenever I want. I can't eat right. I don't know why, but I do know everything that's happened, everything in a few weeks' time, has completely undone everything I ever thought I was."

"No," she said, gently but stern. "Not everything. You can choose."

He nodded, his lungs shaking slightly. "I did choose." It was the most painful confession of all. "I chose to drink when I never used to. I chose to take everything that was offered. It felt… I don't know. It felt freeing somehow. Like, for the first time in my entire life I was in control of what I was doing. No one—no moral code, no best friend, no nun—*no one* was telling me which path to take. And I didn't realize—I thought I was being strong. I thought I was growing a backbone."

"Max, you always had a backbone," Philip interjected. His eyes were glazed with tears in remembrance of the man he so admired. "Everyone told you in school to take shots, to drink, to smoke, and you wouldn't. You said no as many times as you had to to stay true to your own beliefs. It's not the beliefs of the nuns, Max, it's not the belief in every word of the Bible. Our friendship is proof of that. You believe in goodness and compassion and understanding, but you believe a certain set of morals will stop you from losing sight on that, and it has. I mean, you even lost the love of your life because she wanted you to give up a piece of that. You had a backbone your entire life. You're not weak."

"Yeah?" Max's voice cracked. "Then why are we standing the way we are now? Why am I constantly drunk? Why am I missing the most important parts of being who we are and doing what we do? I mean, forgetting about the people who support us, falling on stage. Can't speak properly half the time, or even think straight. I'm constantly hurting myself— accidentally at first, but you can't possibly understand how strongly I considered doing it on purpose, and how many times. Especially writing songs about temptation but from the other side of it— when people asked me about the godly messages of my songs," he scoffed, wiping at his eyes with his free hand. "They're not there anymore. That message…I don't know how to preach it. Not if I don't practice it. And on top of it all, I lost my best friend." He looked to Bonum, "I don't know how this happened. But I'm so sorry for it."

"I know you are. It's not entirely your fault, Max. You made some choices, some horrible ones, and those are rightfully on your conscience. But the turmoil you're feeling, the physical aversions, the troubling mental pain, it's all part of the oppression."

He looked to Philip, trying to remember from his drunken stupor why that word seemed to resound within him, then he looked back to Bonum and hesitantly asked, "Wh-what oppression?"

The door swung open. An eyebrow arched over golden eyes.

Bonum's lips curled in reaction to her presence, and Philip moved himself closer to Max as she stepped into the room.

"Malum," Bonum said.

"Hey, little sister." She grinned, swirling a cherry around in her drink.

"I am not your kin." Her teeth gritted, nostrils flaring as Malum stood next to her, directly in front of Max.

"You were." She shrugged a shoulder nonchalantly.

"You fell," Bonum hissed, her booming voice stronger

and more forceful than Max or Philip imagined it could be.

"I know what you're doing here," she said, exhaling as if it were daunting. "But you can't cast me out, Authority."

"If you know I'm one of the Authorities then you know that I can."

"Ah, maybe, my little warrior sister, you have the ability," she lifted the cherry from the glass she was holding, letting a few drops of vodka fall from it before she brought it to Max's lips. "But you won't."

"Max, do not accept anything from her."

His lips parted to speak, but nothing could come out. On one hand, he loved Malum, trusted her with his body, his music, his life— and that's what really hung in the balance, for how could he eat if she didn't feed him? On the other, Bonum's powerful purity, how amazing he felt in her presence, and how badly it pained him to disappoint her. But he was so famished that his body lurched at the sight of the small offering of food. He looked over to Bonum, eyes pleading for understanding and for forgiveness as he leaned into Malum to take the cherry into his teeth.

"Good boy," she grinned, then she looked to Bonum, "Who will feed your prophet if I'm not around? Who will let him sleep? Maybe that's your plan," she sneered, "A dead prophet is better than a corrupted one, huh?"

"P-prophet?" Max leaned forward, "What does that...." he looked over to Philip who offered only an acknowledging nod with stern eyes. Max shook his head, looking back to the women who stood before him—women discussing oppression, falls, the casting out by Authorities.

Light shone through both their eyes, blanketing the room in the heated fire of the sun and the cooling calmness of the moon. Cosmic eyes. The stars. The heavens.

"Bonum, when you said you weren't quite a guardian angel—" his eyes flooded, all the myths surrounding a lifetime of devotion now standing before him in perceptible, tangible, undeniable reality.

"There are three angelic spheres. Angels belong in the third," she smiled warmly, lifting a hand to his cheek in an effort to lighten the realizations. "The second sphere, it's Dominions, Strongholds, and my faction, the Authorities."

Malum rolled her eyes, "Honestly, why does everyone insist on talking to you like you're a child?" Her smile was punctuated by a scoff, and she shook her head. "I mean, Max, quite frankly, I'm the only person in this room who treats you with any respect. I'm the only person," she moved against him, her fingers slipping down his bare chest in a heated trail. "Who treats you like the man that you are."

"Malum," he said lowly, eyes gazing into hers deeply. His brows furrowed, skin prickling inside the sleeves of his jacket. "If she's an angel, then what are you?"

She lifted her chin, a smirk adorning her beautiful features with malice, "I won't treat you like a child, Max. That's one thing you can always count on me for. We all know what I am. We all know why I've come."

"So you— you did show up around the clubs, the bars, everything for me?"

"You knew that the first time you asked me," her brow lifted, lips never faltering from their arrogant curl.

"So, recruiting people to your side…" he swallowed thickly, heart racing. The magnitude of all he'd done, every commandment broken, every value tossed aside, every sin, seemed a separate entity inside his being which gnawed on his organs, twisted his guts, and threatened to burst out of his lungs. He hadn't sinned for the sake of experience, for the sake of living, or even for the sake of love. He'd sinned because someone designed to be temptation in and of herself was sent to try to make him. He licked his lips, biting down on his lower one, and then he looked to Bonum. "I didn't realize what I was doing. I'm sorry."

"Yeah, well," Malum said cheerily, laying her hand on his shoulder. "You can't go back. You let me in, Max, and I appreciate you for doing it."

Grabbing Malum's wrist and yanking it away from Max, Bonum commanded, "You will not touch the prophet."

Malum snickered, her hand settling on her hip as she turned to face the angelic being. Leaning in, she practically purred, "I did so much more than just touch him."

Bonum looked over to Max; his fallen head, teary eyes. "You haven't reached the point of no return, Max." She took his hand in hers, "You can go on that stage and spread your message of light, and you can tell those kids that they don't have to succumb to whatever pressure is being placed on them today, whatever one was there yesterday, or whatever one will be there tomorrow."

"Or," Malum said, grinning as she looked at him, "you can get up there, sing your songs of sex, drugs, and rock and roll, and finish your part of the deal."

"Deal?" Bonum said, looking to Malum, then her eyes moved back to Max's. "What deal did you make with her?"

"No, I—." His head shook, words stammering, breath catching in his throat.

"Finish your part of the deal, so I can finish mine."

"What deal?"

"I just wanted to eat," the words left his lips in a broken breath as he looked up to Bonum imploringly. "I couldn't eat. I wanted to, but I couldn't."

Philip's eyes widened, moving from his weakened friend to the woman standing before him. "You son of a bitch," Philip said, memories of untouched plates in diners and hotel rooms suddenly making perfect sense. "How could you do that? How could you keep him from eating?"

"Philip," Max said, shaking his head. His worry for his friend forced him to turn to Philip and block Malum from his approach. "Stop," he breathed.

"You're gonna stand between us?" Philip said. "After everything that's been said tonight, you're gonna stop me to protect *her*?" But it was Philip that Max was shielding.

"Please, just don't." His eyes were glistening pools of fear and worry, but he knew what he had to do. He knew who he had to please, not just to eat or drink or sleep, but in this very moment, and most importantly to him, to protect his best friend.

He looked back to Malum, and tried to smile through his tears. "You really are the only one who doesn't treat me like I'm a little kid." He worried he might choke on the words.

"Max," Bonum said commandingly, "You don't have to fear her."

"I'm not afraid," he said shakily. "I want to be a rock god," he looked to Malum. "I want to finish our deal."

Malum eyed him, "Then go on," she stood aside, clearing the path between Max and the door to the stage. "Be the Rock God."

He swallowed thickly, stepping toward it, and passing through its frame, Bonum and Philip on his heels, Malum swaggering out behind them.

Standing before the stage, Max's eyes were on Craig tuning his guitar, tuning Max's, checking mics.

"Max," Bonum said, her hand gently caressing his

forearm on his left side. "Tell them about chastity. Tell them it's okay to keep it. Tell them about connection, and say it's all right to be different. Tell them about the beliefs you hold. Tell them that people are good, and that it's okay to just be good."

Malum smirked from his right side, lifting her hand to his shoulder and gripping it tightly. "To Hell with that," she growled. "Tell them how good it feels to give in. Tell them how good everything we've done has felt. Get up there and be the guy you are, not that doormat you used to be."

Max's eyes fixated on the stage. Craig's eyes practically bulged from their sockets when he saw Philip, who realized his role in this pivotal point in Max's life. He walked past the three of them, turning to face them. He lifted his hand to Max's shoulder, looking over to Bonum on the same side, then over to Malum on the other. "Make the *right* choice," he said, "Please. Brother." Then he licked his lip into his teeth, and moved onto the stage.

Max inhaled deeply, savoring the feel of Bonum's coolness as it penetrated his jacket sleeve and caressed his left arm. Juxtaposed with the fiery heat of Malum's heat on his right shoulder, the two sensations felt like this duality he'd been wrestling with his entire life.

Did the lyrics matter to them? Did they listen to what he said when he stood on that stage? Or did it only matter to them because he had a stage to stand on? And, if it didn't, then did it really matter whose path he chose?

The heavy strike of Philip's drums sounded. Craig's guitar roared.

Max inhaled deeply, ready to take the stage, and when the sound of Philip's bass drum shook inside his lungs, he took a step, and then another. Bonum's hand slipping away from him, Malum's falling from his shoulder, Max climbed the stairs, and stood upon the stage.

He lifted his guitar, placing the strap over his chest, and settled his lips before the microphone.

This first song, he thought, This first song matters.